Through the Heart

**Center Point
Large Print**

**This Large Print Book carries the
Seal of Approval of N.A.V.H.**

Through the Heart

Kate Morgenroth

CENTER POINT PUBLISHING
THORNDIKE, MAINE

This Center Point Large Print edition
is published in the year 2010 by arrangement with
Plume, a member of Penguin Group (USA) Inc.

The text of this Large Print edition is unabridged.
In other aspects, this book may vary
from the original edition.
Printed in the United States of America
on permanent paper.
Set in 16-point Times New Roman type.

ISBN: 978-1-60285-718-6

Library of Congress Cataloging-in-Publication Data

Morgenroth, Kate.
  Through the heart / Kate Morgenroth.
    p. cm.
  ISBN 978-1-60285-718-6 (library binding : alk. paper)
  1. Large type books. I. Title.
  PS3563.O871497T48 2010b
   813'.54--dc22
2009045834

for love

One learns people through the heart, not the eyes or the intellect.

—Mark Twain

Through the Heart

Nora's Introduction

Nora

Kansas

It happened on a Monday morning.

It.

The thing we're all looking for. Love. On a Monday morning.

My mother always called it heart-attack Monday because more people have heart attacks on Mondays than on any other day. (She loved to share cheerful little facts like that with me.)

So it was strangely fitting that it happened then, since love is a kind of heart attack. I'm sure it hurts as much as one sometimes—and the pain lasts for a whole lot longer.

My mother was right about the statistics on heart-attack Monday, but when I looked it up online, even though my mother was right, I discovered that the second most likely time for a heart attack was Saturday morning. That made perfect sense to me—for some people the thought of going back to work on Monday was enough to bring on a heart attack. For others it was the thought of a whole two days at home with the family.

The second one sounded about right to me—especially when my mother told me for the bazillionth time that if I didn't meet a man soon, I

13

would be alone forever, because it was more likely that a woman would get murdered by terrorists than get married over the age of forty. She'd read that fact in *Newsweek* decades ago, and even though I told her that they'd gotten their facts wrong, she seemed to think that since it was in print it was the gospel truth.

Speaking of murders, Saturday also happens to be the day when the most murders are committed. But people tend to worry more about heart attacks than murder. The thing is, they both happen. The only difference is that one is something you can imagine, the other is beyond imagination. Murder is something that happens in the news, in horror movies, to other people—not something that might be a reality in your life. And if people do imagine getting murdered, it is usually by a serial killer or in a terrorist attack. But studies show that between 50 and 75 percent of murder victims know their killers.

In murder mysteries, to solve a murder we look to the past for clues. But if the clues are there in the past to be found, they must have been there all along—we just didn't know how to read them.

My own personal heart attack happened on a Monday. And, right in line with all the statistics (which we often don't like to think about—probably because we all become one at some point), it was on a Saturday that the dream ended.

What might be the strangest fact of all is that my

best friend, Tammy, predicted them both. Sometimes I wonder: if I'd listened to her, would it have made a difference? And then I ask myself, would I go back and change it if I could?

Timothy's Introduction

Timothy

New York

There is no "happily ever after" here.

Am I giving it away? I don't think I am. I believe that all beginnings contain the end hidden within them. You can try to ignore it, but it's there. The sadness is always tucked away within the happiness.

Maybe I'm a spoilsport. It certainly isn't the worst thing that's been said of me. Lots of people have called me a lot of things. They've called me cruel. They've called me unfeeling. They've called me dangerous. The worst thing you could throw at me? I'm sure I've heard it before, though I have to say that all the people who said those things were women. Does it make a difference? I don't know. I just think it's interesting.

But the women who said those things were right. All I can say is—you try growing up having everything. See how you turn out.

When I say I had everything, money is always the first thing people think of. Why do we make such a big deal about it? It's just pieces of paper—even less real than pieces of paper. For most of us, dollars and cents are just numbers in a computer somewhere. But I grew up with a lot, and when I got old enough, I made more. Easily.

Effortlessly. The money doubled and tripled.

It's never just the money though. Since my father had money, he married a beautiful woman. I got her looks. Just a mistake of the genes, an accidental arrangement of features: this chin, that nose, those eyes. But the difference it makes—I think it might have more of an impact than money. It's amazing the effect that a little bit of beauty has on people.

And just to complete the package, I had brains, too, and all the trappings that come with them: the Ivy League degree, Wharton MBA. I can even pull out the SAT scores, if you want to go that far back.

I know you're probably thinking, "Oh poor little rich boy." Believe me, I would dislike me too. But all these things we call blessings, I promise you, we have misnamed them, but we keep chasing after them, thinking they will give us what we want.

For me, there was only one thing I wanted—the only thing I didn't have, couldn't buy, and didn't know how to get. Love. Real love. But how do you find that? How can you test it for genuineness? Is there a glass to test that diamond on?

A lot of people might think I wasn't worthy of it, and I definitely had days when I would have had to agree with them. I wasn't. But I found it. Or rather, it found me. And it found me in the last place I would ever have thought to look. It's a miracle I even recognized it when I found it. But when I did recognize it, guess what I did? Everything I could to shake it. That's what. You try finding real love and see if it doesn't scare the hell out of you. You might even find that you would choose the same path I did. Judge at your own risk.

The Investigation

THE INVESTIGATION

POLICE REPORT,
THE HAMPTONS, NEW YORK

Case number: 3462
Incident: homicide
Report: April 5

The call reporting the crime was logged at 10:27 a.m. It was placed from the location of the crime: a bed-and-breakfast. The dispatcher took the call and notified the nearest patrol car.

The patrol car arrived, and the two officers were directed to a room on the third floor. The body was lying in the four-poster bed, with a knife in its chest.

As soon as the officers established the death of the victim, they secured the scene, cordoning off the entire third floor. They also notified the precinct desk officer, who alerted the detective squad. All witnesses were identified and detained at the scene by the officers.

The crime scene unit arrived and started gathering the evidence. The medical examiner looked at the body and made an assessment.

Death was surmised to have been caused by a single blow that penetrated the heart.

Nora

Tammy's Prediction

The day Tammy made her prediction was a normal day—normal for me anyway.

When she came by the house, I was in the kitchen, about to make a grilled cheese sandwich for myself.

My mother was upstairs, locked in her bedroom. We'd had another fight.

That morning we had made the long drive up to Kansas City for her fifth chemo session. Second round.

I think my mother actually enjoyed our fights. I wish I could say I did. The problem was, they got in the way of what Tammy called my Florence Nightingale delusion. I thought I'd move home and even though the cancer would be awful, it would also be a sort of miraculous thing that would bring us together. I would take care of my mother, and we would become close in a way we never had been when I was growing up.

It hadn't quite worked out that way—not by a long shot.

I was in the kitchen, heating the skillet, when I heard the front door slam and then the familiar holler, "Nora? Hellooo? Anybody home?"

Tammy had been coming in this way since we

26

became best friends in second grade, and Tammy was not one to give up habits easily.

I went to the kitchen door and motioned her inside with a finger to my lips. As if that would do any good.

"Oh, is it puke-your-guts-up day?" Tammy asked.

That was Tammy. She liked to say shocking things. I never did find the thing that Tammy wasn't willing to laugh about. Other people might say they laughed about the bad things, but you always reached the one thing that sobered them up, the thing that made them say, "No, that's just not funny."

That wasn't Tammy. She laughed.

"You know she can hear you," I said, as Tammy crossed the living room.

"You think she'd be surprised?" Tammy shot back, a little louder than necessary, so I knew it wasn't just for me. It was a small house. You could hear everything, especially if you had my mother's ears.

"You've got a point," I said.

That was part of Tammy's magic—my mother had heard the kinds of things Tammy said, and though she always pretended to be outraged, strangely she never gave me a hard time about our friendship. I think it might have been the one and only thing that was important to me that my mother hadn't tried to take away or ruin. I didn't understand it, but I wasn't one to look a gift horse in the mouth.

"You want a grilled cheese?" I asked, closing the door firmly behind Tammy.

Tammy flopped down on one of the rickety wooden chairs with caning so old it squeaked every time you moved.

"God, yes. I'm starving. Robbie had absolutely nothing at his place."

"Robbie?" I asked, starting to butter the bread. "Do I know about this one?"

"Put a lot of butter on mine," Tammy instructed. "I told you about Robbie last week."

"Wait a second. Don't tell me," I said, turning around, my hand still poised in the air as if the bread was in front of me. "You didn't! Not the boy who bags your groceries at the Price Chopper?"

"That's the one," Tammy said.

"Is he even legal?"

"You're asking me that with a knife in your hand?"

I looked at my hand holding the knife, then at Tammy. "Tammy, it's a butter knife. Don't get dramatic."

"Anyway, he's nineteen," Tammy said. "Oh, to be nineteen again."

"You have no shame," I said, turning back to the sandwiches.

"None," Tammy agreed. "It's a useless emotion, along with guilt and regret."

"Hey, you're knocking my staple diet there. Guilt, regret, and grilled cheese." I peeled slices of cheese out of the package. "How many slices of cheese. One or two?"

"Three," Tammy replied.

"Did you tell him how old you are?" I asked.

"Yes," Tammy said. "I told him I was twenty-four."

"Oh, that's good."

I was the same age as Tammy: we were thirty-three.

"Well, it's how old I feel," Tammy replied.

"It's certainly how old you act."

"And how I look," she shot back.

That was true. But a big part of it was that Tammy hadn't changed her look since high school. She had long blonde hair, which she wore most of the time in a ponytail. And she wore the same makeup, the most important item of which was pink lip gloss. But it was mostly her height. Tammy was tiny. She was barely over five feet, tiny all over except one place—her chest. It was comical to watch men when they met her. They'd try to look at her face, but their eyes would be drawn like a magnet down to her chest.

"You're just jealous I'm gettin' some," Tammy said.

"You're absolutely right." I slapped the sandwiches in the pan with the heat turned high.

"How long has it been?" Tammy asked.

"You know exactly how long it's been. Don't make me say it aloud." I pressed the spatula on top of each sandwich.

"What about the guy in Chicago last spring?"

"No."

"I thought . . ."

"No," I said again. "How is it you can find so many men in a town the size of a pea, and I get nothing?"

Our town was actually not so small by midwestern standards, since something like 90 percent of the towns in the Midwest have fewer than three thousand people. Apparently, everyone was leaving the small towns—they called it the rural exodus. I fervently wished I could be a part of it.

"You get nothing because you're not approachable," Tammy said. Then she added, more kindly, "And I'm obviously not picky. You actually want to like the guy. I just want to be entertained."

"What do you mean, I'm not approachable?"

"You're not. You're actually a bit intimidating."

"Me?" I said. "Give me a break."

"You've been stuck in this town too long. You don't even know what damage you could do somewhere else. You're not bad-looking, you know," Tammy said.

"Gee, thanks." I flipped each sandwich. The undersides had turned a perfect golden brown.

"Okay, you're beautiful. You happy?"

"I know, my hair . . ."

My mother always said my hair was my beauty. It was a color you don't usually see: dark red, straight and thick. I never felt like I was beautiful, just my hair.

"No, I'm not talking about your hair," Tammy said.

"You're full of it," I said. "I'm not ugly, but I'm not beautiful."

"You didn't use to be," Tammy agreed. "You were cute. But you've changed."

"That's true. I've become miserable. I guess it must be the drawn, long-suffering look."

"That's exactly what it is," Tammy said. "Speaking of suffering, how's it going with," and she rolled her eyes up to the ceiling.

"Not so good." I checked the other side of the sandwiches, but they weren't done yet.

"Worse than usual?" Tammy asked.

I shrugged.

Tammy knew me too well. She didn't buy the understated reaction. "Oh no. What happened?"

"I asked her again if I could come into the hospital with her."

"Oh, the horror," Tammy drawled, pressing a hand dramatically to her chest. "Wanting to go into the hospital with your sick mother instead of waiting in the car—how could you?"

I checked the undersides of the sandwiches again. They were done. I forked them onto the waiting plates and brought them over to the table and sat down. The chair creaked in protest. Nothing in this house was stable.

"Well, that's pretty much what she said," I admitted. "But you know she doesn't mean it."

Tammy couldn't answer right away because she'd taken a huge bite of her sandwich while it was too hot and now had her mouth open, fanning the air ineffectually with her hand. But she looked like she was about to choke, she wanted to talk so badly.

"Of course *I* know that," Tammy said. "But do you? She's playing you, honey."

"What would you do? Seriously . . ." I paused, as if Tammy could be serious. I decided to rephrase it. "I mean, if she were your mother."

"If she were my mother, she wouldn't have gotten cancer, because I'd have killed her long before this."

Some people might have found Tammy's reactions to be a bit, well, unsympathetic. But I loved them. Tammy said all the things you weren't supposed to say. I remembered when I first told Tammy that my mother had leukemia, and Tammy said, "It figures your mother would get a kid's disease. It's perfect, because she acts like she's five."

I said, "She's not *that* bad."

Tammy gave me a look.

"Don't give me the pity look," I said.

"Hey, if the pity fits," Tammy said, taking

another bite. Somehow she'd managed to eat almost all her sandwich in three bites. I hadn't even started mine. I picked it up, sighed, and put it down again.

"Okay, fine. It fits," I said.

"Face it, Nora, your life sucks."

"I've *been* facing it. If you could tell me how I could run away from it, that would be great. Now, that's some advice I could use."

"Leave," Tammy said bluntly—and not for the first time.

"But how would you get by without me?"

"Please. Abandon me here. I'd love to see you do it."

"All right. Maybe I will."

Tammy rolled her eyes at me. "That wasn't exactly convincing."

"I could surprise you," I said.

"Yeah, right. Okay. Let's settle this once and for all."

Tammy wiped her fingers on her napkin and held out her hand, waiting for me to put my hand in hers. We had been doing this since middle school. It started when Tammy read a novel in which a psychic was able to tell a person's future by taking their hand and asking a question.

Tammy decided that she was a psychic, and she wanted to try it with me as her guinea pig. We tested it by asking when I was going to get my period (Tammy had already gotten hers. It seemed she always managed to hit the important life mile-stones before I did). Tammy had taken my hand and asked the question, and then, she told me, it was as if a date appeared in her head, like it was written on a piece of paper. The date was February 2, five months distant, which when you're in seventh grade feels like forever. So I proceeded to completely forget about it—until February 2 came around, and I got my period that morning in the middle of social studies class. I missed all of the Boer War in the bathroom. I still don't know what it was about.

Tammy had been predicting for me ever since. She predicted my first kiss and my first boyfriend. She told me where I was going to go to college, where I was going to grad school, that I wouldn't finish grad school, and that I would move home. (I remember how much I laughed at that one when she predicted it.)

It didn't work every time. There were days when she didn't get anything; she said it was just like a blank. That's what happened the few times she tried to predict for a couple of other friends. She said it was just a blank. But for some reason it usually worked with me, and when she made a prediction, it was never wrong. Not once.

This should have scared me. I don't know why it didn't. Maybe it just seemed like part of my friendship with Tammy. Her mother was always a little different, what people called "crunchy," with long skirts and always talking about horoscopes and Mercury in retrograde.

But I think it didn't scare me because, deep down, I didn't really believe in it. In some ways, I can't really blame myself for it. Who would believe it—even with all the evidence Tammy had provided over the years? Believing it would mean that nothing is really what we think it is. So instead, in the face of the evidence, I chose to believe that the world is solid and ordinary and familiar. Like everyone does.

As I put my hand in Tammy's, I said, "We've tried it before. It doesn't work for this question." We had already attempted to find out when I might be leaving; Tammy always came up with a blank.

"It hasn't worked yet," Tammy corrected me as she took my hand. Her palms were dry and warm.

We both closed our eyes, and the heat seemed to intensify like an oven as Tammy pressed my hand between hers.

I felt it—or I thought I did—the little spark of electricity going from me to her. It was as if I had all the information about my own life, and I was just passing it along for her to decode.

I opened my eyes. She opened hers at the exact same time.

And she said, "Don't go."

"Don't go? What do you mean, don't go? Don't go where?"

"Don't leave. Stay here with your mother."

"Wait a minute," I said. "You spend the last three years telling me to go, and now you're telling me not to? Are you saying I'm doomed to spend the rest of my life trapped here?"

I was half joking, but Tammy didn't even crack a smile. Her eyes looked far away, as if she was still looking at my future.

"No, that's the problem—I see you leaving."

"On a long journey, right?" I joked.

That's when Tammy said the words I never thought she'd say: "It's not funny. It will look like you're getting everything you thought you wanted. But it's not safe. Listen to me, okay? It's not safe."

"Aw, you care," I said, teasing her.

Tammy scowled at me.

"Come on, you are not the kind of girl who worries," I reminded her.

Finally, at that comment, her eyes refocused on me, and she snorted—and the Tammy I knew was back.

"Oh, that's right," she said. "I forgot for a second—I'm the kind of girl who doesn't give a shit. Thank God. It must be this house. The atmosphere of caring and obligation is suffocating. I've got to get out of here."

She stood up, brushing the crumbs off her shirt—and onto the floor.

"Wait a second. You mean you're not going to tell me any more than that?"

"Not today," she said. "Let's see what happens. Maybe I'm wrong, and you will be stuck here forever. In that case, it won't matter."

"You're such a comfort to me."

"Call me tomorrow, and let me know if anything happens," she said.

"I call you almost every day anyway. But nothing ever happens, so I seriously doubt anything interesting is going to happen by tomorrow."

But I was wrong about that.

Timothy

The Family Dinner

My mother had no soul. That's what I thought when I looked up from the dinner table at her.

I thought that every week when we gathered for the family dinner, or, rather, what counted as family according to my mother.

Andrew, the next oldest after me, always greeted my mother with a peck on the cheek, saying, "Nancy and the kids send their love." Nancy was his wife, but I very much doubted that Nancy and the kids really did send their love—because they were not invited to the family dinner. Ever.

My sister, Emily, had once tried simply showing up with husband number two, but my mother dealt with that situation by refusing to let anyone bring a chair for him. After standing around awkwardly for a few minutes, he left. Emily never even tried with husband number three.

I had never had a wife to be excluded and neither had my younger brother, Edward. In some ways Edward and I were alike, but he was a more extreme version—if you think I'm an asshole, you should see Edward.

Our weekly family dinner wasn't just any dinner. To see it, you'd think we were celebrating some huge milestone like a twenty-fifth wedding anniversary or a fiftieth birthday party, but that was just the way my mother did things—perfectly. The table was set with silver and crystal and china and flowers and silver tureens. The food was prepared by a different chef every week, even though no one ever seemed to eat much.

"Tell me again, Timothy, where is the portfolio now?" my mother asked me, while carving a tiny piece of the chicken. She cut her food into pieces so small I didn't know how she managed to chew them.

Before I could answer my mother's question, Emily jumped in.

"Can't we wait until after dinner to talk about this?" she whined. "Listening to Timothy talk about money makes me lose my appetite."

"Give me a break," I said to Emily. "Don't bring me into it. You haven't eaten since 1986." That was the first time she went into the hospital for anorexia. She was twelve at the time.

"Timothy, don't be cruel," my mother said, but I swear she was smiling. Then she turned to Emily to explain. "Darling, we have to talk about finances. Don't you know what's going on in the market?" she said gently—as if my sister wouldn't know about the financial crisis that was the front page of every newspaper in the country.

Emily was in reality probably smarter than all the rest of us combined, but my mother treated her like an idiot. And unfortunately, most of the time my sister insisted on living up to her expectations. She never had a job, and she had been married three times, once for only three hours. You are probably getting the picture: my sister was not the most stable person.

"I just don't see why we have to talk about it while we're eating," Emily said.

"I promise I won't talk if I actually see you eating," I told her.

"Mind your own goddamned business," she said.

"Anyway, Timothy, you were saying?" my mother tuned back to me.

I managed the family's money, and normally it was a drudgery to report back to my mother, but I had been looking forward to this moment all week.

"We lost fifteen percent of the portfolio's value," I told her.

My mother practically choked on her tiny piece of chicken. It was priceless. Really. An undignified, uncontrolled reaction from my mother; it would have been worth double what we lost just to see it.

She recovered quickly, pressing her napkin to her mouth. Then she said, "Please tell me you're joking, Timothy."

"I wouldn't joke about that," I said truthfully.

I took my job seriously. I enjoyed it, and I did it

well. But I knew that to be good at making money you had to be good at losing it. It was something my mother didn't understand.

"This is not acceptable. This is not how I expect you to take care of your family. Do you want to land us in the poorhouse?"

That was one of her favorite lines: "Do you want to land us in the poorhouse?" But she was the one who was working on that destination. I knew because, managing the family money, I had a window into how much everyone spent. And my mother was frightening in her ability to spend money; that is, if anything could frighten me. If she couldn't do it, then nothing would—that's what I thought anyway.

I cut off a piece of the chicken on my plate and took a cautious bite. It tasted like chicken dessert. Had the chef used cinnamon? It was probably the latest food trend. Whatever it was, it was disgusting. But it had served as the delaying tactic I wanted—making my mother wait for my answer.

"We've lost less than last year's profits," I told her.

But my mother didn't want to hear that the situation wasn't as dire as she was making it out to be.

"I don't want to hear excuses. I want you to get that money back. In the meantime, the rest of you need to limit your spending. Now that we don't have the same resources, we need to think about conserving."

"We could cut back a lot just by scaling back the family dinners," I suggested.

"Family time is *not* where you cut back," my mother snapped.

She glared at me, but I didn't back down. I just stared back. It was like looking straight into the Gorgon's eyes—just in case you wonder why I'm stone.

When she turned away from me, it was clear I was done.

On weeks when the report for the portfolio was good, I had to go into the details of all the trades. Sometimes it lasted the whole dinner, talking about the money we'd made. With the bad news, she never wanted to hear the details. But even when her questions about the portfolio lasted most of dinner, I considered myself lucky. My weekly examination was only about money. The rest of the family had to endure her poking around in their private lives.

Today, after she was done with me, she raked Andrew over the coals about his boys and whether they'd gotten into what she considered the "right" private school. And in her estimation, only one was the "right" one. This was of paramount importance, even though his older boy was just going into kindergarten, and the other was barely pre-K.

After Andrew, Edward got nailed on whether he had finished the draft of his book yet. He wanted to be the next Hemingway. He had the lifestyle and the women part down, but the writing part didn't seem to be going as well. He'd been working on the great American novel for the last twelve years.

Emily got interrogated about how much she weighed. Today she claimed to have gained three pounds. My mother didn't believe her. She sent Mary, the housekeeper, to get the scale from the bathroom and bring it to the dining room. Then my mother made my sister get on it. That's when I knew my mother must really be in a bad mood. She hadn't done that for a while.

My father was the only one who escaped questioning, but he lived with her. Who knew what happened when she got him alone? And I think there was the sense that he let her have full rein as long as she respected his boundaries. Those boundaries did not include any protection for us, his children. They never had.

As all this was going on, I tried the other things on my plate. There was some dark red whipped thing. I think it was made of beets, but I can't be sure. The chicken was out. The only things safe to eat were three tiny fingerling potatoes and seven string beans. The way she fed us, I don't know how my mother expected Emily to weigh anything.

The dinner went pretty much the same way dinner went every week. But what happened at the end was one of those tiny moments that seem inconsequential but that end up changing your life.

After my mother finished interrogating the others, she turned back to me. It was obvious that my report on the portfolio was still bothering her.

"Timothy," she said, "I am going to arrange for you to see Warren. I think he might be able to give you some guidance. At the very least, maybe he can teach you to have a little more respect and concern for your position in this family."

"Mother, I don't think Warren is going to have the time right—"

"You'll take the plane to Omaha tomorrow morning. I think it's best that you be out there so you're available when he has a moment."

I tried again. "Mother, this might not be the best time for me to leave the office. There's a lot going on in the market right now. I need to be here—"

"You're going." The way she said it I knew there was no negotiating with her.

There was only one person who could veto her.

I looked to my father. He sometimes would intercede on money issues since he was the one who had made the bulk of it—in bowling alleys and strip malls and retirement homes. He had the Midas touch when it came to money, if in nothing else.

But today was not one of the days when he was willing to step in. When I looked at him, he just shrugged. "You might as well see what Buffett has to say. It can't hurt."

That's how I ended up going to Omaha first thing Monday morning.

THE INVESTIGATION

VICTIMOLOGY

In the manual *Practical Homicide Investigation*, it states that victimology is one of the most significant factors in death investigation.

Victimology is "the collection and assessment of all significant information as it relates to the victim and his or her lifestyle" (Geberth, p. 21).

Basically, it boils down to a simple question: who was the victim, and what was going on in his or her life at and before the time of the event?

In the inquiry, every detail is relevant. You never know where you will find the meaning in the minutia that illuminates the whole.

Nora

What Happened After Tammy Left

After Tammy left, I got a burst of energy. I think it was Tammy's prediction that I was going to be leaving. I don't know if I believed her, but just the idea of leaving was enough to get me going. I spent the next few hours cleaning the house, scrubbing the black gook off the stove, wiping the food splatter out of the microwave, throwing out all the things in the fridge that were growing mold, vacuuming the huge dust balls that had gathered under tables and in the corners, and wiping the thick layer of dust off the TV and the hall table and the bookshelf.

I didn't often get the urge to clean, but when I did, I loved the feeling of accomplishment. But this time, when I finished and looked around, instead of feeling satisfaction all I could think about was the fact that it was just going to get dirty again.

It all went downhill from there, and late that night I ended up sitting at the computer doing yet another Google search on the survival rates of patients with acute lymphoblastic leukemia, which was the type of leukemia my mother had. It was a macabre activity, but I couldn't seem to help it. No matter how often I looked, the survival rates didn't get any better. For kids, the odds were pretty good: 85 percent survived. For adults it was an even fifty-fifty. I was always trying to find better numbers, as if some words on a screen could change the outcome of my mother's disease.

I was so absorbed in the computer, I didn't even notice when my mother came down the stairs behind me. I just heard her voice say, "Honey?"

Even before I turned around, I could hear that the fight of the morning was over.

I had forgotten to turn on the lamp, so I was working by the light of the monitor, and when I turned around, in the darkness, in her white nightgown and her short haircut, she almost looked like a child. I had a strange sense of unreality, as if our positions were switched and I was the mother. At that moment, I felt a surge of feeling flood through me; I think it's how a mother might love: fiercely, without reason. Love isn't reasonable; I stopped looking for reason in it long ago.

Then my mother turned on the light, and I noticed that her toenails were freshly painted: small, perfect ovals of pink. There was something about those nails that just killed me, the color against her pale skin. It wasn't the big things that got me the most—it was these small acts of bravery.

"Honey," my mother said again, "I was wondering if you could maybe get me some ice cream? And some ginger ale? I think that might help settle my stomach."

"Of course. Of course I can," I said. I got up, grabbed my wallet and my jacket, and said, "I'll be right back." I knew ice cream and ginger ale weren't going to fix anything, but the illusion of being able to make things better, even if just for a moment, felt good.

That feeling lasted exactly ten minutes—until I got to the 7-Eleven and saw the blue Camry with the license plate beginning with "CHI" and the dent over the left rear wheel.

I checked my watch. It was past ten o'clock, so the 7-Eleven was the only place in town still open. I could have driven by, made a big loop in the car and doubled back, hoping I would have wasted enough time that he would be gone—that's the kind of thing I had been doing for the last three years. But suddenly, tonight, the effort of it seemed too much to keep up.

So I parked in the lot and went into the store and picked up a red plastic basket from the stack near the door. I went straight to the wall with the freezers that held the ice cream and picked out a pint of Häagen-Dazs vanilla. Then I headed toward the back of the store where they had the refrigerated cases with the sodas.

Dan was there when I rounded the end of the aisle. And he must have known I was in the store, because when he saw me, there wasn't even the hint of surprise.

We were together for ten years, engaged for two of them, and it was now almost three years since I had seen him. In front of me stood the object and focus of probably 50 percent of my thoughts since I had been a teenager.

That was ironic, because before I fell for him (during senior year of high school), I couldn't have been less interested. He seemed to me just another big, blond football player, handsome in an obvious, ordinary way. For most of high school, I imagined myself to be different. I knew I didn't want the obvious—even if the obvious was good-looking and popular. Dan was a walking caricature of the obvious.

After I fell in love, I couldn't see him that way. He was just . . . himself. And for almost a decade (Tammy called it "the eternity"), that's what he was to me. But now, standing in the aisle in the 7-Eleven, after not seeing him for three years, I discovered that the big, blond football player was all I could see. Except that now his good looks were being chipped away by wrinkles, and he was a little soft around the middle where there used to be nothing but skin and muscle.

While avoiding him these past three years, I had worried about how much it would hurt to see him. But the surprise was that it didn't hurt. It turned out that those three years had turned him into a stranger—a stranger with a baby strapped to his chest. A sleeping baby wearing a pink dress. A girl.

"Nora," he said.

"Hello, Dan," I replied.

"It's been too long," he said.

If anything, I had the feeling that it wasn't quite long enough, so I didn't know what to say.

Then I thought of something.

"How is Stacey?" I asked.

Stacey was his wife—the one he'd broken up with me for, and then married in a shotgun wedding a month later. Six months after that, they had Dan Junior. (And from the little girl strapped to his chest, it was obvious they had decided to give Dan Junior a baby sister.)

His wife, Stacey, had been in high school with us. She had been a cheerleader, and I remember her giggling a lot in the back of the room during the one class I had with her. Dan's life had ended up exactly like I thought it would before I knew him: football player marries cheerleader and joins his father's company. But being right about it didn't give me any comfort, because there was that little detour in the middle where I thought maybe I would marry the football player. When my stereotype turned out to be true, the joke was on me.

"Stacey's fine," Dan said. "She's fine."

One more fine and I wasn't going to believe him.

"Good. I'm glad." I paused. Then, not quite as smoothly as I would have liked, I said, "Well, I wish I could talk, but I need to get going." I took a step back, because it seemed strange to just turn my back on him.

"Don't go yet," he said.

"I'm sorry, maybe we can talk another time," I said, not meaning it.

When I took another step away, he repeated more urgently, "Don't go. Please."

It's hard to walk away when someone says that to you. I found I couldn't do it. So I waited, but Dan didn't say anything else. I shifted my gaze to the baby on his chest. The little girl was sleeping: her head lolled against his chest, her face slack, and her mouth open in that perfect baby pout. Sometimes babies look like strange versions of their parents, but this baby didn't seem to look like either Stacey or Dan. It just looked like a generic baby, with the small button nose, the pouty lips, long eyelashes, and light downy hair.

The silence went on so long that I started to think I might be able to escape after all. I didn't realize that the length of the silence was really just an indication of how uncomfortable the topic of conversation was going to be.

Finally, Dan burst out, "Nora, what happened to us? Remember when we thought we'd never be apart? What happened to that?"

It took me a second for my brain to process the words.

"I don't think this is exactly the time or place, Dan," I said. It wasn't my most inspired response; it was trite and cliché, but it was also true. There were Tostitos on one side of us, and cheese in a can on the other.

He wasn't really listening to me though. "That's what I always hear. I want to know, when is the time and place? Can you tell me that?" He threw out his arms in a gesture that would have been dramatic if he hadn't had a sleeping baby strapped to his chest. As he threw his arms out, the baby's head bobbled—it blinked, and then settled back into sleep.

I glanced down at the baby, I thought quite pointedly, and said, "I can't tell you. I think maybe you should try talking to your wife about that."

Dan didn't seem to notice the glance, and he seemed oblivious to the fact that he might not be talking to the most receptive audience.

He shook his head stubbornly, "But she's the one who always says it's not the right time or place. I want to talk to someone who will listen. Someone who knows me."

He was obviously going to need a bit more of a direct hint I decided.

"Then you definitely have the wrong person," I told him firmly. "It's been a long time, Dan. We don't know each other anymore."

I thought that would surely do it. But it didn't.

"You're wrong," he insisted. "I know you. And you know me. I'm the same person you knew back when we were together. I haven't changed."

I wanted to ask him who that was. Because there was the person I thought I knew, and then I came home one vacation to a man who had cheated on me and was leaving me for another woman. On that day I realized the Dan I thought I knew was gone—had in fact never existed.

"Maybe *I* have," I said. "Maybe I've changed." I wanted that to be true.

"No," he said. "You haven't. I know you haven't. What you're doing for your mother . . ."

I didn't like the idea of him knowing anything about my life. "How do you know about that?" I asked.

"Nora, come on. It's not exactly a big town here. Haven't you noticed?"

"Yes, I've noticed," I said, thinking of all the times over the years I'd seen the dented blue Camry in the parking lot of the Price Chopper, parked in front of the video store, idling outside the hardware store, and I'd kept on driving past what had been my destination.

As if reading my mind, he said, "I don't understand how I haven't seen you more. I think about you. I think about us. What we could have had. I feel like nothing in my life has gone right since we broke up."

How many times had I imagined this moment? I had imagined what hearing those words would give me—not that it would take all the pain away, but I thought it might give me back a sense of not having been so completely and disastrously wrong.

All of a sudden, something in his face tugged out the echo of an old memory—the memory of what I used to feel when I looked at him.

"And?" I asked.

"And I want to spend time with you," he said earnestly. "Could we do that? I miss having you in my life."

Then the baby stirred on his chest—a visible reminder of the intervening years, the betrayal, the hurt: the ocean of hurt.

"What's her name?" I asked him.

"Courtney." He looked down at the baby, and he smiled. It was involuntary, genuine, real. It was a smile I realized I'd never seen on his face. And without knowing why, my heart started to ache.

"How old is she?" I asked.

"Six weeks." Dan caught one of her tiny hands between his fingers. He was still in full confessional mode. "Stacey found out she was pregnant . . . and we thought . . . well, things hadn't been going so well, and we thought it might help. It was so good at the beginning, when we had Dan Junior."

The ache intensified, I observed, almost dispassionately. Now it had an object; it hurt to hear that he'd been happy when I'd been so miserable.

He went on, "But it didn't. I mean, it hasn't . . . helped. At all. Not between me and Stacey. If anything, it's worse now."

"When did you decide that you were going to leave Stacey?" I asked.

The moment I said it, I knew something was wrong.

He shifted from one foot to the other and smiled—but it was about as different a smile as you could get from the one I'd just seen when he looked at his baby. This one was nervous, uncomfortable, apologetic.

"I . . . well . . . the thing is, Courtney's so young. I couldn't leave. Not just yet anyway. When she gets a little older . . ."

I knew what he was saying, but somehow I couldn't quite believe it.

"So what exactly did you mean when you said you wanted to spend time with me?" I asked. What's usually said about cheaters is, "If they do it with you, they'll do it to you." He wanted to turn that around. He'd done it to me, and now he wanted to do it with me. He had nerve—that was for sure. And when we were together, I thought it was the one thing he lacked.

"Well . . . I mean . . . I miss you. My marriage is basically over, even if I can't leave. And I guess I thought you might be lonely too. I haven't heard that you've been dating anyone. It's been a long time. Maybe you've been thinking about me too? I thought maybe you never really got over us."

"You mean you thought that if I couldn't be with you, I wouldn't want to be with anyone?" There should have been emotion in that question. But the emotion had been missing from my life for so long that maybe it was just cleaned out—like someone had taken a big vacuum and sucked it all away.

He said, "I don't know. Not exactly. But . . . well, you're not with anyone else, are you?" Then he added, "I think you know that it doesn't get better than we had."

This was so ridiculous, that I couldn't help it—I laughed. Right in his face. And the words just slipped out. I said, "Oh, Lord, I hope to God you're not right about that. That would be terrible."

He looked incredibly offended. Finally, something had gotten through to him.

For one moment I could see clearly. I'd spent so much time imagining him as the one who had it all together—who had a wife and a family and a good job and a life—but there in the store it seemed very clear to me that even though he appeared to have everything, he in fact had no more than I did. And maybe less.

It was one of those rare moments when all the trappings of life drop away and you see the person standing in front of you, almost, it seems, from the inside out rather than the outside in. If only we could all look at each other in that way. The outside wouldn't even exist. It doesn't anyway. It's just a trick of the mind. Like the illusion created by a magician.

I said firmly, but not unkindly, "I've got to go. I'll see you, Dan."

The ginger ale was just past him, down the aisle. So I slid by, found a bottle, and put it in my basket. Then I circled around and went back to the freezer to put back the pint of ice cream I'd gotten, and which had already started to melt, to change it for a new one. (My mother loved ice cream frozen so hard you practically had to chip it out of the carton. She always kept our freezer on the coldest setting, and it looked like an arctic ice cap with a thick layer of frost and stalactites dripping from the ceiling.) After exchanging the ice cream, I went up to the counter to buy the two items I'd come for. I thought Dan had left the store by then, but I wasn't sure.

The clerk was a woman in her fifties, with hair that had been badly dyed so the gray somehow showed through the too-bright red. I thought she was looking at me funny as she rang up the two items and put them in a bag. And then, when she gave me back my change, she patted my hand and said, "You did real good."

I probably should have been horrified that this

woman had overheard the conversation. But her words were clearly heartfelt, and in that moment they seemed to be one of those kindnesses—so small, so real, so unnecessary, and at the same time so genuine—like my mother's painted toenails.

"Thank you," I said.

Then I took the ice cream and ginger ale home to my mother, and we ate it in front of the television while watching someone win $800,000 on a cable rerun of *Millionaire*. And for an hour or so, even with everything wrong, life seemed perfect.

Timothy

After the Family Dinner

I left the family dinner ravenous. I know that's very Freudian, but it almost always happened that way. After a three-course meal, I would leave and feel absolutely empty. Sometimes I went home like that, but then it always took forever to fall asleep. I understood why they keep watchdogs hungry if they want them to be alert.

Edward followed me out after the dinner, and as I stepped to the curb to hail a cab, he said, "You hungry?"

"Yeah," I said. "Starving."

"Ray's?"

"Sure," I agreed.

We took a cab to one of the dozens of Famous Ray's pizza places—this one near his apartment in the West Village. I remembered the fit my mother had when Edward decided to move to the West Village. In her opinion, the Upper East Side was the only place to live. But Edward was smart. He'd waited to tell her until the purchase had gone through and he'd signed the contracts on the sale of his old place. Of course, he needed me to keep quiet about it, but I was happy to do it, mostly because I knew how angry it would make our mother.

I escaped the Upper East Side by moving down to Tribeca, but I had the excuse that I wanted to be closer to the financial district. That worked for my mother. The money excuse always did.

When we got to Ray's, I ordered two plain slices, and Edward got a slice piled with so much crap on top you could barely tell it was a slice of pizza.

"So, what's the latest?" I asked him as we waited by the counter for our slices to heat up.

"Emily thinks she's found husband number four," Edward told me.

"Good luck to her with getting our mother to say yes to that," I said.

Emily would have to get our mother's permission if she wanted to stay on the payroll. She—or rather her three ex-husbands—had gone through all her money, and now she was on a monthly allowance doled out by Mother.

"She might not need to. This one is loaded," Edward said.

"Really?" I was interested. This didn't sound like my sister's type of husband. "Mother might even approve of him then."

"Oh, I don't think so." Edward grinned.

"What's the catch?"

"He's Colombian."

I snorted. That was why I could stand to be around Edward. At least he had a sense of humor, even if it was a dark one.

"Drug money?" I asked.

"No, I'm not sure where the money is from. Probably graft, bribes, that kind of thing. But maybe drugs too. Who knows." Edward smiled, seemingly delighted at the prospect.

I noticed two women sitting at one of the dirty Formica tables at the back of the restaurant, staring at us.

Edward noticed them a second after I did. His smile got bigger.

"Edward, don't," I said.

He just winked at me and sauntered over to them.

"Hello, ladies," he said.

They giggled as if that was the funniest thing they ever heard. But I knew those two were about to stop laughing, because I knew what was coming next. I'd seen Edward do it before.

He said to the women, "If you ever want to fuck, you can call me," and he flicked two cards onto the table.

The cards he gave them had a phone number and nothing else. Edward had a special phone for the number on that card, so he always knew that a call to that number was going to be a random woman who he had no serious interest in.

Just as I predicted, they stopped laughing. Their faces kind of froze, as if they weren't certain he'd actually said what they thought he said.

Edward didn't wait for a response; he simply

turned and walked away. But I noticed they didn't throw the cards away. That phone of his rang a lot.

When Edward came back, he grinned at me.

I just shook my head at him. "What else is going on with the family?" I asked.

"Andrew's brats got rejected from that school Mother wants them to go to," he said.

"But he wrote the school a check for an obscene amount." Actually, I had been the one to write the check in his name, so I knew, and I knew the obscene amount down to the dollar.

Edward nodded. "And they said thank you very much for the money and no to the nasty little munchkins."

"That should make for a fun dinner next week."

"I think he's waiting until they get them in somewhere else. I say send them to public school. Toughen them up a bit."

Our slices came out, and we carried them over to a table.

"Anything else?" I asked. I figured I might as well get all the information out of him before he hit me up for the favor I knew was coming.

Edward had just taken a bite of his pizza, and I had to wait for him to finish chewing to get my answer. I didn't know how he could eat pizza when it was that hot. Whenever I took a bite as fast as he did, I ended up burning the top of my mouth. Maybe all that crap he got on top didn't get as hot as the cheese.

"Mother got kicked off another board," Edward offered after he swallowed.

I rolled my eyes. "Anything else *interesting*," I amended. Our mother was always getting invited on to boards, and then getting kicked off. "The old man?" I asked.

"Who knows. He plays it close to the vest, you know," Edward said.

I knew.

"Did I dance enough?" Edward asked.

That was the deal. Edward told me the scoop on the family gossip but always in exchange for something. My brother was not one to give away anything that might be potentially valuable for free.

"All right, what do you want?"

"Twenty thousand."

"Are you going to tell me what it's for?"

Edward just looked at me.

"All right," I said. "Stop by the office this week. I'll tell Marie, and she'll take care of it."

"Why Marie?" he started to ask. Then he remembered. "Oh, that's right. Because you'll be partying in Nebraska. You get to dole out the money to the rest of us, so it's only right that you should have to dance to someone's fiddle."

I shrugged.

He looked at me for a second. "You don't care, do you?"

I took a cautious bite. It was the biting that

64

scorched the top of your mouth—when you had to bite down with your front teeth to cut through the crust. You could eat pizza hotter if you used a knife and fork, but no self-respecting New Yorker ate pizza with a knife and fork.

I chewed, washed it down with some soda, then said, "No, not really."

"That's your secret, isn't it? You don't care about anything or anyone."

I couldn't tell if he said it with disgust or admiration. But the truth was, I didn't care about that either.

He went on, and what he said next sounded like a kind of curse. He said, "God help you if you ever do start to care. You won't be used to it, and you'll suffer."

I just took another bite. That didn't even deserve an answer.

Edward took the hint, and we ate our pizza in silence.

Even with two slices, I was done before him. I stood up. "Got to go, Eddie."

He hated when I called him that.

"You're a bastard," he said.

I smiled. That was another reason why I liked Edward. He told the truth.

THE INVESTIGATION

LIE DETECTION

In a homicide investigation, there are two sources of information: evidence and people. The main difference between the two is that evidence doesn't lie.

An investigator working with the second source, people, must be able to discern trustworthy information from information that is suspect.

A June 8, 2007, *ScienceDaily* article reveals new investigative interviewing strategies. Investigators are generally trained to watch for both visual and verbal cues: ability to hold eye contact or body movement indicating nervousness (such as shifting in one's seat) as well as stumbling over words or giving contradictory information.

However, the study "Interviewing to Detect Deception," funded by the Economic and Social Research Council, shows that investigators who pay attention to visual cues over speech-related cues do worse in being able to distinguish truth from lies. Liars often appear less nervous than people telling the truth. The best way to distinguish a liar is to "raise the cognitive load" by asking interviewees to repeat their stories, tell them in reverse order, or give them in more detail.

Investigations are further complicated by the fact that lying is not necessarily an admission of guilt. People can lie for many different reasons. They are not always lying to cover up a crime.

Nora

Sunday Morning, Deirdre's Visit

I was still in my nightgown when my sister arrived. I had just gotten up and was making coffee when I heard the front door. I thought it might be Tammy, except it would have taken a crisis to get her up before noon on a weekend.

When I went out into the living room, I discovered Deirdre coming in with a diaper bag over one shoulder and one of the twins asleep on the other. She looked tired, as if it were the middle of the night, after a hard day, instead of first thing in the morning.

"Is there any coffee left?" was the first thing she said to me.

"I'm only just making it now," I told her.

She looked at me and took in the nightgown. "You're not even dressed yet," she said accusingly.

"It's only seven thirty," I said.

That Deirdre was here so early meant she must have been up well before six, since she lived a good hour and a half away. And she would have had to pack the car with all the things the twins needed. It's always amazed me, not just how much work kids are, but also how much stuff you seem to need to take care of them.

"And I didn't know you were coming," I added.

It was the mildest way I could think to say it, but my sister still jumped all over it.

"What do you mean, you didn't know I was coming? I spoke to Mom this week."

"Well, she didn't tell me," I said.

"I guess maybe she doesn't tell you everything then. You think you're so *close* now, but you're not."

It usually ended up like this, but it was a bad sign that it was starting out this way. Deirdre and I had been close when we were growing up. We formed a united front against my mother and provided some protection for each other. But then she left for college, and she met Boyd (her husband), and I met Dan, and we just didn't see each other much. For a long while it seemed like it was just distance and time that came between us. But it turned into something else when I moved home. For some reason, my sister hated the fact that I was taking care of our mother during her illness. I figured it was probably guilt.

I said, "Mom might not be up for a bit. She had her fifth chemo session yesterday, you know."

"Oh really?" Deirdre acted as if she were completely uninterested. Most of the time I thought it was an act, but sometimes I wondered.

As usual, she changed the subject and said, "I've got to go get May from the car. Here, take Frankie."

When I took him, Frankie was as heavy and unwieldy as a sack of potatoes. You would never guess that when awake he turned into a whirling dervish of energy.

Deirdre returned a minute later with May. While she waited for the coffee to brew, she settled the two sleeping twins into a portable crib she had brought. Then she poured herself a cup of coffee in a travel mug, and before I knew it, was gone, mentioning something about meeting a friend in town for breakfast.

It was nine hours before my sister returned.

My mother came downstairs when the twins were just waking up. But when Frankie hit May and May started to scream, she said, "I don't feel up to this right now. I think I'll go lie back down for a bit," and she disappeared upstairs and didn't come down again. I was relieved. The one thing my sister and I agreed on was that our mother was not good with children, even her own. We knew—we had firsthand experience.

I was exhausted after two hours with the twins. I had no idea how my sister managed. After eight hours I thought I'd figured it out—at a certain point autopilot takes over, and you do it because you have to, because there's no one else.

When Deirdre finally walked in the door, I was in the living room, the twins sprawled out asleep on the sofa. I was sitting on the floor, my back against the sofa, still in my nightgown, trying to find the energy to get up and get some food. I hadn't properly eaten all day.

Deirdre came back looking like a different person. She took after our mother, small boned and birdlike, with dark brown hair that she wore in a bob. This morning her hair had been pushed back in a headband—and it looked like she hadn't even brushed it beforehand. Now it was glossy and perfectly cut and dried. She had arrived wearing gray sweatpants and a T-shirt, and now she had on a red scoop-necked top and jeans. Her nails were polished dark red to match her top. So I knew at least three places she'd been in the last nine hours: the beauty parlor, the nail salon, and the mall.

I was about to say something to her about her disappearing act, but Deirdre looked at the sleeping kids on the couch, held her finger to her lips, and pointed at the kitchen.

I nodded and got up from the floor carefully, so as not to wake them, and followed her.

"So you can't wait to go to sleep, is that it?" my sister said when we reached the kitchen and closed the door safely behind us. She was looking at my nightgown.

"No, I never changed from this morning," I said.

Deirdre laughed. "That's why I wear sweatpants and a T-shirt to bed, so if it's one of those days, no one can tell," my sister told me, giving me a view into her life that I had suspected but hadn't known for sure. I decided not to say anything about her disappearing. Deirdre didn't have an easy time of it. My life wasn't a walk in the park either, but if you compared it to twins and an alcoholic husband, my sister won.

"I need to take some coffee so I don't conk out while I'm driving home," she said as she crossed to the coffee maker. She put in a filter, then opened the jar where we used to keep the coffee.

"It's in the freezer," I told her.

"You're not supposed to put coffee in the freezer." My sister shook her head at me, as if I should have known better. "You're supposed to keep it in the fridge. The freezer destroys the oils or something. You work in a coffee store, and you don't know that?"

In fact, I knew more than that. I knew that everyone agreed on what was bad for the coffee (air, moisture, heat, and light), but no one seemed to be able to agree on whether the freezer or the fridge was better. But I didn't say that. I tended not to say what I thought to my sister. Things went more smoothly that way.

"This is regular coffee, right? If it isn't, it will be your fault if I fall asleep at the wheel and we all die," Deirdre said as she dumped three, then four, then five scoops into the filter.

Not for the first time, I thought that Deirdre and my mother had more in common than just their appearance.

"So why don't you stay here tonight?" I suggested. "You didn't even get to see Mom."

Deirdre shot me a look over her shoulder as she carried the glass carafe to the sink to fill it with water. "You're saying that like it's a bad thing?"

My sister had a point; whenever they spent more than an hour together they always ended up getting in a screaming match. It made a kind of sense—they were too much the same. Even while screaming they both had a vein right in the center of their foreheads that branched above the eyes like a wishbone and stood out and throbbed.

"You didn't even ask how she was," I said.

"No, I didn't," Deirdre said, and ran the water full blast so that I couldn't easily talk over it. When she shut it off, she said, "I don't want to talk about it, okay? We always fight when we talk about it. And I don't want to fight."

"Okay. We don't have to talk about it."

Deirdre didn't say anything else right away. She fiddled with the coffee scoop. The fine grains of coffee that clung to it drifted down to the counter like a mini brown snow flurry. She pushed them together with the side of her palm, and then left them there in a little pile.

"Do you want some food?" I asked, wondering what made her so quiet. "There are some leftovers in the fridge."

"No, thanks. I ate dinner."

Another thing she'd done while she was out. I have to admit, it hurt a little. I knew Deirdre was probably just avoiding our mother, but it felt like she was avoiding me too.

"But you can do something else for me," Deirdre went on.

"What's that?"

As I watched, she pushed her finger into the pile of grounds she'd made. She swirled her finger as if making a pattern. Then, almost abruptly, she said, "I need to borrow some money."

"How much?"

"Not a fortune or anything. Just enough to cover me for a few months. Rent and groceries and diapers."

This wasn't going to go well, I thought.

"Well?" Deirdre demanded, when I didn't answer right away. "Don't tell me you're going to give me a hard time about this. It's not like you've got a whole lot of expenses. Seems to me like you've got it pretty easy living rent free. Bet Mom pays for the food too, right? What do you even need any money for?"

We had never talked about the details of my staying here.

"Actually, Mom doesn't pay for anything," I told her.

She looked at me as if I had started speaking in a foreign language. "What do you mean, Mom doesn't pay for anything?"

"I mean I pay for the food and the mortgage and the bills. I pay for everything."

"Bullshit."

I shrugged.

"Bullshit," Deirdre said again with even more feeling. "How long has this been going on?"

"For three years. Since right after I moved home. You know when she got sick she had to leave her job at the bank. And she told me she didn't have the money, so I paid."

"That's such crap," Deirdre said. "She's got to have something. I mean, I know she was just a secretary, but she was there for years. She must have gotten some retirement or something. Some savings . . . something."

"I don't know anything about it except what she told me. Why don't you ask her, if you want to know." I suddenly felt exhausted. I sat down in one of the kitchen chairs.

"I really need the money, Nor. Seriously."

I wondered if using my childhood nickname was unconscious or some sort of strategy, an attempt to call on the old times, old loyalties, old affection. Whatever it was, I matched her nickname for nickname.

"I don't have it, D. I'm sorry. But I just don't have it."

"You want us to be out on the street?" my sister said, almost desperately. If it was an act, it was a good one.

"You're not going to be out on the street. Boyd wouldn't let that happen."

"Boyd's gone," Deirdre said quietly.

I looked up at my sister. Deirdre was standing there, looking lost. I'd never seen my sister look quite like that before.

"He's left before, and he's always come back," I said.

Boyd was a binge drinker. He sometimes went months without drinking, he went to meetings, he did everything he was supposed to do. Then he'd disappear for a week, sometimes two. Once I think he disappeared for a month, and my sister was convinced he was dead somewhere. When he showed up, he was always full of apologies. He would promise it would never happen again. But it always did.

"No," my sister said. "It's different this time. He's not off drinking somewhere. He left me for someone else. Someone he met in AA. He says she understands him. She'll help him stay clean, unlike me. Apparently I drive him to drink. And he never wanted the twins. He says he can't be sober and handle the pressures of being a father."

"But he can't just leave. He still has to help you. He can't just abandon all his responsibilities."

"Oh, come on, Nor. Grow up. It's Boyd we're talking about. What else has he been doing all his life but abandoning his responsibilities? Sometimes I think he's not even really an alcoholic. I think it just gives him an excuse to disappear, and that every time he leaves, he's really secretly hoping I won't take him back. That I'll drop him like a hot potato, like what happened with all his jobs. His bosses—they could see the writing on the wall. Why couldn't I? But no, I had to go have babies with him because I thought I could get him to straighten up that way. What a joke. Even before the babies, it was too much for him. He had to escape when it was just me. Why did I think that loading on more would make it better?"

She paused for a moment, then she said suddenly, "You knew."

"Me?" I hadn't seen this coming.

"Yes. I still remember what you said to me when you first met him."

I had no memory of it. "What did I say?" I asked.

"Well, you said he seemed fun."

"He was," I said, recalling Boyd's antics that first night I met him. He seemed to take special delight in making me laugh, no matter how outrageous he had to get.

I also remembered how jealous Dan had gotten. He said he didn't like Boyd, didn't trust him, thought I should tell my sister he was bad news. And then, sometime later, he asked me why I never laughed at *his* jokes. That comment in itself would have been funny if Dan hadn't been serious. But that was the thing—Dan was always serious. Then he said (and I remembered this later) that couples should laugh more than we did. I remembered that when he left me for Stacey the giggler.

"But it was what you said after that that I'm talking about," Deirdre said.

"I liked Boyd. I don't think I said anything bad about him."

"You said that he couldn't sit still."

"Oh. Right."

It was true. I don't think Boyd stayed seated in a chair for more than five minutes the whole night.

"And you asked me what it was like to be in a relationship with someone who couldn't sit still. I tried to forget about it at the time. After all, look at who you were with—you weren't the best judge of men."

I thought of the encounter at the 7-Eleven the night before. For once I could wholeheartedly agree with my sister.

She went on, "But I never forgot when you asked me that. And I can tell you the answer now. Exhausting. It's exhausting to be with someone like that. But there were also times he could sit still, and that was almost worse. It was as if he'd run out of gas, and then he'd crash—for days sometimes. And he'd just sit in front of the television, and he wouldn't move. He'd even sleep there. And you know how most of the time you couldn't shut him up? Well, it was like pulling teeth to get a couple of words out of him when he was like that. And the more we were together, the more he seemed to be like that. The other was exhausting, but that . . . that was scary. And I knew it was me. I wasn't fun enough anymore. I didn't make him happy."

"D, I know everyone says this, but it wasn't you."

Deirdre wiped her face almost angrily. My sister never cried.

"It doesn't matter," she said abruptly. "He's gone now. And he's not going to take care of what you call 'his responsibilities.' And if I don't find the rent for this month, we're going to lose the apartment. We're already behind. I really don't know what else to do. I wouldn't ask you if I had any other option. I don't like asking you for this, Nor, but I'm really desperate. I understand that you don't have the money, but maybe you can take out a loan? I tried. They turned me down. My credit is for shit."

It was true, I suddenly realized—Deirdre had a hard time asking for things.

I said reluctantly, "The thing is, I don't think the bank would let me take another loan. I could try; since Mom worked there for so long, they might make an exception, but I think the rules about it have gotten really strict."

"Another loan?"

"I had to take a loan back at the beginning of the year."

Deirdre looked as dismayed about the loan as I was whenever I thought about it. That's why I tried not to think about it. The loan had seemed to be a good idea at the time. The interest rates on my credit card were outrageously high, and Mom seemed to be better, and I thought I might be moving out. It seemed to make sense to take out a loan to pay off the credit card and cover my expenses while I looked for a job. I had to fly back and forth to Chicago a few times while looking for a job, and after I found one, I needed money for the down payment on the apartment. Of course, that was just money down the drain when our mother got sick again and I let the job and the apartment and everything go in order to stay on here.

"God, you're such a sucker. And now you won't help where it would actually do some good. I can't believe you did it for her and you won't do it for me."

"Come on, D, it's not like that. It's not like you both came to me at the same time and asked. I didn't know this was going to happen. I didn't know you'd need money."

"Whatever. You can try to sugarcoat it all you want, but basically you're saying you won't help me."

"It's not that I won't. I can't. I swear, if there were anything I could do, I would do it. Why don't you move home for a bit? I can cover most of the bills here. We can buy what we need from the store on the credit card. I can help out with looking after the kids—"

"Are you kidding me?" Deirdre said. "I would never bring my children into this house, with her. Never. I'd rather go to a homeless shelter than bring them here. In fact, I don't know how you live here. I really don't."

I didn't say anything to that. I always tried to remind myself that she had been older and wilder, and she had taken the brunt of our mother's moods when we were growing up. I remembered once when Deirdre was about nine or ten, our mother had started hitting her hard across the face—open-faced slaps that echoed with the sharp crack of force. Again and again and again. Our mother had hit us before, but this time Deirdre hit her back—and not just a slap. She delivered a dead-on right hook that gave our mother a black eye for two weeks. After that our mother never hit either of us again.

I said, "Mom's different now. She's a different person."

Usually, Deirdre got angry when I said this. But this time she just shook her head. "She's the same, Nor. She's exactly the same. You just can't see it."

"What do you mean, I can't see it? I live with her."

"That doesn't matter. You see what you want to see."

"What is that supposed to mean?"

"Nothing. Never mind. Just forget I said anything about any of this, all right? It's not your problem; it's my problem. I'll deal with it. I'll get the money somehow."

I suddenly missed being kids, when we promised that we would always be there for each other—that we would always rescue each other. Life had shown us pretty clearly that rescue wasn't always possible.

"I'm sorry that Boyd left," I said, feeling useless.

"I'm not. I'm better off without that asshole," Deirdre said. But I could tell she was lying. I could hear it in her voice—the difference between really believing something and wanting to believe something. Deirdre was trying to convince herself of something she didn't feel at all. "You're lucky Dan left you," she said. "You're lucky you're alone. It's better that way. It's not worth it."

My sister was the master of the backhanded compliment. The thing was, Deirdre was only saying aloud what I had been trying to tell myself for years.

After last night, I shouldn't have trouble believing it. I had every piece of evidence that relationships ended in a mess, a car wreck of shattered trust and broken love. But sitting in the kitchen with my sister, with the smell of the coffee brewing and the quiet of the night outside, I finally told the truth. Before this I told myself I had given up, but I hadn't. And now I voiced my hidden hope.

"I could still meet someone," I said.

Deirdre snorted. "In this town? Yeah, right."

"You never know."

And later I wondered if that moment of belief was what drew him like a magnet to me. But if I believed that, I'd have to wonder about the tragedy that was coming along with him.

Sometimes it is best not to know. I think that was why Tammy didn't tell me more about what she'd seen. She knew that sometimes the veil God draws over the future is the greatest kindness he has to give.

Timothy

Timothy Arrives in Nebraska

When I got off the jet in Omaha early Monday morning, I got a message from my assistant telling me that my meeting with Warren was not going to happen until Wednesday morning.

I could have told the crew to turn around and take me back to New York so I could be in the office to follow the surging and plunging market. But then I thought again. In financial panics, people often overreact. I had made some bets the week before, and if I went back to the office I would only second- or third-guess them. I've found, over the years, that the initial gut reaction is the one that pays. I'd read a book about how that split-second gut reaction seemed to tap into some larger intelligence. On Wall Street there is reverence for the man whose gut can be trusted—for the man who has the balls to stand behind his hunches.

My hunches were good, and people were starting to notice. The only reason I cared was that if enough people start listening to you, it becomes a self-fulfilling prophecy. You buy a stock, everyone who trusts you does the same, and like magic, the stock price goes up. Or you sell and dozens of people jump ship with you. Again you're proven right, without even needing to be right.

I decided, not only was I going to leave my bets in place, I wasn't even going to look. So I wasn't going to bother going back to New York. But I had been to Omaha before, and I knew I didn't want to spend two days there, sitting in my hotel room or sitting in some restaurant alone eating steak.

So I did what anyone would do. I rented a car. It was October, but it felt like a summer day, so I got a convertible, threw my bag in the back, and I started driving.

Nora

Nora Meets Timothy

Finally, it was Monday—heart-attack Monday—and I couldn't have been happier to go back to work.

I worked at Starbox on Washburn. Not Starbucks but Starbox. There were fewer than thirty Starbucks in the whole state of Kansas, and they were mostly in the bigger cities. About five years before, at the height of the Starbucks craze, my boss, Neil, decided our town deserved a gourmet coffee shop too. When he designed the store, he used the Starbucks layout, the Starbucks menu, and (almost) the Starbucks name. The only difference was that with the name Starbox, he thought it would be cute to put stars on the ceiling of the store.

I thought it was a miracle that he hadn't gotten sued for copyright infringement. But, then again, there would have been nothing to get. It turned out that the gourmet coffee market was not a gold mine waiting to be tapped, at least not in our town. People preferred to go to Joe's Diner and get a cup of coffee there for fifty cents, rather than coming into Starbox and paying three or four dollars for something that, as one town resident said, didn't even taste like coffee but more like some kind of liquid dessert. The people in our town didn't seem to have a lot of free time; they didn't seem to have laptops they would want to work on while sipping lattes. They liked their coffee simple, and even if they came in to take a look, they just as often left without buying anything. Almost everyone asked me, "What does 'Venti' mean?" I had to explain that it was a large. "So what is a Tall?" they asked. And I told them that was a small. Then they'd shake their heads and ask, "Then why don't you just say that?"

That was a question I couldn't answer.

As a result, a whole hour could, and often did, go by without anyone coming into the store. Then it was just my boss and me.

It was tough for the first year that I worked there. There were times I thought I might go crazy, but sometime in the second year I realized I had started to enjoy it. It happened almost without my noticing. Nothing actually changed, but somehow what had once made me miserable, now I found I enjoyed. I loved the smell of coffee. I loved the hush that descended on the store when it was empty. And I loved the big plate-glass windows that faced the empty lot across the street where the Arby's used to be before they tore it down a few years back. Beyond the empty lot there was the parking lot for the bowling alley, and beyond that I could see the wheat fields that surrounded the town, short and shorn, the stubble a pale dull tan. Every afternoon, when the sun dropped low enough in the sky, the rays streamed in over those fields, sparkling off the roofs of the cars parked for the afternoon bowling league, straight through those huge plate-glass windows.

I loved it, but the sun on those windows drove Neil crazy. He was always trying to get the glass perfectly, spotlessly, transparently clean. He was on medication for OCD, but it didn't seem to be helping. He'd declare the windows clean in the morning, but once the afternoon sun hit, streaks and smudges suddenly appeared, like invisible writing illuminated under ultraviolet light. Neil seemed to think that if only he found the right product, that first wipe of the cloth could produce a pure arc of clarity.

It seemed like every week Neil would come in with some new cleaning solution. This week was no different. That morning Neil came in with yet another bag. He'd been up to Wichita over the weekend, to the Bed Bath & Beyond up there, because he read about a product called Perfect Glass. The label made the claim, "leaves glass looking perfect!" and he'd bought a special cloth that was designed specifically for glass cleaning, also guaranteed not to leave streaks.

He was certain it was going to work this time.

I was not so hopeful. But I didn't mind. Trying to get those windows clean didn't seem more ridiculous than anything else in my life. But by midday, before the sun got low enough to hit the windows, the clouds rolled in. Outside the window, the sky was an expanse of rolling bands of dark and light and dark and light, undulating into the distance as far as I could see.

Even without the sun, Neil couldn't wait any longer. He gave me the bottle and the cloth and told me to get started. The fabric of the cloth felt strange: it was soft and should have felt nice, but it gripped the skin of my hands in a strange way that made my stomach a little queasy. I sprayed a fine mist on the clear glass and wiped it down. The cloth didn't exactly absorb the liquid. It seemed to just smear it across the glass, but with enough rubbing, it eventually dried. I sprayed again and repeated the rubbing. Neil stood behind me the whole time, with his arms crossed, his head thrown back, and his eyes in an intense squint.

After a few minutes, he said, "I think it might be working. It's definitely better. Don't you think it's better?"

"Yes. Sure," I said.

"Are you just saying that, or do you really agree?" Neil asked.

"I'm just saying it. Neil, it's not sunny. We can only see the streaks when it's sunny."

"But it could be working. It could be better. Don't you think it could be?"

"Yes. Sure. It could be."

"You're not just saying that?" he asked, half-hopefully, half-suspiciously.

I opened my mouth to answer, but I was spared from more when the bell over the door jingled.

"Customer," Neil said, unnecessarily. That was the thing with Neil. Almost everything he did was unnecessary.

I put down the cloth and the streak-free cleaner.

"Don't leave that there," Neil said. "What would that look like to customers?"

I thought that it would look like I was washing the windows, but I kept that thought to myself. I just turned back, picked up the cloth and the liquid, and stashed them behind the counter. The man was waiting for me by the time I got around behind the register.

Looking back, I can't find any sense of recognition in that moment. There was no funny feeling, no premonition that this small slice of time, this ordinary Monday afternoon, would change the course of my life. And this man's life. And the lives of everyone who was close to me.

No, all I could remember was that I noticed the suit. It wasn't his face or his eyes or his smile. It was the suit that struck me. Wearing a suit in town was not unheard of, but it was never a suit like this. The suits I saw around town were either black, for funerals, or mud brown, and usually paired with the unfortunate choice of a checked shirt and striped tie in even more unfortunate colors. But comparing the suits I usually saw with this one was like comparing a Volvo with a Lamborghini. The fabric of the suit was gray, with subtle lines that were actually tiny ridges in the cloth. And it had just the faintest sheen to it. He wore it with a pale blue shirt and a dark blue tie, also with the same little ridges in the fabric. It was very simple, but the kind of simple that cost more than a lot of people made in a month.

When I looked up from the suit to his face, I saw what I thought was the best-looking man I'd ever seen in person. He might almost have been too good-looking, with the plastic look of a magazine, but he was saved from that by the deep lines sloping across his forehead and bracketing his mouth.

I said, "Welcome to Starbox. What can I get you?"

The man squinted up at the board. At least he didn't ask the same question everyone else did. Instead, he said, "Is this a Starbucks?"

"No, it's Starbox," I said.

"Ah, I understand," he said. He paused. Then he shook his head and said, "Actually, I don't understand at all. This has been a very strange day."

"Maybe a coffee will help," I suggested. Then I happened to look over his shoulder and catch sight of Neil mouthing something. Unfortunately, I knew exactly what he was trying to tell me.

I sighed and said, "Might I recommend our special drink of the month, pumpkin-spice latte?"

I hoped I put the right amount of lack of enthusiasm into my voice. The special drink was like drinking pureed pumpkin. Neil had gotten the name off the Starbucks Web site, but the recipe was his. And it was disgusting. But Neil thought it was a masterpiece, and he wanted me to recommend it to everyone that came into the store. So far, not one person had taken me up on it. Until now.

"If you think it's good," the man said, "I'll try it."

"Are you sure?" I said, trying to shake my head at him subtly so he would get the message, and Neil wouldn't notice.

But it turned out that the man didn't notice and Neil did. Neil was glaring at me as the man said, "Your recommendation is good enough for me."

I turned around to make the pumpkin spice. I thought maybe if I added less of the pumpkin syrup, it might make it a little less disgusting, but when I tried to put just one pump in the cup, I turned to find Neil standing right behind me.

"Nora, it's four squirts of the pumpkin syrup. How many times did I go over this?"

"I'm sorry, Neil," I said, turning back and reluctantly putting three more pumps of the liquid in the cup.

"Do you want me to make the rest of it?" he said. "Or do you think you can get it right?"

"I can do it," I assured him. "It's fine."

"It's not fine," Neil said. "One squirt is not fine."

I ignored him and went on making the drink. Neil went back around the counter, but I could feel him watching me, ready to pounce if I made another mistake in his recipe.

I finished the drink, fit a travel lid on the cup, and gave a silent prayer that the man wouldn't try it until he was out of the store. Then I brought it over to the register where he was waiting and rang it up.

"That will be $3.82," I said.

The man reached inside the jacket of the beautiful suit and brought out his wallet. He handed me a twenty, then picked up the drink, peeled back the plastic flap of the lid, and raised the cup to me, smiling, and took a sip.

Then his smile disappeared.

"Is everything okay?" I asked.

He bravely summoned the smile back up. "Wonderful," he said, as he put the cup carefully back down on the counter—as if it might leap up and bite him. "But maybe I could get a regular latte as well? Double shot, Venti, with skim."

"Of course," I said.

I packed the coffee grounds into the double espresso filter-cup, fit it into the machine, and ran it. Then I foamed the milk and poured it into the cup, put on the lid, and brought it back over to the counter. I added that drink to the tab and gave him his change from the twenty.

"Thank you," he said, picking up his two drinks and heading to the door.

As soon as he turned to leave, that's when I knew. The feeling was so strong and so eerie, I wondered if it was what Tammy felt when she held my palm and told me the future. I knew he was going to turn around before he did it.

And I was right. In the very next second, he turned back. And it seemed clear to me that the feeling and his turning around went together, but which came first was a chicken-or-egg dilemma I had no way of solving. Did I have the feeling because he was going to turn around, or did the feeling cause him to turn? All I know is that he did turn around and come back to the counter. He put his drinks down and looked at me.

"I wanted to ask you a crazy question," he said.

"Okay," I agreed.

"I wanted to ask if you would come have a cup of coffee with me," he said.

"I . . ." I started to answer and stalled there. I wanted to say yes, but all my brain came up with were the reasons I couldn't. I was working, he was too good-looking, and he was obviously from out of town so what was the point? Those were just the top three. You wouldn't believe how many went through my mind in the space of a split second.

"I'm sorry," he said. "I shouldn't have asked."

"No, it's not that—"

And that was when Neil came up beside me.

"Is there a problem here?" Neil asked.

"No, no problem," the man said. "I was just trying to be friendly."

The other thing about Neil was that he might give his employees a hard time, but he was fiercely protective of us. He didn't follow the policy that the customer is always right—he followed the policy that the person who worked for him, and who he knew and trusted, was to be defended at all costs, which was nice when there was a problem but could be embarrassing in a situation like this, where he got aggressive for no reason.

"I know you're not going to try to tell me that my employee wasn't friendly," Neil said.

"No, of course not," the man said.

Neil said sternly, "We serve coffee here. And lemon loaf. That's it."

"Yes, I know. I'm sorry." The man looked at me and repeated it again. "I'm very sorry." Then he turned around to leave for the second time.

"Your drinks," Neil said.

"Right," the man turned back, picked up his drinks, and walked back toward the door, but when he got to it, he couldn't actually open it because he had a cup in both hands.

I did it without thinking. "Wait," I said. "I'll help you with that." I hurried around the counter and crossed to the door to open it for him—and then I slipped out the door after the man and closed it behind me.

"I would love to have a cup of coffee with you," I said. "But could you wait for me for just a minute? I need to go tell my boss I'm leaving."

The man gave me a strange look, but all he said was, "Sure. I'll be right here."

"Okay. Great. Thanks. I'll be right back," I said, and turned around and went back in the store.

"What was that about?" Neil demanded as I came back inside.

"Neil," I said. "I want to ask you a favor."

Neil looked at me. Then he looked past me through the plate-glass windows at the man, still standing there on the sidewalk with the two drinks, one in each hand. And then Neil surprised me.

"Go on," he said. "I'll see you tomorrow."

"Thank you," I said. "Thanks."

"Just do me one favor, okay? Don't go to Joe's."

"Okay, I won't," I said as I slipped back out the door.

The man was still standing on the sidewalk, waiting for me. "My car is just over here," he said.

He led the way down the street to where a con-vertible BMW (with a rental license plate I noticed) was parked, with the top down. He clicked open the locks and turned around. "Will you hold this?" he asked. He handed me one of the drinks, then turned to open the car door for me.

I got in, and he went around the other side to the driver's seat.

"Will you be cold with the top down?" he asked.

"No, it's beautiful out," I said. And it was, despite the clouds. It was one of those Indian summer days when the breeze off the plains still smelled like summer and cut grass and heat.

He put the cup he was holding in the cup holder between us, and I did the same.

He held out his hand.

"I'm Timothy," he said.

"Nora," I said, holding out mine.

He took my hand for a moment, then let go.

"So, Nora, tell me where should we go in this town of yours?" he asked.

"We're just going a couple of blocks," I said.

"All right."

He started the car and pulled out slowly into the street. As we passed by the store I glanced over, and there was Neil at the plate-glass window, with his rag and his bottle of 100-percent-guaranteed no-streak glass cleaner. I saw him lift the bottle and spray, then lift his arm to wipe the special cloth across the glass. Suddenly the sun burst through the clouds, lighting up all the streaks and dust that clung to the glass. Then Neil swept the cloth across the glass, and he left behind a rainbow arc of pristine, transparent glass.

THE INVESTIGATION

CRIME SCENE

Forensic scientists, when talking about their jobs, often quote the renowned French criminologist Edmond Locard: "Every contact leaves a trace."

When the crime scene crew came in to work the room at the bed-and-breakfast, they found hair from seven different people, dozens of fibers, and even more latent prints. So many people had passed through the room and left traces of themselves.

There is invisible but undeniable evidence of everyone's passing. But, unless there is a tragedy, no one bothers to look.

Nora

Nora Walks Out on Timothy

I took him to Joe's Diner. I had promised Neil I wouldn't, but what was I going to do? There was no place else to take him, not at three o'clock in the afternoon anyway, unless we went to one of the fast-food places out near the highway.

Starbox was always empty, and Joe's was always crowded. Maybe it was because Joe's diner made sense. It belonged to Joe. It was a diner. There were no sizes for coffee in the diner, because they would refill your cup till you burst.

We slid into a booth at the back, and the busboy came over with menus and water.

We both opened our menus and looked, even though I knew exactly what was on it. Nothing had changed in all the years I had been coming to Joe's. Not even the prices. Joe didn't like changes. He was always complaining about how the prices everywhere went up so much. So he decided not to raise the prices in his diner— as if he thought that somehow other people would take a cue from him and do the same. As a result, for the last ten years the town had had to hold a raffle to raise money to save Joe's from foreclosure. But every year the raffle managed to scrape together enough money, and

Joe's kept on serving a meat-loaf dinner for $2.50.

Timothy looked at the menu, and I looked at him.

"What's good here?" he asked. Then he looked up and grinned. "Oh, wait. Forget I asked. I've discovered your recommendations aren't exactly trustworthy."

"I can't be held responsible for the pumpkin disaster," I said. "You can't ask an employee their opinion on the things they're selling. Half the time, if they told you the truth they'd lose their jobs."

"So who's responsible?" he asked me.

I raised my eyebrows at him. "Well, who's left?"

Our waitress came over to our booth. It was Jeanette, who had been in my class in high school. She'd been working at Joe's since she graduated, and she was a terrible waitress—well, whenever I came here with Tammy or my sister or my mother, she was a terrible waitress. She took the job description literally, at least the part that had the word "wait" in it; we always had to wait for at least fifteen or twenty minutes before she even came over to take our order.

It was different this time though. I knew immediately that something was up when she appeared within three minutes of our sitting down and said perkily, "Hey there, Nora. How are you?"

"I'm good, Jeanette. Thanks. How are you?"

"I'll be better when you introduce me to your friend here," she said. She sure didn't waste any time, I thought.

"Jeanette, this is Timothy. Timothy, this is Jeanette."

"Timothy, a pleasure. How did you all meet? Are you together?" she asked suggestively, looking from me to Timothy.

Jeanette was not a subtle person.

I opened my mouth to answer her, when Timothy beat me to it.

He looked up at her and smiled. "You want to know how Nora and I met? It was fate, Jeanette. That's the only way I can explain it. Do you believe in fate?"

Jeanette seemed dazzled by him, standing there staring at him and clutching her pad to her chest. I didn't blame her. He had turned the full force of his attention and charm on her, and she was like a deer in the headlights.

"Yes, I do," she said.

"I thought you might," he said, nodding approvingly.

I wondered what he would say to me if I told him that I thought fate was a bunch of baloney. It's true, I did. Isn't that funny? Even with Tammy's predictions, I believed firmly and completely in the randomness of events. Now that I look back, it doesn't make any sense at all. But at the time I thought it was just logical and practical—hardheaded of me.

Jeanette hesitated, then said to Timothy, "Can I ask you a question?"

"Sure thing. Shoot."

"Do you ever worry that you might miss it? That you have to keep an eye out or fate might just keep right on going by?"

"Miss it? Not possible. If it's supposed to happen, there's nothing in the world you can do to stop it. Like what happened with me and Nora," and he reached over and took my hand from where it had been lying on the table between us.

And then, oh, the look that Jeanette turned on me. As if she were starving and I had a feast in front of me and wouldn't share. It was a relief when she looked back at Timothy and I was able to quietly pull away my hand. I didn't like what he was doing; he seemed to be both mocking her and flirting with her at the same time.

"Do you have any friends who believe in fate?" Jeanette asked. "A twin brother maybe?"

"You don't need to find someone who believes in it; you're still ruled by it whether you believe in it or not. And you wouldn't want either of my brothers. Trust me on that one."

"I'm not so sure," she said. "I'd like to check that out myself."

"They don't live around here. But listen, I have a question for you."

"Yes?"

The way she said it, she probably would have told him anything. Her darkest secret even. But all he said was, "Do you have any specials that you'd recommend?"

"We have specials," Jeanette said, "but nothin' I'd recommend. They're always some mess Joe puts together with the ingredients that are about to go bad, or what's worse, something he makes up when he's feeling artistic. Stick to the menu, and you'll be just fine."

"Hamburgers?"

"Delicious," Jeanette assured him. "Bloody?"

"Perfect."

Jeanette turned to me. "Nora?"

At this point I was annoyed with both of them.

"Coffee and a piece of apple pie," I said.

Jeanette didn't write it down. Instead she said, "You sure about that pie? You know how much Crisco Joe puts in the crust?"

"I'm sure about the pie," I told her.

I wasn't so sure about anything else though. I was feeling more and more uncomfortable every moment the little show went on between Timothy and Jeanette. I felt like the intruder, as if I were sitting and watching someone else's date.

"Okeydoke." She pivoted, and the way she walked away was just an invitation to watch her backside.

I watched for a second, then turned back to Timothy, sure I would find him still watching her.

But he was watching me. And laughing.

"I didn't take you for the jealous type," he said.

"That's not jealousy," I told him. "That's disgust."

"Oh, bringing out the big guns."

"Were you trying to prove something?"

"No, of course not."

There was something in the way he said it. Dismissive. Condescending. Just shy of rude.

I slid out of the booth and stood up.

"I think I'd better go," I said. "I thought you were . . . I don't know. Anyway, I should probably get back to work."

Still, I waited a moment for what he would say.

"You're going to leave me to eat my hamburger alone?" he said, but he said it in that same voice he'd used to talk to Jeanette. It was mocking, slick banter. That was all.

"I have a feeling you're almost never alone. I think you'll be fine."

And I left.

Did I come close to escaping fate that Monday afternoon when I walked out of Joe's Diner?

You can play "what if?" games until the Resurrection, but how can you escape fate? Maybe you don't believe in fate. But fate doesn't require belief. As Timothy said, you're ruled by it whether you believe in it or not. If it exists. I'd say it's up to you to decide, but you don't even need to decide. Just live your life, and when it's over, then tell me. Do you believe?

THE INVESTIGATION

STATISTICS

The Human Side of Homicide reports that currently a quarter of all murderers are women, and their victims are usually someone close.

Timothy

What Timothy Thought When Nora Walked Out

I'll admit it. I was sure she would come back.

I sat there. I sipped from my water glass. It was barely an inch below the lip, but that waitress came back with the water jug to fill it up. And she bent over to show me her tits. They weren't bad, not great either, but there was something sexy about the pride she had in showing them.

I flirted with her and waited for the other one to come back. That's how I thought of her—as the other one.

There was no strike of lightning for me. It might have seemed like it, but there wasn't. I was just bullshitting about fate. I'd been in the habit of talking that way to women for years. They loved it, and it kept me from having to answer questions. They just went off into their dream world; I could see them construct the image right before my eyes. "This is the guy who believes in fate." "This is the guy who believes in love." "This might be the guy I've been waiting for all my life." And then they don't even bother to get to know me. They think they know already, and then they just look for evidence to back it up.

So at the time I was sure it was just more of my

bullshit. But later I looked back and asked myself, why did I get off the highway? And why there? I wasn't really hungry. I didn't need gas. I wasn't in the mood to explore. There was no reason. I just did it. And when I was driving through town, I saw the sign for Starbucks, though it wasn't a Starbucks, and I just thought I'd get myself a coffee.

I walked in and there was that girl. I found out later that she was over thirty, but there are some women who are women and some women who are girls. One isn't better than the other. They're just different. This one was a girl.

Anyway, she was just a girl with beautiful hair. I couldn't really see it well, but I could imagine what it looked like down. It was the kind of hair that when you see it down, it's almost like seeing the girl undressed.

I have to admit, it annoyed me that she didn't even seem to notice me. Oh, I suppose she did notice in a way, but she looked at me like you'd look at something through a window. That was why I asked her to come get a coffee. I wanted to crack the glass. And I thought I had shattered it pretty good when she came running out of the coffee shop after me. It was the kind of thing I was used to. That proved to me she was just an ordinary girl—a girl with beautiful hair and a mysterious look but underneath that obviously the same as all the others.

So when we got to the diner, I acted with her the way I acted with all women: never awful but just rude enough that they knew exactly what the deal was. Yet they always chose to ignore my clear signals. They saw what they wanted to see.

Until now.

This was the first one who watched me, listened, and got it. And walked out. Not because she wasn't interested. Not because she was playing a game. It was because she understood me.

She was the only one.

Nora

What Nora Thought After She Walked Out

Should I lie and say that after I walked out on him, I never gave him another thought?

The truth was that even as I was walking out, my brain was screaming at me, "What are you doing? Did you even look at him? Do you have any idea what you're walking out on?"

That was what it was like to be inside my head that afternoon. I don't think another thought got any play time in my brain. That's the downside of working a job that doesn't require you to think— it leaves you at the mercy of whatever thoughts are tormenting you. I hadn't realized how peaceful I'd become over the past few years. Or maybe I was just empty. There was nothing to want. There is great peace in that. Boredom too. But also peace.

But I have to tell you—when it came back, it came back with a vengeance. By the time I left work my mind had him at Jeanette's place in a bad soap-opera scene. I had myself so convinced that I even drove by Jeanette's house on my way home to see if his car was parked outside.

I know it undermined my bold move in walking out on him. I wish I could take credit for strength and self-respect, but since I'm confessing, I might as well go all the way. I didn't walk out on him thinking that I wouldn't let a man treat me that way. I didn't look at the situation and realize that, no matter how good-looking he was, if he was flirting with another woman right in front of me on what had to be considered a date, he would only bring me misery—no matter how much I wanted him.

No, it wasn't like that at all. Even if I can see the truth in that kind of reasoning, I still wanted him. And seeing how much Jeanette wanted him only made me want him more. If I had any question in my mind about how desirable he was, I could see the answer reflected in Jeanette's eyes.

So why did I walk out?

All I can say is that I didn't do it.

It was like when you jump onto the tracks in front of an oncoming train to save a person who has fallen, and after it's over, there was no sense of *you* having done it. Suddenly I found myself getting up and walking out, when no part of my conscious brain wanted to do it.

Because, truthfully, I can't say I'm any different from Jeanette in her search for a man. The only difference between us is that I don't try so hard. In fact, I don't really try at all. So who, between the two of us, is the more honest?

How could I escape being like Jeanette when it had been my mother's favorite theme for my entire life? I know it was out of love, on her part. It was because she equated a man with stability, security, and happiness. She had raised two girls without any help, and her life had been hard, but her belief made my life harder. Practically every day when I got home from work, she would say to me, "How are you ever going to get a man when it looks like you've been digging ditches all day?" (The coffee grounds left black lines under my fingernails.)

I hated the way she said "get a man." It wasn't "meet a man." It was always "get a man." Like you might go to the pound or the pet store and get a dog. But in the way my mother said it, it was clear that it wasn't something that simple. It was more like a hunter getting the big game: hard to track, tough to bring down, requiring time and planning and patience and strategy. But then, of course, the hunter hangs the prize trophy on the wall. That's how I imagined it. I would go out, "get" a man, and hang his head on the wall—because there was never any discussion about what my mother thought I should do with the man when I got him. Just the getting. That was of paramount importance. Without that one accomplishment, my mother always seemed to imply, life wasn't really worth living.

I had a feeling that Jeanette and my mother would be in perfect agreement. And I'm sure neither my mother or Jeanette would have walked out on Timothy. And when I walked out, I thought that would be it.

But he walked right back in.

THE INVESTIGATION

STATISTICS

"Who kills whom?" This question is posed in Martin Daly and Margo Wilson's book *Homicide*.

To try to answer the question, Daly and Wilson did an analysis of the murder cases in Detroit in 1972. In that year 512 cases of homicide were solved: 243 were unrelated acquaintances of the murderers, 138 strangers, 127 "relatives," and in 4 cases the relationship was unknown.

The fact that 127 perpetrators out of 512 were "relatives" means that one of every four victims was related to the killer. Of the 127 victims who were related to their killers, 32 were blood relations, 10 were in-laws, 5 were step-relations, and 80 were spouses (36 women were killed by their husbands and 44 men were killed by their wives).

Nora

Nora Says Yes to a Date

He walked back into Starbox first thing the next morning. No suit this time. He wore a pair of slacks and a long-sleeved T-shirt, but both looked crisp and perfect in the way that clothes usually only look in the movies.

I watched him come in, my face (I hoped) a blank.

He didn't smile either. He was very serious as he walked up to the counter and said, "I'd like a pumpkin-spice latte please."

I nodded. "To stay or to go?"

"To stay?" When he said it, he made it a half question.

I just nodded again.

I took a mug, and even though Neil wasn't in yet, I made the pumpkin latte as if he were standing there watching me: four full squirts of pumpkin syrup.

When I was done, I brought it back to where Timothy stood waiting and put it down on the counter.

He picked up the mug, and he drank the whole thing. What was even more impressive was that he didn't even flinch. He put the cup down, took a napkin out of the dispenser, and wiped the edges of his mouth with it.

Then he said, "You were right yesterday about me trying to prove something."

"You're still trying to prove something," I pointed out, flicking my finger at the cup.

"You're right again."

"So?"

"So . . . do you think you could make me an espresso? I think I might need a palate cleanser."

I laughed. And then I made him a double. I brought it back over to him, and he picked it up and tossed it back expertly, like he did it every day of the week—which he probably did.

"That's better. Thank you."

He paused, running his finger around the rim of his empty espresso cup. Then he said, "What I'm trying to say is that I'm sorry for how it went yesterday."

"Just saying sorry might have been easier," I said. "You didn't need to drink the pumpkin latte."

The wince he had suppressed while drinking showed itself then.

"Now you tell me. I don't remember you saying anything about that before you made it and put in down in front of me."

"You seemed very determined."

"I was. I am."

He let that sit out there for a minute.

Then he said, "Can I take you out for another cup of coffee? Maybe a slice of apple pie loaded with shortening?"

"You ate my apple pie, didn't you?"

"I did," he said. "It was delicious."

"I know."

"It would have been even better if I could have eaten it in peace."

"Jeanette?" I guessed, though it wasn't really a guess.

"Good Lord," he said, with feeling. "Like getting thrown into the lion's cage before dinner."

"No one but yourself to blame for that," I pointed out. "You encouraged her."

"Because I thought you would be there to protect me."

I raised my eyebrows at him.

"I miscalculated," he admitted.

"And that doesn't happen often," I guessed.

"Almost never."

"And the times someone has walked out on you?" I asked.

He thought for a second. "Never."

"Well, it's not a party trick. It was a first for me too," I said.

"I know," he told me. "I can smell a strategy a mile away. You never expected to see me again, did you?"

"No."

"But you don't seem upset that I'm here."

"No," I said. "I'm not upset."

The understatement of the century.

"So can I take you for a coffee?"

116

Don't get me wrong, I was happy to see him, but for some reason I was also glad to be able to turn him down. "I can't. I'm here alone this morning. I can't leave the store. And even if Neil were here, I couldn't just leave like that again."

"Then can you come sit down with me at one of the tables?"

I shook my head. "Sorry, but I'm supposed to stay behind the counter, or if the store is empty, I can clean the tables or the windows."

"I'm not used to people telling me no," he said, but he softened the remark by smiling as he said it.

"You're taking it well."

"I'm on my best behavior right now," he admitted. "So is that no a real no or a no to coffee?"

"It's a no to coffee."

"What about dinner then?"

"Yes." I said it calmly, but if my insides were outside, I would have been doing backflips.

"Good," he said with obvious satisfaction, though not, I noticed, much surprise. "You'll need to give me your address and tell me what time to pick you up."

"Why don't we meet at the restaurant?" I suggested.

"I like to pick my dates up."

"You might like it, but it's not going to happen."

He didn't like that. I could see it in his face. It's

not that he showed it exactly. But something went still.

He took a moment, as if he were deciding which tack to go with. I think he chose honesty, but it's so hard to tell. And if you chose honesty as a strategy, is it still honesty?

"You're going to make me suspicious. What are you hiding?" He said it lightly, but I could tell he wanted a real answer.

But I wanted to hide everything for as long as I possibly could. If I could hide it all forever, maybe I could leave it behind as well.

"If I told you, I wouldn't be very good at hiding it," I said.

"Do you have a husband or boyfriend at home?"

"Sadly, no. It's much less interesting."

"I prefer less interesting. So no skeletons?"

"No boyfriends or husbands anyway." Maybe I should have dissembled more. Played the game. Been more mysterious. Pretended that there might be someone in the wings. But I couldn't do it.

"So you're a woman who walks out, without other prospects. I was sure that you walked out on me because there was someone else."

"No, there's no one else. But it can't be so unusual for a woman to walk out without other prospects."

"Unless she's just not interested . . . ?" he suggested in a half question.

I just looked at him.

"It's unusual," he assured me. "Most people don't want to be alone. But it seems like you don't mind."

That's when I told him my first lie. "Not really," I said.

"Well, tonight I hope you won't mind the company. But since I am a bit old-fashioned, and you won't let me pick you up at your house, would you meet me here, and then we can drive together to whichever restaurant you choose? My one request is that it's not Joe's Diner."

"You're afraid of Jeanette," I said laughing.

"Terrified," he agreed.

The rest of the day seemed very long. But finally the sun dropped in the west, and its rays slanted across the empty lot and through the windows into the store. The rays, as they reached the windows and then made their way across the floor of the café, told time like a sundial, and at this time of year, I noticed, when they reached the counter it was time to go home.

I had a couple of hours before I had to be back at the store to meet Timothy, so I took the long way home, which is to say I drove past our street and out into the plains. Just outside of town, there's a turnoff from the main road onto a gravel road that goes out into the wheat fields and dead-ends at an old grain silo. I took that turnoff, drove to the end, parked the car, and walked out into the fields.

The weather had changed drastically from the warm summery temperature of the day before. It had turned cold overnight, and out there, with no protection, the wind whipped through the stubble in the fields and through my jacket. I stayed out there as long as I could stand it.

It's only now that I can look back and see the truth—that those were my golden moments. It was out there that I found what I was looking for. And it was when I was most alone—the thing I was most afraid of. Will you believe me if I tell you that the thing we fear most is the thing we want most? No? Well, I wouldn't have believed it either. I couldn't see it, even with the evidence right there in front of me.

I stayed out there, alone in the fields, longer than usual. I stayed until the sun went down and the temperature dropped even more. Then, when my nose and fingers were numb and I was almost shivering, I walked back to the car and drove home to my mother's house.

I went straight upstairs to take a hot shower, and then I took the time to blow-dry my hair, which I almost never do since it takes forever. I dug out the makeup that I hadn't used for ages. It had been so long, in fact, that when I tried to use the mascara, I discovered it had dried to a solid inside the container. For the first time I realized how much I had let slip in the last three years.

I put on the nicest dress I had, which was also the only dress I had. I'd bought it for the one date I went on in Chicago in the spring, and I hadn't worn it since. Then I put a pair of heels in my bag and put on jeans underneath the dress and an overcoat on top of it. I knew if I went out in a dress and heels, and my mother saw me, there was no way I was going to get out of the house without an interrogation. And I wasn't ready to be questioned—especially since I didn't have any answers.

Even with my disguise, getting out of the house proved to be tough. It was like my mother had radar for the times when it was most inconvenient for her to be difficult.

She was sitting, watching TV, when I went downstairs.

"I'm going out," I told her.

She turned to look at me, and I felt like she had X-ray vision, as if she could see right through the coat to the dress underneath.

"Where?" she demanded.

"Meeting Tammy."

"Tammy is more important to you than your own mother?"

"Of course not," I said.

"Good. Then stay in with me tonight. I'm feeling low. I've been alone in this house all day. I need some company."

"Mom, I'm sorry. I can't tonight."

"Why not? You see that girl all the time. Why do you need to see her tonight?"

I spent practically every night with my mother, sitting on the couch watching TV. I couldn't even count the number of nights she told me I should be going out instead of sitting around, that my life would be over before I knew it, and I'd still be sitting there on the couch alone because she wasn't going to be there forever.

"I promise I'll stay in tomorrow night," I told her.

"I'm not talking about tomorrow night. I'm talking about tonight. Are you going to stay with me *tonight*? That's all I'm asking you. I don't think it's so much."

I realized that if I had really been going out with Tammy, I would have given in and stayed in with my mother. I knew it and she knew it. So by saying no, it was as good as saying there was something I wasn't telling her. The only thing for me to do was to get out of the house as quickly as possible.

"Sorry. Not tonight, Mom," I said, heading for the door. "I'll probably be back a bit late. See you tomorrow." And I hurried out, not waiting to hear what was sure to come. I could hear her through the door, but, mercifully, I couldn't make out the words.

I drove far enough away for it to be safe to pull over, wriggle out of my jeans, change my shoes, take off the bulky coat, and put on some lipstick. Then I drove back to town and pulled up behind the now familiar convertible. Tonight the top was up, and the rear window was so small, and it was so dark, I couldn't see if he was inside.

He wasn't. He was standing underneath the Starbox awning. As soon as I turned off the car, he came over and opened the door for me.

He smiled at me as he took in what I was wearing, but didn't say anything. Most men will say something on the first date: "You look nice," or even "I like that dress." Something. But he didn't say a word. He just escorted me over to the passenger side of his car and opened the door for me. Then he went around to his side and slid into the driver's seat.

I gave him directions for the few blocks we had to drive to get to Mike's Italian.

"Mike's?" he said when he heard the name. "People like to name their restaurants after themselves here, don't they?"

"It works," I said. "I bet Neil would be doing a lot better with his place if he named it Neil's. People would feel more comfortable."

Mike's was actually a fancier place than its name implied. Fancy for our town anyway. There were white tablecloths, linen napkins, candles, and fresh flowers on the tables.

Well, usually it was one of the fancier places. I hadn't been in ages, so I didn't know that, to help business during the week, Mike had started up a Tuesday family night. Kids under five ate for free.

I realized the change when we walked into the restaurant and, instead of the murmur of adult voices, two little boys were doing laps around the tables like it was a track meet. Rising above their yells was the ear-splitting shriek of a baby. What's more, there was brown paper on the tables instead of white cotton, and crayons in shot glasses instead of fresh flowers and candles.

Timothy looked over at me. "Is this another test like the pumpkin latte?" he asked me.

"It's not usually like this," I said. "Why don't we—"

But before I could finish my sentence, Mike had discovered us at the door.

"I have a very quiet table," he said immediately, reading the looks on our faces. Then he herded us into the restaurant, arm outstretched, as if in welcome, but I swear it was more blocking tactics to keep us from making a break from the door.

As he ushered us across the room, he said, "And the kids, they have early bedtimes. A lot of the families will be finishing up soon."

I looked around. Most of them didn't even have food in front of them yet. But it was too late to escape easily.

Timothy caught my eye. He was laughing, and he shrugged as if to say, "Why not?"

We managed to make it across the dining room and into a little nook that was quieter and a little recessed from the rest of the restaurant.

As we sat down, Mike pulled off the paper tablecloth and returned a minute later with a real tablecloth and two candles. He lit them both with a lighter from his pocket, winked, and disappeared.

Timothy looked across the table at me.

"You are full of surprises," he said.

"Believe me, this is as much of a surprise to me," I told him.

"It's not just the restaurant. You also had this hidden." And he reached out and lifted a lock of my hair from where it had fallen forward over my shoulder. He brushed it back, saying, "You attract a lot of attention with that hair."

"That's why I usually wear it up," I said. "But I think I'm safe from attention here."

"Do you?" he asked curiously.

"In a room filled with families and screaming kids, yes."

"A man doesn't stop being a man when he gets married and has kids," Timothy said.

I had a sinking feeling in my stomach. He spoke with such authority. Of course I'd already checked the ring finger and found it empty. Was he *that* guy—the one who refused to wear a wedding ring? Or, worse, the kind who took it off when he went away on business trips?

My face must have showed something of what I was thinking because he said, "My brother is married and has two kids. That's how I know."

I wasn't used to being read so easily. I thought about whether I could get away with denying I'd been thinking that very thought. But I didn't have a chance because he went on.

"And, just so you know, I think every man in here watched you as you crossed the room. And there's one over there to your right who is looking at me like he wants to kill me."

"Don't be silly," I said.

Then I looked over.

It was Dan.

He was sitting at a table with Stacey and his two kids—and Timothy was right. If you could kill someone with a look, Timothy would have been dead at that moment. Dan was so intent on Timothy, he didn't even notice me looking at him.

"Is there something I should know about?" Timothy asked.

"No," I said. "Nothing."

"The wife doesn't think it's nothing," he observed.

I looked back over. Stacey was looking at Dan almost as ferociously as Dan was looking at Timothy. I had the thought that without the social veneer, in a more primitive time, I didn't know what might have happened.

"I'm sure it has nothing to do with me."

"Mmm," he said. It was a sound of agreement, but it wasn't agreement.

He seemed to study me for a second. And the way he looked at me—how can I explain it? It felt like no one had ever actually looked at me before him. I thought they had, but in comparison it felt like they were looking through me or over me or around me. He looked right at me.

His eyes narrowed a bit, considering. Then he said, "Is this false modesty? Or is this real? I have to admit, I can't tell."

"It's not modesty, false or otherwise. It's reality."

He snorted as if he didn't believe me.

There was a reason for that—it turned out I was wrong. Not about the modesty, but about the fight between Stacey and Dan being about me.

Right after we ordered our drinks, I noticed Stacey talking heatedly to Dan. And a moment later she started furiously bundling the baby's things into a bag. Then she scooped the baby up in her arms, and grabbing Dan Junior's hand, she hustled them out the door, leaving Dan alone at the table full of barely touched plates of food.

I still didn't think it had anything to do with me, until I saw Dan get up—which I expected—but instead of following Stacey out the door, he stalked over to our table and stopped right in front of my chair.

"What do you think you're doing?" Dan said to me.

I pushed my chair back. I didn't like the way he was standing over me.

"Dan, I'm having dinner. Do you mind?"

He seemed to take the question literally. "Yes, I do mind. Do you even know who this guy is?"

"I don't see how that's any of your business."

"It should be yours," Dan said. "What are you thinking, going out with a guy who's already hit on half the women in this town?"

Timothy spoke then. "What on earth are you talking about?" He sounded calm and reasonable.

"I'm not talking to you," Dan said, not even turning around.

"No, but you're talking *about* me," Timothy said. "And, quite honestly, you're talking nonsense. I've been in this town for a total of about thirty hours. So I have no idea when I might have been seducing all these women. Or who would have told you."

"You can't hide things in a small town," Dan said. "Even if you're only here for a day. My wife's good friend said you were all over her yesterday. And now you're out with Nora tonight."

All of a sudden something clicked in my brain. I remembered that Jeanette and Stacey had been really good friends in high school.

Timothy caught my eye and smiled.

"Is he talking about who I think he's talking

about?" he asked me.

"I think so."

"The lion's cage?"

"At feeding time," I said.

"Jeanette," we both said at the same time.

"You know about it, and you still agreed to go out with him?" Dan said, as if personally out-raged.

"Dan, he was flirting with her. Flirting isn't a crime. It doesn't mean you can't take someone else out to dinner."

"He might have told you it was flirting, but it was a lot more than that—I can tell you."

I looked back over at Timothy.

"After eating my hamburger and your apple pie, I got back in my car and drove to the highway and checked into a motel. I went to the Burger King next door for dinner, and I came to see you first thing this morning."

I looked back up at Dan. "Not that this is any of your business, but are you saying you heard something different?"

"Well, not . . ." Dan floundered, then tried to recover by asserting angrily, "It was a whole lot more than just innocent flirting. He practically propositioned her."

The way he said it make it sound as if the crime were attempted murder. Had he forgotten that just last weekend he'd pretty much done exactly that to me in the aisle of the 7-Eleven? And if he hadn't forgotten, how on earth could he be so righteous?

"Dan, you're being ridiculous."

He ignored my words. "I know what you're doing," he told me.

"What am I doing?"

"You're trying to make me jealous."

I tried again. "Dan, you're married, and you have two kids. Go home to them, okay?"

"Don't tell me what to do."

Suddenly this was familiar. I had totally forgotten that he was like this, but whenever he realized he was losing an argument, he started sounding like a five-year-old. It used to drive me crazy. I felt like I had a child instead of a boyfriend. I had spent a good part of the last three years thinking about him, but I never once remembered this. All the good times, all the wonderful things, yes. But this had been erased from my mind as if it never happened. Why is it that when you sit around thinking about your ex, you don't remember these things? The things that drove you crazy and now you no longer have to deal with?

"Okay, don't go home," I said. "I really don't care. But let me have my dinner in peace."

Dan just stood there, glaring at me.

"I believe Nora asked you to leave," Timothy said. The words were mild, but his tone was not.

Dan finally pivoted to face Timothy, but at that

moment Timothy picked up the menu and started reading it. He didn't even look up at Dan. It's hard to fight with someone who's not even looking at you.

Dan stood there for a moment, looking increasingly awkward. Then he turned back to me.

I was expecting . . . I don't know what I was expecting. But it wasn't what he did.

He looked at me intently, and he said, "You look beautiful." Then he turned around and walked away.

I didn't know what to do with that. I really didn't.

I also didn't want to look around the restaurant, because I was afraid to find that everyone was watching. I looked anyway. There were a couple of people who were so intently not looking at us that I knew they'd been trying to follow the little scene, but the rest were busy with their children, trying to get them to sit down, to eat, to stop hitting each other, that they had no time for someone else's drama.

Then I looked over at Timothy. I was expecting to share a smile over the ridiculousness of what had just happened. But he wasn't looking at me either. He was still studying the menu—in a way that let me know he was angry.

I waited a moment, and he still didn't look up.

"Are you okay?" I finally asked.

He shut the menu and finally looked up at me.

Suddenly I felt the reverse of what I felt with Dan. Not that I was with a child, but that I *was* the child.

"You told me no husband, no boyfriend, but you should have mentioned that you had a lover."

"Okay, how about this—I have no husband, no boyfriend, *and* no lover," I told him.

"Someone doesn't act like that unless you're sleeping with them."

He sat back in his chair and crossed his arms. It was as if he were erecting a barrier between us.

"Not only am I not sleeping with him, before Saturday night I hadn't even spoken to him in three years."

There was no hint in his face that he was softening.

He said, "I don't know if I believe that. And even if it's true, he wants you back."

I leaned forward across the table, trying to make him believe me when I said, "I don't care what he wants."

"You're not going to go back to him?"

"Not tonight anyway." I was too used to being sarcastic with Tammy and getting her to laugh. It didn't work with Timothy at all.

He gave me a withering look, and it was all downhill from there.

I think the way he acted during our dinner was his version of my leaving the day before. The only difference is that he didn't get up and walk away from the table. At least not in body. I tried asking him questions, but he gave me yes or no answers, or ignored the questions altogether. Eventually, I gave up, and we finished the meal in silence.

We were done faster than some of the families who had been there when we arrived. At the end of it, he paid. I tried to offer, but he just made a little brushing motion with his hand, like he was sweeping crumbs from the tablecloth. Then he drove me back to the store, walked me back to my car, opened the door for me, and said good night.

I didn't ask him if I would see him again. He didn't ask to see me either. There wasn't even a kiss on the cheek.

I think it might have been the worst date I've ever had. Not that I've had that many, but it was still a doozy—even without many others to compare it with. So you'd think I would be relieved that I wouldn't have to suffer through another date like that. But "relieved" is not the word I'd use to describe what I felt.

It was barely past ten when I got home, but the lights were all out in the house. Just to be safe, I pulled on my jeans, changed my shoes, and then put on my jacket and went inside.

I shut the door softly behind me and leaned against it for a second. Back here. Again.

Always back in this house.

It was just a house. Dark. Quiet. So why did I feel like I couldn't breathe in it?

After a moment I turned on the lights—and discovered that my mother was sitting there on the couch. She had been sitting there in the dark, no TV, no music. Just sitting there.

"Mom, what are you doing? Are you okay?" I asked her.

It was as if I hadn't spoken. I know she heard me because she shifted on the sofa, but she didn't even turn her head to look at me.

"I'm going to bed," I said. "I'll see you in the morning, okay?"

Still nothing.

"Do you want the light on or off?"

No answer. But I knew what she wanted all the same.

I turned the light off and left her sitting there in the dark.

THE INVESTIGATION

ASSUMPTIONS

In piecing together the story, the investigator needs to beware of assumptions. The same event can be seen from another perspective in a completely different way.

The FBI has a saying: "Any assumption is the death of a good investigation."

Timothy

What Timothy Thought During the Date

I was stunned when she got out of her car.
Really.

I had no idea. She'd looked like an average pretty girl in her uniform in the coffee place. And she'd acted like an average pretty girl, and I mean that in a good way. Really beautiful women have a self-consciousness about them: they're always aware of the effect they have on people. It's not their fault—they really do have an effect on people. So it's just something they learn to expect, to defend against, to use, to deflect. Sometimes they get savvy, and they try to cover the fact that they're aware of your reaction to them, but I can always spot it. It takes one to know one, after all.

This girl had none of that about her. And yet when she stepped out of the car, she was something out of myth—a creature so beautiful, and yet somehow, amazingly, unaware of her beauty. The important element isn't the beauty. It's the being unaware of it. How could she have existed in the world without knowing?

I can't describe to you her hair. I had noticed it before, and I thought I knew what it would be like when it was down. But it transformed everything. Her face, her eyes, her body—everything changed with the hair. I thought I had such a good eye for spotting beauty, and it had been right in front of me and I hadn't even noticed it. It humbled me. And I have to be honest, that was a new experience for me. Humble gets a bad rap. I'm here to tell you, if I could live that way, I think it's all I'd need to be happy.

I always compliment my dates. Always. I try to find one true thing that I like. And if I can't, I compliment the thing that I dislike the most: Gold lamé shoes. A fuzzy purse that looks like a hair ball. Orange lipstick. There is a certain admiration in my horror. So I draw on that.

But this time, I swear to you, I couldn't say a word. So I just opened the car door and helped her in.

She didn't even seem to notice that I didn't say anything. When she got in the car and told me where to go, she seemed both quiet and relaxed. I don't think I'd ever experienced quite that combination of traits—at least not in a woman. With a guy, sure. You could sit there for half an hour without saying anything, and he'd barely even notice. If that happened with a woman, you could be sure that she was either pissed at something or upset, usually both.

But she only told me how to get to the restaurant. A right and a left and we were there. The whole downtown was about the size of one New York City block. There was also the strip just outside town, off the highway, with the motel where I was staying, the McDonald's, the Burger King, the gas station, and the Dunkin' Donuts.

The main part of town was actually quite picturesque. It was what you imagine a small town looks like. And the restaurant looked like it was right in step with that: a green scalloped awning that said just "Mike's" and an old-fashioned glass-and-wood door. It looked perfect for a quiet dinner—until we opened the door and walked into chaos. It was like walking into a five-year-old's birthday party after the cake has been served and the sugar is coursing through those little five-year-old bodies. I should know: I had spent about ten minutes at my nephew's birthday party a month before.

By this time in my life, I had come to the conclusion that I didn't like children. It's not a popular opinion, but I think it's one that more people have than will admit to. What I don't understand is how those very same people are convinced that they will like their own children. Or rather, that their children will be different. I am not so sure of either.

When we walked into the restaurant, my first thought was that this was some kind of message—she had taken me here to make it clear that she loved children and wanted some as soon as possible, and she was already picking out names for the ones she was planning we would have together. That's what went through my head after we went through the door. It's not exactly logical, but I have to tell you that this is the level of paranoia in the older single man going out on a first date. And it is not completely unfounded. I could tell you stories . . .

But one look at her face and I knew it was unfounded in this case. When we walked into the restaurant, she looked shocked. Appalled really.

I said, "Is this another test like the pumpkin latte?"

"It's not usually like this," she said. "Why don't we—"

But it was too late. The host had spotted us and caught us at the door.

At that point I was really quite enjoying her discomfort. She seemed so composed before, but I was very happy to have her off balance. I admit, it made me more comfortable.

But then we walked across the dining room, and I swear to you every male in the place looked up and watched her. It's not that I wasn't used to that with the women I went out with. That was part of the pleasure of it. Half the time the women weren't worth the bother, but the other men didn't know that, and their envy was what I fed on. I loved having something they wanted.

But for the first time, I felt something else. She seemed so naive, and I wanted to keep it that way, but I thought all it would take would be for her to look up and notice, really see how they looked at her, and it would be gone. That innocence would disappear. And then she would be like all the other women. Something priceless would have been lost.

Maybe that's what people love about their children. They see that pureness. That innocence. It's irresistible. And then the kids grow up. Thinking about that, I was sure I didn't want kids. How do you get over the heartbreak of seeing something perfect spoiled?

When we sat down at the table, I looked across at her. "You are full of surprises," I told her.

I have always prided myself on being honest. But at that moment, I realized that I usually congratulate myself on being honest when I'm telling someone something unpleasant, something they don't want to hear. And there is great power in that. Being honest about positive things—that lays you open. Of course, she didn't hear it the way I meant it.

"Believe me, this was as much of a surprise to me," she said. And she left it at that. She didn't do the thing that women so often do when they make some mistake and then get overly apologetic.

"It's not just the restaurant. You also had this hidden."

I have to admit, I think I said it just to have an excuse to reach out and touch her. To feel that hair. It was as heavy and silky as it looked. Like a doll's. "You attract a lot of attention with that hair."

"That's why I usually wear it up. But I think I'm pretty safe from attention here."

"Do you?" I asked.

"In a room filled with families and screaming kids, yes."

"A man doesn't stop being a man when he gets married and has kids," I told her.

It never made sense to me that this fact always seems to surprise women—that they somehow think a man will get married and then never notice a beautiful woman again, that he'll never desire anyone other than his wife. How can you ever have a true relationship without understanding that instinct doesn't get snuffed out by two words in a ceremony?

And, unfortunately, it looked like her opinions were the same as the others'. She frowned at me, but then I saw her glance at my hand, and I realized she wasn't frowning at the general concept; she was thinking that I was talking about myself.

"My brother is married and has two kids. That's how I know," I said. But then I added, "And, just so you know, I think every man in here watched you as you crossed the room."

I looked around at the men, and then I noticed him. I couldn't believe my radar hadn't picked up on him before. A big guy. Blond. You could tell that he'd been good-looking at one point, but he was starting to lose it, as men often do when they settle into career and family, start eating too much from the boredom of it all, and then compound that by watching too much television as a way of trying to escape the trap of "have to's" and checklists their life has become.

This guy was sitting there, glaring at me like he wanted to strangle me, and I knew the girl I had sitting across from me wasn't as free as she claimed to be. There was a man in this room to whom she belonged. I could see it in that glare. It was unmistakable.

I said, "And there's one over there to your right who is looking at me like he wants to kill me."

"Don't be silly," she said.

I am not used to people accusing me of being silly. I didn't like it.

Then she looked over, saw what I saw, and her face changed.

"Is there something I should know about?" I asked.

"No. Nothing."

I also don't like it when people lie to me.

"The wife doesn't think it's nothing."

"I'm sure it has nothing to do with me," she said.

I looked at her, trying to figure out how deep the lie went. Had I been wrong about everything? I didn't think so. I wasn't given to romanticizing about women, and I had known a lot of them.

I considered for a moment, then I just asked her, "Is this false modesty? Or is this real? I have to admit I can't tell."

"It's not modesty, false or otherwise. It's reality," she said.

Then the guy who had been sitting there glaring at me charged over and demanded to know what she was doing. She answered him calmly. She said, "Dan, I'm having dinner. Do you mind?" He seemed to take the question literally. "Yes, I do mind. Do you even know who this guy is?"

I could feel the possessiveness radiating off him in waves. But from the way she was talking to him, I could see that she didn't feel the same. He hung on stubbornly for a little while, and finally he gave up and left. And then I accused her of lying to me. And when she told me she hadn't, I pretended not to believe her.

But that wasn't the truth.

The truth is, I got scared. Not easy to admit, but there it is. I didn't think she was lying. I wasn't an idiot; I knew she hadn't just been born. She had a past. Okay, so it wasn't all the time that the past charged your table on your first date, but I thought she handled it better than I could have imagined. And her composure just scared me more. I suddenly had the sense that this girl I found in the middle of nowhere, Kansas, was the real thing.

And I realized I wanted nothing to do with it. You can't play with something like that. It's like playing hopscotch near the third rail. And once I touched that rail, nothing would be the same. In the moment I realized that, I was gone.

Nora

The Day After the Date

There was a part of me—okay, all of me— waiting the next morning at work. I was waiting for him to walk in again. He'd done it once. Why not again?

Well, I don't know why not, but he didn't. Instead Tammy stormed in at around eleven.

I was behind the counter, and Neil was sitting at one of the tables with his laptop, doing the ordering.

"Hey, Tammy," Neil said when Tammy burst through the door.

Tammy ignored him and marched up to the counter, glaring at me the whole way.

"I thought we were friends," she said furiously.

I blinked. "Yeah, well, I didn't want to tell you, but I've actually just been pretending for the last twenty years or so."

"You suck," Tammy said, trying desperately to hold on to her anger and not quite managing it.

I knew she must have heard something about my date. "I'm sorry I didn't tell you," I said.

"I had to hear it from Jeanette down at the Box last night."

Tammy was a bartender at a local bar, the Box, during the week and at a strip club, prosaically named Pussy's, on weekends.

Tammy went on, "What was even worse is that Jeanette assumed I knew all about it. I had to pretend I knew what she was talking about. Thankfully, I think she was drunk enough that I might have pulled it off, but talk about embarrassing."

"I'm sorry," I said again. "It was very wrong of me." I made my best effort at exaggerated remorse.

"Shut up. Just shut up." She scowled at me. Then she said, "Is it true you stole Jeanette's fiancé right from under her nose? Some guy named Timothy, from out of town?"

I burst out laughing.

"Okay, I guess that's a no." Tammy leveled a finger at me. "But you are going to tell me everything later. Come by after work."

That meant I was going to have to talk about it, and I didn't want to. I felt like if I talked about it now, it would mean this was the end of the story. I didn't want to think about the fact that it almost certainly was the end of the story.

But Tammy wasn't asking, so there wasn't a chance to say no. She spun around on her heel and marched out again.

I glanced over at Neil. He had his glasses up on his head, had stopped doing the accounts, and was staring at me.

"What?" I demanded.

"Nothing," he said, putting his glasses back down and going back to his laptop.

The rest of the day was impossibly long. Time stretches when you're waiting for something—especially something that doesn't come.

I went to Tammy's that night and told her the whole story. I had to go all the way back to Saturday night and the run-in with Dan. I also had to stop a few times for cursing breaks—Tammy's, of course. She's always hated Dan. And I have to say, it didn't look like she was shaping up to like Timothy much either.

"Just give him a chance," I pleaded.

She gave me a look, and I caught myself. "I mean, if he comes back," I added quickly.

"Nora, I wouldn't get your hopes up."

I don't know what my face looked like, but it must have showed something of what my stomach did when she said that because she shook her head and said, "Oh, baby. Take my advice. Get off that train, and now."

"Did you see something?" I asked her. "Do you know he won't be coming back?"

"You know I only see things when I'm holding your hand."

So I made her do it, but she couldn't see anything.

I left feeling worse than before I arrived. Sometimes talking doesn't help. You just get caught in the loop of wondering and worrying and wanting.

It wasn't better when I got home. My mother

still wasn't talking to me, but that was almost a relief. It was too early to even try to get her to forgive me, so I just went up to my room and spent the rest of the night there, in the narrow twin bed that had been mine since I was a child. It was more like a hammock, with the sag in the middle of the mattress. I should probably have bought another, but I never wanted to think about how long I might be there. At some point I heard my mother come up to bed, and I don't know how long it was after that, but eventually I fell asleep.

I got up the next morning. I worked. I waited. I wondered.

What was he doing? And, more importantly, was he thinking of me?

Timothy

What Timothy Did After He Left Kansas

I left, and I didn't think about her.

My ability to do that was almost frightening. I just got busy and got on with life. I met with Warren. I flew back to New York. Then my mother called in a panic because while I was away the market had been cresting and troughing like a ship in a hurricane, and she was worried I hadn't been playing close enough attention.

I hadn't been paying attention at all.

But it turned out that was the best thing I could have done. The market has its own intelligence. I trusted that. Other people choose to trust family and institutions like marriage and church. Those things I don't trust at all—but the market I trust, not necessarily to go up and up and up without ever a down: that doesn't make sense. No, I trust it to find its own equilibrium, despite the idiocy of many of the people who trade it.

I was back in the office by Wednesday afternoon, and I spent the whole afternoon on the phone. In case you were wondering what people do on Wall Street, most of them just talk. They spend twelve hours a day on the phone, talking. They are paid spectacular salaries to gossip. Other people crunch the numbers—the researchers, the quant guys—but the ones who do the things that might be recognizable as work aren't the ones who get paid.

I have to admit that I loved the drama of the so-called economic crisis. Every day brought some new development. The jobless data, the housing foreclosures, the details of the bailout—they were like snapshots of a situation that was still developing. And from those snapshots everyone was trying to predict the future. There were all sorts of doomsday predictions, like the whole globe going into a recession, or another Great Depression, or that the financial system was on the verge of collapse.

But it turned out that our portfolio was positioned just right, and we made back almost all we had lost. When I thought the gains were almost maxed out, I changed tactics and took a more conservative stance. The wild swings were far from over, and though there was money to be made in this market, there was as much, or more, to be lost. And if you looked at it like gambling (which it was), then I wanted to be the casino. Casinos very carefully fix the odds so they win at least 51 percent of the time. That 1 percent is small, but the amount of money that flows through adds up to millions in profit. That's the position I wanted. I didn't want to be the reckless gambler who is in for a quick, easy fortune and ends up losing everything.

All in, it was a very good week. It's a sad truth that the taste of success is much sweeter when you know that so many around you are sitting down to a very bitter meal of failure.

I told myself that my road trip into Kansas had really been about getting away from work—about giving the portfolio the space to work rather than following the hourly fluctuations too closely and ruining the strategy I'd crafted. Beyond that, there was nothing to it. It was just a jaunt where I'd met a pretty girl who I'd made up a whole story about. I told myself that the wide-open spaces of the West must have gotten to my brain, and I slipped quickly back into my old routines.

Friday came around, and I went to meet my trader and best friend, Marcus, at Cipriani Wall Street, just like I did every Friday. It was a ridiculous place to go and have beer. A Budweiser cost more than ten dollars when you factored in the tip. But that was sort of the point.

Marcus was already there when I got there. Who am I kidding? Marcus was always there first. That means he always got his beer before I did. Once I tried to get him to order me one so it would be waiting when I got there. He just laughed and said he wouldn't want my beer to get warm. That was the closest he ever came to complaining about the way I was always late, but he wasn't a sucker. He wasn't about to have a beer waiting for me when

I arrived. Wait, I forgot. Once he did have a beer waiting for me. I started drinking it, and it didn't taste right. He'd gotten me an O'Doul's—alcohol free. I didn't ask him again.

That day I wasn't too late, and I was able to catch the bartender just as Marcus's beer was arriving.

"A Stella, please," I said.

Then I turned to Marcus. He had ordered a Peroni. "Who orders Italian beer?" I demanded.

"I think you stayed too long in the Midwest," he replied.

"That's very geographically prejudiced of you. I think the trading floor might be rubbing off on you."

Marcus was a trader at Goldman Sachs. I think everyone has heard the stories of the macho trading floor, the cursing, the hamburgers for breakfast, the pornographic e-mails that make the rounds of nearly every computer. Traders take pride in being incredibly politically incorrect.

Marcus was an exception. He had organic granola for breakfast every morning. He never cursed. He was the only man I've ever known who didn't admit to watching porn (though I'm not sure I believed him). If it sounds like Marcus was a bit of a prig, you would be right. But he was a prig against the grain. No amount of teasing about his granola and the perfectly pressed dress pants he wore to work every day ever seemed to ruffle him. He probably got more porn in his in-box every day than the rest of the trading floor combined, from people who were trying to yank his chain. But he just deleted it without a word. I had never seen Marcus upset. Come to think of it, in some ways Marcus reminded me of me—which is probably the reason I liked him.

"I was thinking we might grab a table today instead of eating at the bar," Marcus said.

I knew what that meant. His wife was going to join us.

I said, "I can't stay for dinner tonight."

"Come on, Tim. You always do this."

"If I always do this, then why are you surprised?" I asked him.

"You're my best friend. I would like you to get along with my wife at least well enough to have dinner with her."

"Okay, if it was your idea, I'll stay," I said. "Was it?"

Any other guy would have lied to get what he wanted. But Marcus just smiled and shrugged. "Okay, escape if you want."

"Why do you let her push you around like this? You know women don't respect men they can boss around."

"So now I should take marital advice from the perpetual bachelor?"

He had a point.

"The thing is, women like to be included every once in a while in the guy events, otherwise they get suspicious," he said.

"I wouldn't put up with it."

"That's obvious. And that's also why you're a lonely, miserable bastard," he told me.

"Better than a smug bastard," I said.

Marcus had just gotten married the year before. Even I had to admit that his wife was perfect: American father, French mother, grew up in Europe, summers in the States, gorgeous, smart as a whip, and a successful artist. Her paintings sold for a fortune. Exotic, talented, completely self-possessed—and there was no way in hell I was having dinner with her and Marcus.

"She's going to think you don't like her."

"I don't care what she thinks," I said.

"I have to tell you, Tim, I don't envy the women who date you."

"I'd be worried if you did."

"Very funny. But I actually think that's part of the reason Celia wanted to come."

"I don't follow."

"Well, she feels left out of our Fridays, so a couple of weeks ago I told her some of the stories—"

I groaned. "No, tell me you didn't."

"What?" He pretended like he didn't know what I was talking about.

"Marcus, what did you tell her?"

"Nothing really. Just some stories. Like that blonde last month who came up to us—"

"Oh, good Lord."

"It's okay. I'm not even sure Celia believed me. I think she wanted to see for herself."

"That's it. There's no way I'm going to be put on display like some sort of zoo creature," I told him. I stood up just as the bartender came back with my beer.

"You're not even staying for one beer?" he asked.

There was something about the way Marcus was looking at me. I sat back down.

"Okay. I'll stay for one beer."

His face cleared, and he said, "Good, because I wanted to tell you about the rumor I heard today."

"What's up?"

Working on the trading floor, Marcus always did have the best stories.

"I don't even know if I believe it. And there were no names attached, but I heard someone has been fudging the books and is about to get busted. And I've heard it's big."

"How big?"

"Billions."

"Billions? Someone is pulling your leg."

"Maybe. But the source is pretty solid."

"Who is it?"

He just smiled.

"Come on, spill it," I said.

I think I would have gotten it out of him, but Celia arrived before he could finish. I had my back to the entrance, but I knew she'd come in from the faces of the men farther down the bar who were facing the door.

Marcus got up from his seat. He still did that— got up when a woman arrived or left. I stayed seated. She came around me and kissed Marcus. Then she turned to me and gave me a frosty smile. "Hello, Timothy."

"Hello, Celia."

She gave me an air kiss. "How are you?"

"Good. Good. You?"

"Not bad. Working on my next show. I have one at a new, bigger gallery coming up in the spring."

"That's great. Congratulations."

"Thanks."

She eyed me.

I smiled at her. It was a smile calculated to annoy her. And it worked. I saw it in the way her face froze.

Marcus did too.

"I was just telling Tim about a crazy rumor," he said quickly.

"Is that right?" she said, obviously not interested at all.

I said, "I have to get going, but, Marcus, you can tell me the rest of it on Monday."

"So you're going?" Celia said.

"Yeah, I'm heading out."

"Why am I not surprised?" she said.

Marcus and I looked at each other—and he shrugged apologetically.

This is what it was like to be married. Where was true love, outside of books and movies and songs? If I was tempted to believe, all I had to do was look at Marcus. He thought he'd found the perfect woman. And I knew better.

THE INVESTIGATION

A CONTROVERSIAL VIEW OF VICTIMS

Victims may also play a role in their homicide ... In about 55 percent of all homicide cases the victim and killer knew one another, and the homicide often arose out of conflicts in their relationship. Lester and Lester (1975) point out that victims may be as strongly motivated to be killed as their killers are to kill. Viewed in this light a homicide may not be an isolated event; it may be an expression of an integral pattern of a relationship. An additional feature of the victim-precipitated homicide is the fact that in this type of homicide one can see a close relationship between suicide and murder.

—From *The Human Side of Homicide*
by Bruce L. Danto, John Bruhns,
and Austin H. Kutscher

Nora

What Nora Did After Timothy Left Kansas

The disaster that was dinner with Timothy happened on Tuesday. The rest of the week was an eternity.

Then I came home on Friday to find Deirdre and my mother sitting in the kitchen. Together. And they weren't fighting.

When I pushed open the door, they both looked up at me like I was the last person they expected to see. I don't know who they thought it might be.

I was annoyed. I'll admit it. I was annoyed, even though I'd been trying for the last three years to get my sister and my mother to sit in the same room without fighting. For the last three years, I seemed to be the only one who was aware of the fact that they might not have much more time left to spend time together. I would have thought I'd be ecstatic to walk in and discover my mother and my sister deep in conversation. But I wasn't. The moment I walked in the room and saw them I realized I didn't just want them to make up—I wanted to be the one who brought them together.

It didn't help that my mother took one look at me, turned to Deirdre like *she* was her best friend, and said, "Call me later." Then she stood up and left the room without another word or even a glance at me. Apparently, the time since Tuesday night didn't feel like an eternity to my mother.

My sister said, "You're home early."

"Actually I'm not. This is the time I get home. I didn't know you were coming. Where are the twins?"

Deirdre seemed almost embarrassed. She couldn't quite look me in the eye when she said, "A friend of mine is looking after them. And, actually, I need to get back. It's later than I thought. I lost track of the time."

"You're going now?"

"Yeah," and she got up and pushed her chair in as if to prove it. "I just came by to see Mom," she added awkwardly. "See how she was doing."

The fact that she tried to explain what she was doing there only made me more suspicious. Deirdre never bothered to explain herself.

"That's a first," I said.

"So?" There was an edge to her voice—her way of warning me that if I kept on in this direction I was going to have trouble.

"I'm just saying it's a new thing."

"Maybe I've come before and you just didn't know it."

That made me stop and think for a second. It was true I had no idea what happened here during the day. And if I'd been five minutes later, and

Deirdre had left, I never would have known she was there at all.

Then I remembered our conversation the Sunday before. I felt a little guilty that I'd been so immersed in my drama that I'd completely forgotten her problems. But once I remembered her money issues, I realized what Deirdre must have come back for.

"So did you find out if Mom has any money?" I asked.

"I didn't come back for money."

I didn't believe her. "I thought you were about to lose your apartment."

"Yeah, well, Boyd came through. He's giving me enough to get by."

"You were so sure he wouldn't help." It was my way of saying I didn't believe her.

She shrugged. "I was wrong. So sue me."

"So you didn't ask Mom for any money at all?"

"Why do you want to know?"

We were both standing—since I'd never sat down and she had gotten up as if to leave—and now it felt like we were facing off. But for once I didn't feel like backing down.

"Well, maybe because I've been footing the bill, I'm deep in debt, and I'm kind of curious if she was telling me the truth."

Deirdre rolled her eyes as if that was just the most ridiculous thing she ever heard, but I guess she decided to humor me because she said,

"Okay, fine, then yes, I asked her for money. But she told me the same thing she told you."

"Did you believe her?"

Deirdre finally erupted. "God, I don't know. I've got enough problems—I don't need to worry about yours, okay?" Then, abruptly, "I've got to go."

And that's exactly what she did.

The weekend brought another trip to Kansas City for chemo session number six. But this one was a silent trip. I was still enemy number one, according to my mother.

Sunday was a wasteland.

I was waiting for Monday.

It came and went. And the week slid by.

Another Monday came and went.

And another.

It got bitterly cold. The wind blew down from the Canadian steppe. We had our first snowfall, just a dusting. Then we had a real early season blizzard that closed down the streets for a day.

My mother started speaking to me again. I don't even know when. It came as a gradual thawing as the world around us froze.

I didn't see Dan, and I didn't even have to avoid his car. I wondered briefly if he might be avoiding me now. But then I asked myself if I cared, and the answer was no, so I didn't think about it again.

Life went back to normal. My heart had long stopped racing every time the door to the coffee shop opened. What had happened with Timothy was almost like a story in a book I'd read—he was like a character I'd dreamed of but who wasn't quite real. Though isn't that what all our loves are?

How can I call him a love? Love after five minutes in a diner and a painful hour sitting across a table from each other not speaking?

Well, why not?

Timothy

Another Family Dinner and a Visit from His Sister

At the first family dinner after I got back, the theme was red. My mother loved to match: red tablecloth, red napkins, red flowers, red wine, beet salad, rare steak, red velvet cake.

It wasn't just the table and the flowers and the food. She also wore red. She was dressed in a red Chanel suit. And that wasn't the end of the matching either. She also liked to match designers. Chanel suit meant Chanel shoes and Chanel belt and Chanel bag and Chanel scarf and Chanel coat.

A man shouldn't know these things.

It turned out that she chose the color specifically for me. She announced it at the beginning of dinner. She tinged her wineglass and said, "This night is to help everyone understand the position we are in now as a family. Unfortunately, thanks to Timothy, we are now in the red."

I hadn't told her about what had happened that week. I'd been saving it.

She turned to me. "Timothy, do you have anything to say to that?"

"Yes," I told her. "I'm afraid I have bad news."

Her lips pursed, but she looked almost perversely pleased. My mother does love a good tragedy, once she embraces it. Who doesn't like the image of himself, or herself, suffering terribly? Not the actual suffering, mind you. Just the image of it.

"I'm afraid, after this week you've chosen the wrong color."

"The wrong color?"

She wasn't pleased anymore; she didn't understand, and she didn't like that.

"It should have been black," I told her.

"Black?" There was a long pause as she took that in. "You mean . . ."

"It was a good week," I said.

"Why didn't you tell me this before?" she demanded, sounding almost angry.

If I had been expecting her to be happy, I might have been disappointed. But I knew that she wouldn't be. She didn't like surprises, my mother. Even good ones.

I also knew that she couldn't resist the idea of money—it turned her giddy. So her bad mood would only last until she saw the spreadsheet.

"Do you have a printout for me?" she asked a second later.

I reached under my chair for my folio and pulled out the weekly report I'd put together.

She had her hand out waiting, and I gave her the paper.

She took it, looked at it, and smiled. Then she started grilling me. She wanted a blow-by-blow account of every successful trade. That took us through the appetizer and into the main course. But when she heard I had taken profits and had pulled back, she went from giddy to furious in a second.

"Just when we have a chance to actually make some money, rather than simply making back what you lost, you get scared?" she demanded. "I honestly don't know what I was thinking, putting you in charge of managing the money. I would do it myself, if I had more time."

I looked over at my father. He was silently cutting the last of his steak (rare and very red). He didn't even look up. It was actually my father who had put me in charge. And he might let my mother have her way in all other things, but he would never in a million years let her take over managing the money. That was understood.

Eventually, when we got to dessert, my mother moved on from me to the rest of the family, but she didn't have enough time to really rake them over the coals. It gave me another reason to feel good—I felt like I had spared them.

But, as is so often the case, other people often don't see things the same way. My sister, for one, didn't see it quite in the same light, which I discovered a few weeks later when she came to see me in the office.

My sister never came to see me in the office. Or maybe I should amend that—my sister never came to see me at all. I had never thought about it much, but we had no real relationship. I sat with her at the dinner table every week, and I heard about what she was doing from my brother Edward, but when we saw each other, she and I rarely even exchanged more than hello and a polite kiss on the cheek. And it had been that way for as long as I could remember. In the family order, it was me, and then Andrew came a year later. Then my mother took a few years off before having Edward and then Emily. I was five years older than Edward and just over seven older than Emily. I went off to college when Emily was eleven, so I wasn't there for the years she spent in and out of hospitals and clinics for the eating disorder that set in at puberty.

I have to admit, other than having a laugh about her crazy marriages, and thoroughly enjoying the fits my mother had over her, I never really thought about my sister. She might as well have been a stranger. In fact, she was.

I got my first sense of this when my secretary, Marie, knocked on the door of my office and told me Emily was outside and wanted to see me. I swear to you, for a good ten or fifteen seconds, I searched my memory for an Emily I had slept with and who might have gone so far as to find out where I worked and shown up there. Then I realized that she meant my sister Emily. That's how unexpected her visit was.

"Tell her to come in," I told Marie.

Emily entered a few seconds later. Even though she was thirty-five now, in some ways she looked like the twelve-year-old I remembered. For one, she was about the same size. She had been tall even back then, and she still had the straight-as-a-board, pre-puberty body. She wore a blouse with a ruffle at the collar, like a girl. And she wore her hair like a girl's too: long and straight, pinned up with a simple barrette.

I got up and came around my desk to kiss her cheek. "Hi, Emily."

"I hope I'm not bothering you," she said.

"No, I can take a break."

She sat down in the chair across from my desk—not over by the couch. So I went back around the desk and sat down.

She didn't look at me right away. She looked down at her lap. She placed her hands on her legs, then spread her fingers out, as if inspecting them.

I waited.

"I've met someone," she said without looking up.

"Really? Who is it?"

She looked up at me then. "Don't pretend. I know that Edward told you about him."

"I didn't know if you were talking about the

same man," I said. "It's been at least a week since I talked to him." I couldn't help teasing her.

She looked at me levelly. "I guess I deserve that. And I don't expect you to believe this either, but Alejandro is different. This time it's real."

"Okay," I said. I didn't believe her.

"We're going to get married."

"Congratulations," I said, though I have to admit, my tone was a little dry.

She heard it.

"Fuck you," she said.

"That's better," I said. It annoys me when people aren't honest and try to play nice because they want something from you.

"You're such an asshole. I wanted to come in here and have a civilized conversation."

"You wanted to write the script for how it was going to go," I corrected her. "I don't like reading from a script, at least not one that someone else writes for me—especially since I gather that you're not here for a social call. I'm assuming you want something."

"Edward told me it didn't matter if I came in and cursed you out. He said you'd do what you were going to do."

"You should have listened to him. So why don't you tell me what you want."

"Fine." She obviously still wasn't happy that things hadn't gone her way. "I told Mother about Alejandro, and that we were going to get married."

"And how did she take it?" I asked—though I knew already without her even needing to tell me.

"She said that if I went through with it, not only would she cut off my money, but that I would never have another cent and I'd be taken out of the will."

"Big guns. Did you go to Dad?"

"Yes."

"And?"

"He said if Alejandro loved me, he would provide for me. *Provide* for me. What, are we living in the nineteenth century now?"

"Well, couldn't he? Edward told me that the guy—Alejandro is it? Anyway, Edward said that he had money."

She was silent for a minute. Then she said, "Yes, but what if it doesn't work out? What if I'm wrong?"

"You're risking a lot," I agreed.

"I don't think it would be healthy for our relationship to have me completely dependent on Alejandro."

"What does he say?"

"He says he'll always be there for me. But that's what men always say. And then they're not. How can I trust him?"

"I don't have any insight on that one. So why did you come to me? Are you hoping I could change her mind?"

"Do you think you could?" she asked.

"No," I said.

"No," she agreed.

I waited.

"I thought you could help me another way." She looked at me for a few seconds, waiting.

I didn't say anything.

"You're not making this any easier for me," she burst out.

It was always people like my sister—victims—who thought other people should always be making things easier for them. Well, that's what she'd had her whole life, and it didn't seem to have helped her any. I just looked at her.

"Okay, I get it. I wanted to ask you if you could give me some money. A lump sum, not a huge amount, just something that would make me feel secure."

Enough to make her feel secure—I'd like to know what that amount is. Of all the people I've come across, none of them, no matter how rich, seemed to have that magic number—the one that would make them feel secure. Security, as far as I could tell, came from a different place altogether. But I had a feeling my sister didn't want to hear that.

"How can I give you money if Mother said no?" I asked her.

"Oh, come on. There have got to be ways. You could pretend to buy some stock, and then write down that you've sold it at a loss."

"You want me to cook the books."

"I just want you to help me out a little. It's not a big deal."

"It's a big deal to me. And I'm not going to do it."

"So now you're this really moral person who's not going to do anything wrong?"

"No, I'm just not going to put myself in a dangerous position in order to give you money because you spent all of yours."

"Then give it to me from your own money. I know you have bags of it," she said, and she couldn't keep the bitterness from her voice.

"Emily, I started out with the same amount as you did. If I have more now, and you've blown through yours, is that supposed to be my problem? Even if I did give you money, it wouldn't be enough. You'd be back here in a year, asking me for more. You're like our mother in the way you go through the cash."

"I'm like Mother? *Me?*" Her voice climbed in disbelief. "My God, you've got to be kidding me. You're the one who's like her. Exactly. You look like her; you sound like her; you're obsessed with money like her. Don't you wonder why she gives you all the attention and none to anyone else? Because you're just a reflection of her."

Up to then I had been mildly amused by the scene, but at that point I started to get annoyed. "If it were up to me, you could have one hundred percent of her attention, Emily," I said. "If she ignored me completely, nothing would make me happier."

"Oh really? Then why don't you just fax her the update at the end of the week? I've heard her ask you to do that, but you never do. You always bring it with you. Why is that?"

"I thought I was actually doing you a favor, taking up her time and letting the rest of you off the hook."

"You have got to be kidding me. You mean you've been telling yourself you're the hero of the family? That's what's been going through your head? You're sicker than I thought."

"Me? I'm sick?"

She didn't seem to hear me. She just barreled on.

"And clueless. You're good at money and absolutely nothing else. You have no idea what's actually going on. You bring that stupid spreadsheet with you every week because if you didn't it would become embarrassingly obvious that there is absolutely nothing else going on in your life. There would be nothing else for Mother to talk to you about."

"You don't know anything about my life," I told her.

"Don't fool yourself, Timothy," and the contempt in her voice was so real, it penetrated even my thick skin. "It doesn't matter if you've got this girl or that girl or twenty of them. They might as well be blow-up dolls, for how real they are to you. We all know it. Even Mother. That's why she doesn't bother asking."

"You're just pissed because she doesn't butt into my life."

"See, you still don't get it. She doesn't butt into your life because you don't have one. You don't have a life; you don't have friends; you don't have anything but money. You know, I've just decided I'm going to go and marry Alejandro anyway. Even without the money. And that terrifies me, but not doing it terrifies me more. Because I worry that I might end up like you."

"There are things about me you don't know."

"Yeah, right. I would love it if that were true. But the sad fact is, you're the one who doesn't know. You don't know about yourself, or anyone else for that matter."

"Yes, I do. I know more than you think. I knew about Alejandro, didn't I?"

"You only know what Edward tells you, and he doesn't tell you shit. He and I talk about what bullshit he's going to feed you this week. It's a game for us. We laugh at you."

I didn't believe her. I said to her, "Maybe I don't know the details, but I don't give a crap about those."

She looked at me pityingly. "You don't believe me. Okay. How about this? Edward has been writing books for years now. He has four pub-lished, under a pseudonym of course, so Mother won't know. His fifth is coming out this spring. And, Andrew, he's gay. He and his wife still live together, but she knows and he's got his own place downtown where he stays half the time. Dad, he has a house down on St. John. We went down last year. Me and Edward and Andrew and Dad's mistress. The woman he's really been with for the last twenty years, and you've never even met her."

She had to be lying. That's what I told myself. She must be lying. But then why did I believe her?

She stood up. "I'm sorry, Timothy, but I thought it was time that someone told you the truth."

Then she turned around and walked out.

THE INVESTIGATION

MOTIVE

In the chapter "Homicide and Human Nature" in the book *Homicide*, it states that "People who kill in spite of the inhibitions and penalties that confront them are people moved by strong passions. The issues over which people are prepared to kill must surely be those about which they care most profoundly" (Daly, Wilson, p. 12).

Nora

Timothy Comes Back to Kansas

You probably think I'm going to tell you that it was a total surprise when he came back. But it wasn't. Or maybe it was and I'm just rewriting the story in hindsight. But I'll tell you how I remember it.

I was standing behind the counter. I had a cranberry muffin stashed away on a lower shelf, and I was picking at it. I had a piece of it in my mouth—a piece that had a cranberry, so it was both tangy and sweet at the same time—when I got a picture of Timothy. I could see him walking down the street outside, headed toward the store. I closed my eyes to see it more clearly. In my mind I could see him approaching the store. I could see him reaching out for the door, and even as I saw it in my mind, I felt the rush of cold air as the door opened. When I opened my eyes, he was there standing in front of me.

Did that actually happen? Or did it happen in one of the dreams I had about him, and I just rearranged it in my head? I don't think so, but I can't know for sure. Dreams and memory blur together for me now, so I can't really tell them apart. Can you tell the difference? Are you sure?

When I opened my eyes, he wasn't smiling. He

177

seemed almost angry. But a different kind of angry than the last time I'd seen him. Before he'd been a cold sort of angry. This was more agitated angry. Upset maybe.

"Well," he demanded. "Aren't you going to say anything?"

I smiled at him. "What can I get you?" I asked.

He didn't smile back. "This," he said, and he reached over the counter and cupped the back of my head with his hand. I could feel his fingers twining into my hair. When he leaned over, there was no way I could have escaped. But I didn't want to. His lips were softer than I could have imagined. All he did was gently touch them to mine. He left them there for a lingering second, but just as I started to lean forward into him for more, he pulled back. Then he was smiling. And he turned around and walked out again.

Oh, did I mention that Neil was there?

As Timothy walked out, he gave Neil a little nod.

After the door closed behind him, Neil looked over at me and shook his head. He said, "I've always wished I could do something like that."

"Neil!"

"What?" he said, as if he had no idea why I was angry. Then he made it even worse. He said, "Do you think he's coming back?"

Timothy did come back, but he took his time.

He waited until almost the end of the day. I was just locking up to leave when he came sauntering up.

"Hello," he said.

I was so angry I almost couldn't speak. But I managed to get something out. "Where have you been?"

He kissed me again. Then he pulled back and looked at me intently. "Now I know why I couldn't forget about you."

"Why?" I asked.

He shook his head at me silently, and I knew it wasn't going to be that kind of relationship. It wasn't going to be something logical. Women like to talk about it, to try to figure it out, to pin it down and capture it with words. He wasn't going to do that. He didn't even try.

"Come on." He took my hand and led me to his car. It was another BMW rental, but not a convertible this time.

"Where are we going?" I asked.

"Back to my hotel."

I stopped.

"Come on," he said.

I shook my head. "It's a small town."

"And it's a short life," he countered.

I still hesitated.

"Do you want to?" he asked.

That was a question I didn't usually ask myself. I asked what other people wanted. I asked what I should do. What I shouldn't do. But what I wanted?

The answer was surprising.

"No. I want to go have a cup of coffee, and I want you to tell me what your last name is."

"Coffee and my last name. That's what you want?"

"Yes. I haven't seen Jeanette in a while. Don't you want to say hello?"

It wasn't until much later that I found out he'd already been to say hello to Jeanette. That was where he had been most of the day. So he said no to going to Joe's. At the time I assumed it was because he was scared of Jeanette, and I remember thinking it was sweet and funny. Our conclusions are based on nothing: partial truths and assumptions.

We agreed to go for a drive instead. I unlocked the door to Starbox, made us two large lattes, and we got into his car and drove out of town. It was getting dark already as we left, and soon we couldn't even see anything, but he kept driving. And we talked. At first we talked about his life in New York, and his work, and then he started telling me about his family. He started off by describing their family dinners. He told me about the color themes: the matching food and outfits that his mother liked to coordinate. Then he told me how, at a recent one, his mother had made his sister, who had been battling anorexia for years, get on a scale in front of everybody to prove she hadn't lost more weight.

So I told him how, before we went to dinner last time, I'd put on jeans and a coat over my dress to sneak out of the house to meet him. And how it totally hadn't worked, my mother had known anyway, and it felt like this elaborate game of unspoken things that everyone knew but no one talked about.

He was silent for a bit after I said that. At first I thought he was thinking about the fact that I still lived at home with my mother. Because in telling that story, I had to admit that detail—but I didn't tell him that I'd been at school and that she got sick and that that was why I'd come home. I didn't tell him that I was working at the coffee shop because I needed to pay the bills and in our tiny town that was the only job I could get. I felt like it would sound like excuses, and I didn't want to make excuses. I knew it wouldn't matter anyway. It wasn't like he was going to move to Kansas, and I certainly couldn't pick up and move to New York.

But when he spoke, it was clear he hadn't actually been thinking about me at all. He had been thinking about the phrase I said: "unspoken things that everyone knows." He told me that there were unspoken things in his family, and not everyone knew about them. He paused again for a long time. Then, with the hesitation of confession, he told me the story of how his sister had come in to see him and spilled all these secrets about the family that he didn't have any idea about. He admitted that he didn't even know his sister well enough to know if she was lying.

And with that story, I got a peek underneath the facade. Before I had seen him as good-looking, confident, magnetic, and a bit of a jerk. I have to admit I was attracted to that man, but I didn't trust him at all. But then I caught a glimpse of the man underneath that facade—the uncertainty, the insecurity, the questioning, the honesty—and that man . . . That man I knew I could fall for. And in the moment that I realized I could fall for him, I knew I already had.

We drove all night, and we told each other stories. A lot of them were stories about our families. I told him how diabolical my mother had been in punishing us when we were very young. My sister was claustrophobic, and, knowing this, my mother would lock her in the closet. But it was also a punishment for me at the same time; I would have been fine in the closet, but having my sister in there screaming and not being able to help her, that had been the perfect brand of torture for me. And my mother knew it. When I was bad, my mother didn't threaten to do anything to me, she threatened to lock my sister in the closet. And she even did it once when I lied about having done my homework. My mother found out I had lied, and she locked my sister in the closet for three hours. I never missed a homework assignment again after that. It was probably why I'd done so well in school.

Timothy's stories were like something out of another world, like something I'd seen on a TV show, with money and fancy schools and fancy clothes and alcohol and drugs and no parents in sight.

When it got really late, and I realized we weren't going to be getting back anytime soon, I borrowed his cell phone to call my mother. She didn't pick up, so I just left her a message that I was staying over with Tammy.

I don't know how, but we got back exactly when I was supposed to be at work. I hadn't slept, I was in the same clothes, but luckily it was a uniform (a black polo shirt and khakis) and I wore it every day, so there was no real way to tell that I hadn't changed.

Still, when Neil walked into the store, he took one look at me and said, "You didn't go home last night."

"What do you mean, I didn't go home last night?" I said.

"Which word didn't you understand?" he asked.

"I just don't understand why you'd think that," I said, still trying to evade.

"Because you're wearing the same clothes." Then he added, after a moment, "And your mother called me at three o'clock in the morning."

"Oh no."

"Oh yes."

"Neil, I'm really sorry."

"I didn't tell her anything." He answered the question I'd thought but hadn't asked.

"Thank you."

"I mean, other than the fact that a stranger came into the store and kissed you," he said. He saw my face and he said, "I'm kidding. I told her I wasn't here when you closed up yesterday. But are you sure you know what you're doing?"

"Nope," I said. "No idea."

"Well that's good. At least we're clear on that."

"No offense, Neil, but look where my plans have gotten me so far."

That's when I saw Tammy's car pull up across the street. She got out and hurried across the street, but she spotted me through the windows. She glared furiously at me through the glass till she was inside and could say, "Okay, what the hell?"

"Hi, Tammy," Neil said.

As usual, she barely glanced at him.

"Let me guess," I said. "My mother called you."

"What were you thinking? Your mom's not well, and you go and disappear on her? Just never go home? I'm sorry, but what is that?"

"It's called being selfish," I said.

"Yeah, I know," she shot back.

"So why did you ask?"

She stared at me.

"Joking. Anyway, I did call her. She just never checks the stupid machine. But what's the deal? Why are you so upset? I don't understand."

"You think I understand getting a hysterical call from your mother at three o'clock in the morning?" Abruptly Tammy turned toward Neil. "Would you understand that, Neil?"

"As a matter of fact—" Neil started to say, but Tammy cut him off.

"Oh my God," Tammy turned back to me, "You weren't out last night with him, were you?"

"Him? . . . What, you mean Neil?"

"I'm sitting right here," Neil interjected. "Please remember that when you speak."

"Then who?" Tammy demanded. "Please not Dan."

"Dan . . . Dan Marker?" Neil said. "But he's married."

Tammy gave me a look that said, do you believe this guy?

What I couldn't believe was that she couldn't figure out who I'd stayed out the whole night for.

"Timothy," I told her. "Timothy came back."

For a second Tammy didn't even remember; I could see the blankness on her face. Then it hit.

"You mean the guy. The one . . ." I could see her mind filling in all the blanks. Of course Tammy

jumped straight to the thing she was most interested in. She said, "Oh no, you didn't."

"No, I didn't," I said.

"Well, for God's sake, why not? You waiting for
the engraved invitations to go out? What on earth
did you do all night then?"

"We went for a drive."

At that point, Neil inserted himself back into the
conversation. "All night?" he said, obviously not
believing me.

"Not that it's any of your business, but yes, all
night."

Tammy and Neil exchanged looks.

"Okay, fine. Discuss amongst yourselves, but
leave me out of it."

And I heard the door, and my first thought was
relief that a customer was coming in and that
would break it up. But when I looked over at the
door, I saw my mother.

"Mom," I said. I didn't even feel panic right
away. There was just surprise. She'd never once
come to visit me in the three years I had worked
there. I think it was because she was ashamed.
Her daughter with a degree from Kansas State,
and who came so close to a PhD in economics at
Chicago, spent her days making lattes.

I haven't really mentioned the degrees, have I?
That's because for three years I've done my best
to forget about them. Early on, after I moved
home, I discovered that it was my past that made

186

my present situation so hard to live with. If I didn't have the degrees and all those years spent studying so hard, then—other than the fact that I didn't make enough money to cover all the expenses—it seemed like there was nothing wrong with working at Starbox. It was only when I thought of all that work, the studying, the expectations, and I looked at where I should have ended up, and where I was now, that I got depressed. When I let go of the past—when I let go of the fact that life hadn't turned out the way I had expected—life became bearable.

But I don't think my mother saw it in quite the same way. And that was why she stayed away.

My mother stood there and looked at me, in my polo shirt and khakis, standing behind the counter.

"I just wanted to know if you were still alive," she said. She turned to Neil and Tammy. "Do either of you know what happened to her last night? I'm sure I'm not going to get a straight answer out of her."

Tammy and Neil had both been enjoying themselves at my expense a second before, but now they looked like they wished they were anywhere other than there.

"Okay, I can see that neither of you idiots is going to say anything," my mother said, dismissing them with a shake of her head. She turned back to me. "Will you be home tonight?"

I thought of Timothy. I thought of him coming

back. I thought about how I didn't have any idea how long he was staying—or what he intended. I had found out more about him during the car ride: his last name, for one. His name was Timothy Whitting. And he lived in New York City. He was in finance. He managed money, but he was fuzzy about exactly what he did. I'm pretty sure he didn't talk a lot about it because he didn't expect me to understand anything about it.

The thing was, I hadn't asked him what I really wanted to know, like how long was he staying and why'd he'd come back. Or had he ever been married. Or in love. Or if there was someone else in his life. It could be that he was in town only one more night.

All this flashed through my mind, and still I said, "Yes, I'll be home."

My mother nodded, then turned on her heel and walked out.

Silently Neil got up and came around the counter. He said, "Why don't you go sit down with Tammy, I'll make us some drinks."

I stared at him. "You've never let me sit down during work before."

"Well, you've never gone and done something like this before."

"Like what?"

"Like . . . I don't know. This," he said, and shooed me to sit down.

When Timothy came in about twenty minutes

later, Tammy, Neil, and I were sitting with our drinks, at one of the tables. I caught a glimpse of him coming through the corner of my eye. I saw the stride, the assurance in it, and then caught the falter in his step when he came in and saw that I wasn't behind the counter but, instead, sitting down at a table like I was a customer.

I turned back just in time to catch Tammy's first glimpse of him. Her eyes widened a bit, but then she looked over to me and caught me watching her. She pulled her face back to normal.

"Timothy, this is my friend Tammy," I introduced him as he came up to the table. "And I'm not sure if you've really been introduced to Neil before. He's my boss."

Tammy held out her hand, and Timothy took it. Then Neil's.

There was an awkward silence.

"What brings you out here?" Tammy finally said.

"I came for Nora," Timothy told her.

"All the way out from New York City?" she said, an edge of disbelief to her voice.

"All the way," he agreed.

"How long are you staying?" she shot this next question at him like a bullet.

I held my breath.

"I'm not sure," he admitted.

"What, you don't have a return ticket?"

"Not exactly."

"What does that mean? Did you buy a one-way?"

"No."

"Then that means you have a return ticket?"

"No, it doesn't." He was disagreeing with her, but his voice was mild.

"Okay, you're going to have to explain that one to me," Tammy said. A fist had crept up to her hip, her usual combat posture.

"I flew out on a private plane," he said.

"You have a plane?"

"My family does. Yes."

"So is it your parents' or something?"

"Well, we all have shares in it."

"So you're, like, really rich then, is that it?"

"Tammy!" I said. She was just engaging in her favorite sport—baiting people to see if they cracked—but in this case I had been the one who cracked. I knew I deserved the look she shot at me.

But to Timothy's credit, he looked like he was actually enjoying the game.

"Yes, you could say that I'm really rich."

"Brag about it, why don't you. Jeez," Tammy said.

And he laughed.

"Okay, I like him," Tammy announced to me.

Timothy turned to me as well. "Can I borrow your friend for business meetings? She'd be the perfect secret weapon to knock them off their game. There aren't many people who aren't afraid to break the rules."

There was such admiration in his tone, I actually got a pang of jealousy at Tammy for evoking it. It was also because I was suddenly very aware of how rarely I broke the rules—instead I was friends with someone who did. I let her do the work for me, and I told myself that because she was my friend, it said something about me as well. Maybe it did, but it still didn't make me a rule breaker.

"I'll break any rule you can think of," Tammy said. Then she looked over at me and winked.

"I'll keep that in mind," he said.

"Well, back to business," Neil announced.

Timothy turned to me. "I don't want to keep you from your work, but I wanted to find out about later."

"Later . . ." I took a deep breath. When I opened my mouth, I had no idea what would come out.

The force of habit won.

"I can't today," I said.

"Can't . . . ?"

"Can't meet you." I watched it sink in, saw the play of emotions—the surprise, the hurt, the decision, all in a split second. Something in him closed. The expression was the same, the voice, the tone, but it was as if something had been shuttered.

"Okay," he said.

Tammy leaped in. "If you want to come by the Box, I'll give you some free drinks. I read somewhere that rich people love free stuff even more than poor people."

He turned his smile on Tammy. "You heard right. I'm going to go back to my hotel and get some sleep, but if you'd tell me what and where this Box is, I'll certainly stop by later."

He glanced over at me, and he held the smile in place, but it wasn't the same; it wasn't the way he'd looked at me the night before. Then he turned to go.

"Timothy," I called after him.

He turned back.

"Promise me you won't leave without saying good-bye."

He looked surprised. "Who said anything about leaving?"

"Just, promise me, okay?"

"I promise," he said.

Nora

The Next Day

He came in the next day. I was so sure he was
going to tell me he was leaving. I was waiting for
it. I'd gone home knowing it. I'd lain in bed
thinking about it. I'd finally fallen asleep, and
then the thoughts blessedly went away, but I'd
woken with it. Sometimes when I wake up there
is a second or two when I'm free of my life. It was
not one of those mornings. It was there the
moment I opened my eyes.

The craziest thing was that *I'd* done it. It was all
me. I'd said yes to my mother and no to him. I'd
sat with my mother on the couch, knowing he was
out meeting Tammy. I could have gone. I could
have made an excuse and gone out. But I didn't.

He walked into the store around noon the next
day. So the whole morning, of course, I was
thinking about how late he must have been up
with Tammy. And, yes, I thought about the possibility of *that* too.

All morning only two customers came in, so I
made a total of two lattes in three hours, and the
rest of the time I fidgeted and waited for someone
to come by and tell me what was going on. Neil
wasn't even there to annoy me and take my mind
off things.

Finally, Timothy came in with a bag slung over his shoulder.

God, he was handsome.

"So when are you leaving?" I asked him.

His smile disappeared.

"What's all this talk about me going? Yesterday you were talking about saying good-bye, and today you're asking me when I'm leaving. Are you trying to give me a hint?"

"No, it's just that you have your bag."

He shook his head at me. "Nora, do you think I could fit all my clothes in this? This is for my work. I have papers and my computer," he explained patiently, like you would speak to a child. "See, I was in the hotel, doing work, and I figured I could come here and work instead. I saw the sign for Wi-Fi up in the window. Would that be okay?"

I felt really silly. But also incredibly happy. I tried to cover both by saying casually, "Yeah. I guess that would be okay."

"Oh, and just so you know, even if you did want me to leave, you're not getting rid of me that easily."

Then he turned around and went over to a table by the window. He pulled out his laptop and started setting up.

I made him a double-shot Venti latte and brought it over.

He looked up at me. "Thank you."

He kept looking me straight in the eyes, and it was doing funny things to my stomach.

"Are you sure your boss won't mind me working here? I'm not going to get you into trouble?"

"It's a coffee shop," I said. "It's supposed to be somewhere that people come to do work or read or hang out."

"Really? Because it doesn't have that feel."

"I know. It doesn't. I couldn't even tell you the last time someone came in and sat down here."

"Join me?" he said. "Just for a minute?"

And I did. It was my first rule breaking, though I wasn't sure if it counted because Neil had let me do it the day before.

"How was the Box last night?" I tried to ask casually, but my heart was beating fast.

"Well, it was an experience. Your friend Tammy is something else. You two aren't a whole lot alike, are you?"

"No, not really. I wish I were more like her."

"Really? Why?"

"I don't know," I said—because to tell him why I wanted to be more like Tammy would mean admitting all the things I didn't like about myself. And if he didn't notice them, I certainly didn't want to point them out. "She doesn't let things get to her," I said, coming up with a generic answer, which was also pretty much true.

"Tammy has her own problems," he said.

I wanted to ask him what he thought those problems were (since he claimed he could see them after one night, and I couldn't after more than two decades), but Tammy came in right at that second.

"Heeey, Tito," she cried, when she saw Timothy sitting across from me.

I looked at him.

He shrugged. "At some point last night, she just started calling me Tito."

"What do you mean, at some point?" she cried. "Only after you did five tequila shots." She turned to me. "This man is an animal."

"This man is too old for that," Timothy said.

"Did he tell you about what Chrissy Rorden did?" Tammy said.

"No."

"I thought I would spare her that one," Timothy said pointedly.

"You're kinder than I am. Hoo, boy, I need some coffee. Don't worry, I'll get it," she said, when I started to get up.

Neil would have had a fit seeing her behind the counter, but I let her pour herself a cup. Then she came to join us at the table.

About five minutes later a customer came in, so I had to get up, and as I was making her macchiato the customer said, "So you can bring your laptop to work here?" glancing over at Timothy.

"Yes, sure."

"Is there a limit to how long you can stay?"

"No, I don't think so."

"Well, I might just come back later to do some work."

Timothy stayed all afternoon, and the woman actually did come back with her laptop. Then someone else sat down and read the paper. We hadn't had three people sitting in the place at the same time the whole three years I'd worked there. I think it was just the sight of someone sitting with work spread out on the table, obviously at home in the place, that made the store seem more inviting.

When Neil came in, he almost did a double take. He came up to me at the counter. "What's up with the crowd? You giving away free coffee today?"

I shook my head. "No, they just . . . came."

"Huh." He turned around and eyed Timothy. "Who came in first?"

"He did."

"Figures," Neil said. And then he said, "Do me a favor, why don't you try to keep him around."

Timothy

Timothy Asks Nora to Come to New York

I stayed in that tiny town in Kansas for a month. I spent my days in the coffee shop, doing my work from my laptop (though after a couple of weeks, so many people started to come there that one morning, when I slept late, I arrived and there were no tables left). I kept waiting for Nora to start seeming ordinary. But it didn't happen. How could it be that a girl who lived at home with her mother and worked at a coffee shop would turn out to be the one that I couldn't get out of my head? I couldn't even tell you exactly what seemed different about her, except that she didn't seem to have the need to fill the space, to talk at every pause to make sure there was never a moment of silence. That first day when I came back and we went for a drive and ended up driving all night, we talked a lot, but a lot of the time we were just quiet.

There was also the fact that I could never predict what she was going to do. I was so sure she liked me after that night driving, but then I went to see her the next day, and she told me she couldn't see me that night—and it wasn't her playing hard to get. It wasn't any of those games that I know so well and that never work. Men might be slow about some things, but those games we can spot from a mile away.

I could tell she was worried I might leave—and still she didn't see me. I swear she was like no woman I had ever met.

So I stayed. I told myself I would stay until it wore off. And it didn't. I never saw myself hanging out in a tiny town in a grungy motel for a month, but I did. I ignored the phone calls from my mother, and then from my father. I sent them reports every Friday, and I can't tell you how happy I was to miss the family dinners. I was a little concerned about not being invited to Nora's house, but she'd told me enough stories to know that her family situation wasn't exactly easy. I might have been more judgmental, but my family situation wasn't exactly normal either, so it made a kind of sense to me. I knew I would want to keep her away from my family for as long as I could. I just assumed she was doing the same.

I kept waiting, but I didn't tire of her. So finally I decided to do it—I decided to ask her to come to New York with me.

I wouldn't call myself a patient person, and generally once I decide to do something I do it as soon as possible. Unfortunately, I decided in the morning, and then I had to wait all day, because I didn't want to ask her over the racket of the espresso machine. But at five, which was the posted closing time, the store was still full.

I had taken to helping Nora sometimes behind the counter. I barely recognized myself—I had never in a million years imagined I would voluntarily work behind a counter serving coffee. But I have to tell you, I make a mean macchiato. Nora didn't use enough chocolate. She wouldn't listen to me, until I made her one my way, and she had to concede. I never would have thought I would enjoy hanging out in a coffee shop. Though I knew it wasn't the coffee shop. It was her.

Five o'clock came and went, and then six. Finally, the last of the people wandered out, and Neil put the Closed sign up. Nora was just putting the metal spouts for foaming the milk in to soak. A thick layer of milk residue coated the metal, and if you didn't soak them, it was impossible to get them clean. I was wiping down the counters, and Neil was loading the dishwasher.

I turned to Nora. "Do I get you for tonight?" I asked her.

Just from the shape of her smile I knew the answer was no. When her answer was no, she always smiled but with the corners of her mouth turned down. I had noticed a little dimple that appeared in her left cheek with that same smile. It was my only consolation for the no's that came too frequently. I was not used to people saying no, and I had gotten a lot of practice that month with Nora. But I had a feeling the novelty might be wearing thin.

I hadn't planned to ask her standing in the middle of the coffee shop, but suddenly I didn't want to have to share her anymore. I didn't want to have to ask if I would have her for the evening. I wanted to have her all night long in my bed. I'd had her in my bed, but she always slipped out from between the sheets and got dressed and left. I wanted her there in the morning when I woke up. I wanted her.

I said, "Come back to New York with me."

"What, you mean for a visit? Like a week or so?"

"No. I don't mean for a visit. I mean I want you to come to New York to live with me."

I was so sure she would say yes. But that was the thing with Nora. I was so often wrong.

Nora

Nora Gives Timothy an Answer

Timothy asked me to go to New York with him. He asked me every day for a week. Every morning when he came in he said, "I'd like a double-shot Venti with skim and for you to come to New York with me."

Whenever he came up for a refill, he'd say, "Could I get another, and can I get you to come to New York with me?"

I couldn't go. Of course I couldn't go. But there wasn't an easy way to say no. I didn't want to tell him the reason I couldn't go. I had waited too long to suddenly say, oh by the way, I'm here in Kansas and living at home because my mother might be dying. But even more than that, I didn't want his pity. I preferred him to see me as someone who had chosen a quiet life in her home-town rather than as a victim, someone who'd had her life taken away from her by circumstances and was stuck here with no way of getting out.

At the same time there was a tiny voice inside me saying maybe I could go. Maybe I'd done enough. I asked myself: could I let myself off that hook?

I didn't know the answer. Not the true answer. I knew I wanted to go, but I also knew I would be miserable in New York if I felt like I'd abandoned my mother. Where does responsibility end? That's the question I was left with. And it was complicated. It wasn't just the emotional support but also the fact that I was the monetary support. I paid for the house and the food and the electricity and the phone. And there was also the loan I was paying off. And I wasn't really managing. Even if I could somehow justify leaving my mother, I didn't see how I could move to New York, get a job there, cover my expenses, *and* pay for my mother back here. I would have gladly taken the risk for myself, but it didn't seem fair to make my mother dependent on it too. What if Timothy said he would support both me and my mother, and then we got in a fight and Timothy decided to throw me out or simply to stop paying? I couldn't risk it.

The more I thought about it, the more I knew the answer had to be no. But I didn't say no. I said, "I don't know." And when he asked me when I would know, I just repeated myself. "I don't know." I didn't even know what I was waiting for. A miracle maybe.

Well, I got it. It turned out my miracle was Neil. And I found out that miracles are not always easy to handle.

It happened just when I had finally decided I had to tell Timothy no. I couldn't see any way around it. But I didn't want to do it when the store was filled with people. And I hadn't quite decided what to tell him. So I waited until we were in the midst of the closing-up routine that we'd established. Timothy always stayed to help. Closing down a store owned by an obsessive-compulsive was a little more work than you might think.

"You know what I'd really like to do tonight?" Timothy said, as he was throwing away the one cookie and two croissants left over from the day. Everything else had sold. Some days lately we even sold out.

"What's that?" I asked.

"I'd like you to come back to New York with me," he said with a grin.

I was in the middle of cleaning the glass doors of the food case. I stopped and put down the rag and tried to smile. Then I remembered he said he always knew when I was about to say no because of my smile.

He stood up slowly from where he had been crouched behind the food case. Then he said, "Nora, please."

"Timothy, I'm sorry."

"Think about it some more," he urged. "You don't have to decide today."

"It's not fair to you," I said. "When I've thought about it and I know I can't."

"Can't forever? Or can't just right now?"

How could I put a time limit on it? It would be trying to figure out how long my mother was going to live. And if she died, then I'd get to go off to New York? It's not the kind of thing you can speculate on.

"I can't," I said again, but I didn't explain. It just seemed like too much.

He looked at me very seriously then. "I assume you know what that means?"

"Yes," I said.

What can I tell you about the look that passed between us? Words seemed to flatten things, to trivialize them. Neither of us felt a need to say anything else.

But apparently Neil did. And he said, "Excuse me, but is what I think is going on really going on?"

Timothy and I both looked over at Neil. I'd actually forgotten that Neil was around. But there he was, standing among the tables, leaning on a mop.

Neil was frowning at me. "Are you really telling him you're not going to go to New York?" Then he turned the frown on Timothy, "And you're going to take that as an answer?"

Timothy answered him. "What else am I supposed to do? If that's what she really wants."

"Oh, give me a break," Neil said. "You know that's not what she wants, and, given her situation, I'd think a smart man like you would be able to figure out why she's saying no."

"Her situation?" Timothy echoed.

Then it got awkward.

Neil looked at me. "You didn't tell him?"

I shrugged uncomfortably.

"Oh, good Lord," Neil said.

"What?" Timothy demanded. "What didn't she tell me?"

"I should have known," Neil said, looking at me.

"You're killing me, Neil," Timothy said. "What didn't she tell me?"

"She didn't tell you the reason she's here."

"Here?"

"Here. Here in this town. Here working in a coffee shop. You never wondered?"

"No. I just assumed she liked it here."

"I do like it here," I said. And at this point, that was actually true.

Neil shot me a withering look. "Don't give me that shit. It's not what you would have chosen. Not in a million years." He turned back to Timothy. "Her mother got sick. Cancer. Nora left school and moved home to take care of her. She's been stuck here ever since."

"How long?" Timothy asked.

It was Neil who answered. "It's been three years. They're in the middle of the second round of chemo now."

"Why didn't she tell me?"

It was funny that Timothy kept asking Neil the questions. But I was glad, because I didn't want to answer.

"Because she's an idiot?" Neil said. "Who knows? Maybe she's incredibly proud and stubborn and doesn't want anybody's pity or sympathy or, God forbid, their help."

"I'm standing right here," I said.

It was as if I hadn't even spoken. Neil went on. "In a million years, she shouldn't be working here. She's so much better than this job, but God forbid anybody else knows that. God forbid anybody knows that she's got a master's in economics from Chicago, and she would have had a PhD if she didn't have to leave and come back here."

"She *what?*" Timothy said. He looked at me. "Nora?"

That was a blow. Timothy had talked to me some about his job, thinking that I didn't know anything about the financial market. He'd even spent a half an hour explaining how interest rates worked. At the time I told myself it didn't matter. That he'd never find out because he'd get bored and go back to New York any day.

I bit my lip. "I didn't want you to think . . ." I trailed off. I knew it would be a relief for Timothy to know, but this part of things was harder than I'd thought, even though I wasn't even having to explain it myself.

Neil filled in for me again. "She'd do anything to avoid someone thinking that she's bragging, or that she might think well of herself, or, even worse, that you might actually get to know her. It's much safer to hide."

"Neil," I said, "enough."

Neil spread his hands as if I were exhibit one. "See. It drives her crazy if people ever try to mention it."

"I swear to God, Neil . . ."

"Okay, okay. I won't tell him any more" Neil said, finally.

"Wait, you mean there's more?" Timothy said.

"Well," Neil turned back. "I'm pretty sure she's the only one supporting her and her mother. And I don't know how she manages—"

"Neil!" I said. "Stop."

He turned to me. "Did you ever think that maybe this is the reason you're still single?"

"Now you sound like my mother."

"Well, maybe you should listen to your mother for once. She might have a point."

"Make up your mind. First I'm practically a saint; now everything is my fault and I should listen to my mother."

"You're a saint and a pain in the ass at the same time." Neil turned to Timothy and said, "I'm sorry."

"Why are you apologizing to him?" I demanded. "You should be apologizing to me."

Neil sighed heavily. "No. You mean well, Nora, but this time you're a little confused. I think you should be apologizing to Timothy."

I hated when Neil was right.

I turned to Timothy. "I'm sorry."

He nodded. Then he said, "I think I'm going to go."

"You don't want to get dinner?" I asked him. "Maybe talk about things?"

He shook his head. "Not tonight. I need to think about things."

"See you tomorrow?"

He just smiled at me. And then I knew what he meant about knowing when a smile meant no.

THE INVESTIGATION

According to *Practical Homicide Investigation*, the duties of an investigator are as follows: Observe. Describe.

Nora

A Week Without Timothy

He didn't come back for the whole rest of the week. And Neil took a few days off too, so I was alone in the store. Well, alone with all the customers, but I couldn't exactly talk to the customers about this.

So I called Tammy, and she came over, and I told her what happened. She just looked at me, shook her head, and said, "I don't know why you didn't tell him in the first place."

It wasn't exactly the response I was looking for. I was looking for something more sympathetic. Don't ask me why I thought I was going to get that from Tammy. What I loved about Tammy was that she wasn't like that. But I somehow forgot, and so I responded by demanding, "Why didn't you say anything to me about it?"

"You're not gonna put that on me—no, sir," Tammy said shaking her head.

I tried again. "Okay, then just tell me what should I do now?"

"You're not gonna put that one on me either," she said. And she escaped soon after that. Tammy was not that kind of girlfriend. When it was a problem I had created by myself, she left me to solve it the same way.

I hadn't told my sister about Timothy, so I couldn't turn to her. The crazy thing was that the person I probably could have talked to about it most easily was Neil, and I kept waiting for him to come in, but he didn't. And finally he called and told me that he might not be in for a few days. Neil never took that many days off, so I figured he was avoiding me too. I felt like I had the plague.

What happened was that the time alone gave me a chance to experience what life would be like after Timothy left. Maybe you think I'd know exactly what it was like because I'd been living it before. But that's not the same at all. Before, I didn't think I had a choice. This would be after I'd had a chance at something different and turned away.

Except Timothy hadn't left yet. I knew because I called the motel every day to find out if he was still there. Wednesday, Thursday, Friday—no sign of him, but he was still checked in. I thought about going by his room; believe me I wanted to, but something stopped me.

Saturday, as always, I got up early to drive my mother to Kansas City, and when we got back, she retreated to her room. I tried reading a book. I tried cleaning the house. I tried playing solitaire on the computer. I couldn't settle into anything. Finally, I gave up. I went upstairs, knocked on my mother's bedroom door, and told her I was going out for a bit. Then I got in the car and drove to the motel Timothy was staying at, out along the highway. I parked in front of his room and walked up to the door and knocked. I could feel my heart thumping as I waited for him to come to the door. But there was no response. I knocked again. Still no answer. I couldn't look in the window because the drapes were drawn.

I went to the office to see if I could get some change to use the pay phone and call Timothy on his cell, though I usually avoided the office because one of the reception clerks was a guy I'd gone to high school with. Every time I went to visit Timothy and he was there, he leered at me.

Sure enough, he was there when I walked into the office. Before I could even say anything, he said, "I'm surprised to see you here."

I thought that was strange.

"I came to see Timothy Whitting," I said.

Then I realized what had happened; I knew before he said it.

"He checked out this morning," he told me.

I knew how bad I looked from the pity in his eyes as he said it. I felt my face flush.

"Oh," I said. "Okay. Thanks."

And I turned around and left.

I got back in my car and drove back to my mother's house. Then I went inside, climbed the stairs, undressed, and got into bed. It was the middle of the afternoon, but all I wanted to do was sleep.

And I did. I slept through the afternoon, the evening, and I was still asleep when my sister arrived the next morning with the twins.

Actually, I didn't even wake up when she arrived. I didn't wake up until she was standing over my bed. She didn't even knock. At least I don't think she did. All I know is that the first thing I remember is Deirdre standing there saying, "God, I can't believe you're not up, Nora. You're getting so lazy."

I cracked open one eye. "It's Sunday. And I'm sleeping in," I told her. "I'm not even sure if I'll get up at all."

"Of course you're going to get up. I need you to look after the twins for me while I go run some errands."

"Not today," and I rolled over and turned my back to her.

"Come on, I'm serious," she said, poking me in the shoulder.

"I'm serious too."

There was a little pause. I wondered if that might do it. But she was just taking a little breather before the real attack.

"I drove all the way down here, and now you're not even going to help me?"

"If you wanted help, you should have called me and asked."

"What, because you've got so many other better things to do? I have to book you ahead of time

214

now? Now you've got a boyfriend, or whatever, and your family means nothing?"

My sister hadn't been down in the last month since Timothy came back. So my mother must have told her what little I had said. And at that moment, Deirdre sounded exactly like our mother. Usually guilt worked like a charm with me, but it was as if some magic cloak had descended upon me, and I felt no guilt whatsoever.

"All I know is that I'm not getting out of bed, and I'm not watching the twins today, and if you want me to watch them for you in the future, you're going to have to call and ask me."

"I don't think I like what having a boyfriend is doing to you," my sister said.

"That's funny. I was just thinking I like what it's done very much."

"Okay, come on now. Get up and come take care of the twins."

I closed my eyes.

"Nora, I'm warning you."

I wondered what she was warning me about?

"I can't believe this. You're seriously not going to help me out here?" she demanded.

"That's right. I'm seriously not going to help you out here," I said, my eyes still closed. I felt so peaceful. I was waiting to see if anything she said changed my mind and made me want to get up. So far, not even close.

"I think you must be the most selfish person I know."

Nope, I thought. Colder. Waaay colder.

"You do all this stuff for Mom, and you won't do this one little thing for me?" she tried again.

"I'm rethinking the stuff for Mom," I said.

"What is that supposed to mean? Don't tell me you're thinking of doing something stupid."

"Depends on your definition of 'stupid.'"

"As long as you don't leave her. Mom depends on you for everything."

I had to open my eyes and look to make sure it was still my sister standing there. It was the exact opposite of what she had been saying for years. And I decided to point that out to her.

"That's a bit different from what you've been saying for three years. You've said the whole time that I don't need to be here and I'm just playing the martyr."

"Well, I've changed my mind. I think *you* were right."

"And I've changed mine, and now I think you were right."

"You can't leave. Do you hear me, Nora? Fine, don't help me with the twins, but you have to stay here with Mom."

"I'm not going to do anything right now except go back to sleep. So unless you want to stand there and watch me sleep . . ." And I closed my eyes again.

I guess she didn't, because she left. And I did go back to sleep, minutes after she left the room. I slept most of the day. I got up to use the bathroom, drink some water, and then I just went back to sleep. I slept right through the night, without a single dream.

Nora

Monday Morning

You'd think after all that sleep, I would have woken up easily, but I was deep in sleep when the alarm went off, and I was still groggy when I got into work. I felt like I could have slept another week. I had just made myself a cup of coffee, and I was taking the chairs down off the tables, when Neil came in. I hadn't seen him since the last time I'd seen Timothy—would probably ever see Timothy, I realized.

"Morning," I said.

"What happened to the 'good' part?" Neil asked.

"Just trying to be honest."

He looked more closely at me. "You look terrible."

"Gee, thanks, Neil."

"No, what I mean is you look tired."

"I *am* tired," I said. And that was the truth. I wasn't just tired; I was exhausted. I had slept for thirty-six hours, but I felt like I wanted to crawl into bed and sleep for weeks.

"Why don't you leave the chairs for a second and sit down?" he suggested.

"It's okay. I'm fine. And we need to finish setting up to open." I pulled down another chair and centered it under the table just the way Neil liked. I was amazed he had done so well with letting people come in and actually use the chairs, and not having to push them back into perfect alignment. At first whenever someone left the store, he had gone over to the table and pushed in the chair and aligned it—and he'd taught me to do the same—until Timothy pointed out that it might make customers a little uncomfortable and less likely to come in and stay next time. And, miracle of miracles, Neil listened to him.

Now Neil pulled out the chair I had just perfectly centered and pointed for me to sit down.

I sat.

He took the other chair off the table, and he sat down next to me.

"Tell me what's wrong," he said.

"Timothy's gone."

"Timothy's not gone."

"Yes, he is," I insisted. "He's gone. I went by the motel on Saturday, and he's checked out. He didn't even say good-bye."

"Did you ever think that maybe he didn't say good-bye because he was coming back?"

"No. He's gone," I repeated.

"You're really optimistic today," Neil observed ironically.

"I'm just being realistic. I didn't tell him the whole truth, he got upset, and he left. I would have thought he'd at least say good-bye, but maybe I deserved it. I don't know."

"And maybe he's not gone," Neil said again.

"Why do you keep saying that? I told you he checked out."

I couldn't keep the edge from my voice, but it only seemed to amuse Neil. He said, "Well, I guess I'm saying that because I can see him parking the car out front, that's why."

I jerked around and looked through the window, and Neil was right. Timothy had just pulled into a space in front.

I turned back to Neil. "You knew," I accused him.

"Not only did I know, I told him to take off for a few days to give you a chance to think about things and see what life might be like without him."

I felt breathless and shaky and angry and relieved all at the same time. "Neil!" I said, but I didn't get a chance to yell at him because Timothy pushed the door open and came into the store at that moment.

Timothy looked—different. It took me a minute to figure it out; he looked happy. Really happy. His face was open and he was smiling in a way I don't think I'd ever seen him smile before.

I stood up and he came over and kissed me as if it hadn't been days since he'd seen me. Then he sat down at the table as well, and I saw him look at Neil, and his smile got bigger. I looked over at Neil, and Neil was grinning back at Timothy.

"What's going on?" I demanded.

"Sit down for a second; there's something we want to show you," Neil said.

"What?"

"Sit down and we'll show you," Neil repeated.

I looked suspiciously over at Timothy. He was sitting there, still grinning.

I sat down.

"Okay, now tell me what the hell is going on."

Timothy bent down and pulled a manila folder out of his bag. He put it on the table and pushed it across to me.

I looked at it, and suddenly I felt very strange.

"Open it," Neil instructed me.

Timothy didn't say a word. I realized he hadn't said a word since he'd come into the café.

I opened it. There was a legal-looking document inside. I saw it was from the bank where my mother had worked and where we had our accounts and our mortgage. I looked a little more closely. As far as I could tell, it was saying that the mortgage was paid off.

"What is this? I don't—"

"Just keep going," Neil said.

I turned over that page. The next one was more familiar. It was a record of my loan, the interest accumulated, how much I had due—but at the bottom of the page, for amount due, that read zero as well.

I had almost a sick feeling. I know that sounds strange. But when things that have been weighing you down for so long suddenly vanish, it gives you a strange feeling of being weightless in a way that's completely disorienting. I've heard that the astronauts usually throw up before they get used to no gravity. I think I know what they feel.

I turned the page. It was my student loan.

The next page, my credit card, which I had gotten through the bank.

The next page. It was my bank account. The week before I'd had two hundred dollars in it. Now there were fifty thousand.

"It was Neil's idea," Timothy said, speaking for the first time.

"Not exactly," Neil said modestly. "Timothy asked me if I could think of any way he could help you, and I just suggested that maybe if some of the financial pressure was off you—"

Timothy picked up the thread, "And I thought it was a great idea, but I didn't see a way to do it without asking you first, and I knew you'd say no—"

And then Neil took on the next part, "But since we set up the direct payment into your account, and you approved me for that, I said I thought I could help. We had to talk to the bank manager as well, and he took some convincing, but he eventually saw things our way."

"So that's where we were last week," Timothy finished.

They were so pleased with themselves, but, looking at them, all I could feel was a rising anger that I couldn't fight off. All the time I'd been worried sick, they'd been running around concocting schemes of how to fix my life—without even asking me.

"What on earth were you thinking?" I demanded.

The tone of my voice instantly wiped the smiles off their faces.

Timothy looked down at the table and didn't answer. It was Neil who replied. "We were thinking that with this you could go to New York and not have to worry so much about your mother. We were thinking she'd be taken care of, and that with your bills paid, you could hire someone to drive her on the weekend, and you could come back and see her as much as you wanted without having to ask for money. You know, we kind of thought we were solving all your problems. Don't worry. I don't expect you to say thank you."

Listening to him just made me angrier. "That's good, because you'd have to wait a long time. Why didn't you ask me about this before you did it? Because you knew I'd say no, right? But you did it anyway. And what exactly does this solve? Will you tell me that? You think you can throw some money at me, and I'll just say that's great— now I can leave my dying mother and run off to New York?"

I couldn't hold it back, but even as I said it, I could see the damage I was doing on Timothy's face. The open, excited grin was gone, and now it was like my every word was a blow. He managed to look up at me, but I could see the effort it cost him.

"Nora, I'm sorry," he said simply. "I thought I might be able to help. It wasn't just about you coming to New York. I thought it might make things a little easier. I didn't mean . . ." He trailed off. "I messed up. I'm sorry."

And then he smiled, but it was such a different smile from the one he'd come in with that it just about broke my heart.

Then he went on. "I booked a flight back to New York this afternoon. I've got to head to the airport now. But if you change your mind, and you decide you might want to come to New York, well . . . you know how to reach me."

He waited for a minute, but I felt like I was frozen. I wanted to say something, but I swear I couldn't have gotten a word out if my life depended on it.

He smiled that awful, sad smile again and stood up. He held out his hand to Neil. Neil stood and shook it. Then he picked up his bag and turned around and walked out.

As the door closed, I felt a little gust of cold air against my face.

I didn't want to even look at Neil. I knew what was coming, and I knew I deserved it.

When I finally got up the courage to look over, Neil was frowning at me. But what he said was not what I was expecting.

He said, "You are so selfish."

"Selfish?" I echoed.

"Yes, selfish," he retorted.

"I thought you were always going on about how I did too much," I defended myself.

It hadn't touched me when my sister called me selfish, but for some reason when Neil said it, it stung. When he spoke again, I knew why. It's because when my sister said it, it wasn't true. But when Neil said it, it was.

"You of all people should know how good it feels to give to others. And if you keep that all to yourself, and don't let the people who care about you give to you, then, yes, I call that selfish. Timothy just wanted to help you. This was the only way he could think of doing it. The money was nothing to him. It's a drop in the bucket. And you should have seen how much fun he had doing it. He was like a different person. And he was so excited to see your face when he showed you . . ."

"You can't put this all on me. That's not fair," I protested.

"Isn't it?"

"Neil, I can't take money from him. Especially not this kind of money. Tell me, how do I give it back?"

I didn't realize Neil had mischief in him, but there was no mistaking it when he looked at me, smiled, and said, "I really don't know. I guess if you really feel like you have to give it back, you'll have to go hunt him down in New York and try to figure that out."

Nora

Timothy Leaves the Second Time

It was not a good week after Timothy left for the second time. I knew there would be no walking back in again. This time it was up to me.

I tried to talk to Neil about whether I should go to New York, but he was too smart for me. I think he knew I wanted him to convince me that it would be okay for me to go—and he also knew an impossible task when he saw one. So whenever I tried to bring it up, he'd say, "Nora, you know what I think, but it's your decision. I don't want to fight with you about it."

That left me to decide. Before, when I'd been asking myself if I could possibly go, the money question was always the deciding factor; it just wasn't logistically possible. Now, all of a sudden, that obstacle had been removed. I knew I couldn't give the money back. Even if I did all the complicated steps I would need to recoup it, and I was able to convince Timothy to take it back, I knew it would be like a slap in the face for him. It would be like throwing a gift back in his face. I'd hurt him enough already. It was just my pride that didn't want to accept it, and after I'd calmed down a bit, I could see that, though it was still a bitter pill to swallow. If someone had told me before that all my money problems were going to be solved, I would have thought I would be so relieved. But it didn't feel like that.

Because even though the money problem was solved, I was left with the much tougher question of what was the right thing to do. And I had no idea how to answer that question.

It turned out that it was answered for me that weekend when my mother and I made the weekly drive down to the hospital.

My mother and I always left the house by around seven, but every week the sun was lower in the sky when we left. That Saturday, as I opened the door, the first rays streaming over the horizon flooded the doorway with light. I paused a moment on the stoop. In the distance the wheat fields stretched as far as the eye could see. There were no clouds, just the huge expanse of sky, so pale it didn't even have a color, and the tiniest sliver of light, shooting out rays so bright I couldn't look straight at it. The sun lit up the harvested stubble. On most days a wind blew across the open fields, but this morning it was completely still and breathtakingly quiet—in the way you only find very early when everyone else is sound asleep, and you feel like you're the only person alive.

The door opened behind me, and my mother came out and stood beside me for a moment in silence. Then she said, " 'I stood upon the hills, when heaven's wide arch was glorious with the sun's returning march.' "

"What's that?" I asked.

"Longfellow. It was the poem I memorized for my elementary school graduation. And I still remember every word. Isn't that strange?" Then she went on, as if to prove it: " 'If thou art worn and hard beset with sorrows that thou wouldst forget, if thou wouldst read a lesson that will keep thy heart from fainting and thy soul from sleep, go to the woods and hills! No tears . . .' "

Then she added, with barely a pause, "I guess we're out of luck. No woods or hills here. So are we ready?"

My mother was just being literal. She meant that there were no woods or hills in this part of Kansas. I didn't think she had ever said a truer thing in her whole life. If I wanted to keep my heart from fainting and my soul from sleep, I would have to go somewhere else.

I went down the steps and cut across the lawn to the driveway. The grass was coated with a sparkling layer of white and crunched as I stepped on it. It was one of my favorite sensations: the delicate resistance under my feet.

"Why don't you ever use the walkway?" my mother called over from where she was picking her way along the flagstone path. "You're going to wear away the lawn right down into the dirt."

I silently crossed over to the path.

I remembered that when my mother first got sick, three years ago, and I put my life on hold to move home to take care of her, I had made a vow that I would stop arguing with her. I should have known I was in trouble when I told Tammy about my plan, and she just about bust a gut laughing. "Do you think you're suddenly going to turn into Jesus or something?" she said. "Because that's the only person I can think of who might be able to keep from arguing with your mother. And honestly, put your mother and Jesus in a room together, and I think even he would break eventually. She's like frigging water torture."

"Look at Eleanor's lawn," my mother went on. "The grass is so long it's almost gone to seed. That's such a shame. One house can bring the whole neighborhood down."

I looked over to Eleanor's lawn. There were exactly three stalks over near the curb that Eleanor's husband must have missed when he mowed.

We reached the car, and I stopped to dig in my bag for the keys.

Then my mother's critical gaze moved from the neighbor's unkempt lawn to me, and she found a problem there as well. "Did you even brush your hair this morning?" she asked.

Of course I knew the answer to the question. It was no. But still I automatically raised a hand to my head as if to check.

"It won't matter," I said. "It's not like I'm going to see anyone."

My mother's eyebrows went up and her forefinger came out and started wagging in the air: a sure sign that a cliché was coming my way.

"You never know who you might meet and when," my mother said.

"But I did meet someone," I said.

I had told my mother that much. She wasn't a stupid woman. She wouldn't have bought the lie that I was going out with Tammy five nights a week.

I found the keys in my bag and clicked open the locks.

"So does that mean you're not going to do something about your hair?" my mother asked tartly.

I opened her door, then looked up across the car at her. "Mom, it doesn't matter. Honestly. Don't you think it's just a little more important to be on time for your appointment?"

"The hospital isn't going anywhere," my mother said.

I opened my mouth to argue. But then I thought about whether I wanted to listen to comments about my hair for the next three hours in the car, and I shut my mouth, turned around, and started back to the house. I wasn't sure if it was capitulation or self-preservation; it was a slippery slope.

"The grass," my mother reminded me, as I was about to cut across the lawn again.

I changed course and took the pathway.

"And don't do that awful braid. Wear it down," she called after me. "You're always putting it back. I don't know why you don't try harder. If you did, you might be married by now . . ."

I wasn't sure if my mother stopped talking or she just got out of range.

I took extra care with my hair, not just running a brush through it, but using some gel and a couple of passes with a straitening iron that had been my sister's, because I had a feeling that if my mother started in on me again I might not be able to hold back. It seemed I did a good enough job, because she didn't comment when I returned to the car. That was as good as it got. There was never a compliment. The only reward was the ceasing of the constant drip of criticism. Tammy was brilliant with her metaphors: it was exactly like water torture. And the power of water over time—it was water that carved the Grand Canyon out of solid rock.

It was three solid hours on the highway. Mile upon mile of wheat fields and sky, and after the sunrise, the clouds moved in: big billowing cumulus clouds that sat low in the sky and mush-roomed up, making me feel like an ant crawling across a huge expanse. My mother didn't want the radio on, so I drove with the sound of the road under the wheels and the wind and the occasional truck that roared past.

After taking the exit ramp, it was only a short drive to the hospital. I usually let my mother out at the front, then I pulled around to the parking lot and waited in the car.

I didn't wait in the car out of choice. I waited in the car because my mother never let me come inside. "You do enough," she always said. "This, at least, I can spare you."

It was so important to her to feel like she was sparing me that I had to actually put up with more to maintain the illusion that I was being spared. If I thought about it too much, my head started to hurt. The layers of pretending, all in the name of caring. It never ended, and I wasn't sure that anyone ended up better off in the final tally. I had decided the best way to deal with it was not to think about it.

I hadn't been able to resist bringing it up a few times in the past, but every time it ended in an awful fight. The last one had been a few months before, at the time when I ran into Dan in the 7-Eleven.

Maybe it was all the comments leaving the house, maybe I had bit my tongue one too many times and it wasn't even ten o'clock, but this morning I decided I wasn't going to sit in the car again. I decided this time I wasn't taking no for an answer.

"I'm coming in with you today," I announced as I pulled into the parking lot. "I'll let you off at the front, park the car, and then come meet you inside."

"I told you, I don't want you to see me like that," my mother said. "I want to spare you that. It's important to me."

"It's worse waiting in the car, sitting here wondering what's going on. I never know if you're telling me the truth about what the doctor says."

"I'm telling you the truth. And anyway," she went on, "the doctor isn't going to be in today. There's another doctor covering for him. My doctor went skiing in Colorado. He'll probably come back with a broken leg or something. Why people want to put those things on their feet and go down a mountain, I don't understand."

"It doesn't matter," I told her. "I can talk to the other doctor. Anyone. Or I'll sit in the waiting room with you. Just so I don't sit out here in the car feeling like you're keeping me from what's really going on in there."

My mother's frown returned. "I told you how I feel about this. Do I have to go through it again?"

"But Mom—"

And then my mother kicked it up a notch. She went from relatively calm to furious in a split second. It had been like this the whole time I was growing up. It took a long while for me to figure out that it was my mother's way of keeping me from crossing her. It was very effective. Even after I figured it out, it still worked. I'd almost always rather give in than have to go through the battle that was required to get what I wanted.

"I can't believe you're doing this," my mother practically spat. "And you've chosen *now* to talk to me about it? You have a strange way of showing me that you care. I swear to God, you're the one who's going to be the death of me, not this cancer. The cancer I can handle. But you . . . it's too much. I told you what the doctor said about stress. I can beat the cancer, but not if you're going to act like this."

When I started out, I had been so certain that this time I wasn't going to take no for an answer. Now I wondered what I had been thinking. I was no match for my mother. I never had been.

"All right," I said, wearily.

"All right what?" my mother demanded.

"All right, I won't come in."

"I don't believe you. Now I'm going to sit in the waiting room the entire time, wondering if you're going to pull some stupid stunt and come in anyway. Do you have any idea how bad this is for me? Especially right before a treatment?"

"I'm sorry," I said. "I won't come in. I promise."

My mother opened the door, but she didn't get out yet—not without a parting shot. "Sometimes I think I wouldn't have relapsed if I'd had more support from you. You say I never tell you anything, but you just don't listen. I told you what the doctor said about how important it is to have family around and supporting me, didn't I?"

I felt inexpressibly tired. I knew I couldn't do it anymore. I'd had the thought before, and yet I kept doing it. I wasn't sure if it was guilt that kept me there or love. Maybe I didn't know because growing up in my house there was no distinction made between the two.

"I'm sorry," I repeated.

My mother didn't answer. She just looked at me a long minute and finally shook her head. Then she got out of the car and shut the door. It wasn't hard enough to be called a slam, exactly.

I watched my mother go in through the automatic doors, and I sat there a moment longer. Then I pulled the car around, parked, and sat watching the people come and go through the hospital doors.

Usually I read while I waited. I'd brought Jane Austen's *Persuasion*. Austen's heroines always got their happy endings, but today that wasn't going to work. I couldn't help remembering that even though all the heroines in Jane Austen's books got happy endings, the author herself did not. Jane Austen died young and unmarried and childless. There are books, and there is life, and I often thought, thank goodness for books because sometimes they're what makes life bearable. But sometimes even a book won't do it.

So I just sat there, watching the entrance, waiting for my mother to emerge. On good Saturdays, she walked back out to the car. On bad days, a nurse pushed her out in a wheelchair.

That Saturday was one of the bad ones.

When I saw the automatic doors slide open, and my mother appear in the wheelchair, I started the car and pulled around under the carport. Then I got out and went around to the other side of the car to help the nurse get my mother out of the wheelchair and into the front seat.

"It feels cold in here," my mother whispered. "Is it cold in here, or is it just me?"

"No, it's cold in here," I said. "I'll turn on the heat as soon as the car gets warmed up."

We drove in silence until I pulled onto the highway. Then I finally asked, "Did the doctor say anything to you today?"

"What?" my mother asked, coming back as if from a million miles away.

"Did the other doctor say anything?" I asked again.

"I told you, my doctor is away."

"Then the doctor that's filling in?"

"No, not really."

"Nothing?" I glanced over to see if I could read my mother's face. I could always tell when my mother was worried because there was a little crease between her eyebrows that would deepen—despite the Botox treatments, which even through the chemo, she kept up religiously. That was my mother for you: second round of chemo and still going for Botox. But when asked about it, she simply said, "Just because I'm dying, doesn't mean I can't still look good. Besides, without hair I have nothing to hide my forehead."

I had to admit, my mother looked better than she ever had. It's a strange aspect of leukemia that often you don't look sick. And during the first round of chemo, two years before, in anticipation of her hair falling out, my mother went to the hairdresser and got a pixie cut. It was one of those magical beauty moments that just worked—after the haircut her dark hair framed her face and accentuated her features: the upturned Irish nose, her pointed chin. It gave her a delicate, impish look that suited her. She looked a good ten years younger than her actual age, fifty-four. My mother never tired of telling the story about how, once, when she went out with Deirdre, someone had mistaken them for sisters.

"The doctor didn't say anything at all?" I asked again.

"Nothing new," my mother amended. Then she reached over and turned on the radio and was suddenly very intent, looking for a radio station.

I let it drop. My mother pretended to leave it all in the hands of the doctors, saying they knew best and she'd do whatever they recommended and beyond that it was in God's hands, but I could go on the computer and look at the history of Web sites that had been visited and see what my mother was searching on the Internet. I could see that she was looking up the same things I was: every week there would be some new search into chemo and it's effects, it's success rates, the probabilities of second rounds, the different techniques, and the indications of white blood cell counts. The searches meant that even though she pretended not to worry, she was lying. Once I tried to tell her how much easier it would be if she were just honest and talked about these things, and she nodded and said, "Of course," and "I understand," and absolutely nothing changed.

We drove back with the radio tuned to the news, some talk show about investing money, which was completely useless, because to invest money you had to have it in the first place.

The one thing the radio program was good for was exactly what my mother had intended: it stopped me from talking or asking questions. We drove home with the radio going the whole way, and when I pulled into the driveway, my mother got out of the car before I could get out and around to help her. Once inside, she simply said, "I'm going to go rest a bit in my room," and then she climbed the stairs and shut the door of her room behind her.

And I knew. I couldn't do it anymore. I didn't know what was right or what was wrong, but I knew I couldn't do it. I had made my decision; I was moving to New York.

Timothy

Back in New York

The first thing I did after I booked my flight back to New York (commercial since I had long since sent the plane home) was to send an e-mail to let the other woman in my life know that I was coming back.

I knew she would be anxious to see me. I didn't realize she would be waiting for me in my apartment. But I knew she was there the second I walked in. The foyer was dark, but I could see down the hall, and there was a strip of light under the bedroom door. I tossed my keys on the hall table, took off my coat, and hung it up, and I was about to go back to the bedroom to say hello. Then I thought better of it.

I went into the kitchen and flicked on the light. My apartment had a view looking uptown, and I could see the Empire State Building. It was red.

Red sounded like a good idea—a really good bottle of red. I uncorked a bottle, poured my glass half-full, swirled it to give it a little air, and then took a sip.

I had to admit to myself that there had been things I missed. Living in a motel out by the highway hadn't been exactly easy for me. I stood by the window and looked out at the lights of the city and took another sip. And I waited.

I heard a rustle from the bedroom.

Eventually, she came out in my robe.

I heard her walk down the hall, and when I knew she had reached the kitchen, I turned around. She looked incredible, even wearing a man's robe. For conventional beauty, my best friend's wife was still the most beautiful woman I'd ever seen.

I took another sip of wine. Then I said, "Hello, Celia."

"You bastard," she said. "You knew I was here."

I didn't contradict her. "Would you like some wine?"

Instead of answering, she took my wineglass out of my hand. "Let me taste it first," she said, but she didn't take a sip. She set my glass down on the counter, moved in closer to me, and raised her face for me to kiss her.

I want to take a moment here to say what I had intended. I had intended to tell her that I'd fallen in love and that it was over between us. In fact, I was looking forward to it. But when she looked up at me like that, I kissed her.

One kiss and it was over for me. I didn't pick up my wineglass again. I picked her up instead. Not to go to the bedroom, not even to the couch. I picked her up and put her on the kitchen counter. I laid her down there and opened the robe, and, as I suspected, there was very little underneath. The lingerie she was wearing made her seem more naked than if she'd been wearing nothing.

What can I say? I loved Nora, but the sex with Celia was out of this world. It always had been. It was forbidden and illicit—and irresistible. At one point I thought I was in love with Celia. I met her after she started dating Marcus. I remember wondering how on earth he'd found her first. Of course, the answer was that he went to gallery openings and crap like that, while I never bothered.

I won't bore you with the short, sordid story of how I started sleeping with my best friend's girlfriend. Or how, for months after that, every time I saw her, I tried to convince her to leave him.

She always said no to me. But when Marcus asked her to marry him, she said yes. She explained to me that I was not the kind of man a woman should marry. I was the man you should have an affair with. Marcus was the kind of man you should marry.

At the time I thought it was my first heartbreak. Now I can see that it was just my ego that got bruised. I comforted myself with the thought that I didn't want to marry a woman who would cheat on her fiancé—and with his best friend no less. (I know, it doesn't say a lot about me either, but you have to remember that I was used to that vision of myself.) The funny thing is, it was a very good reason not to marry her, but when I was using it, I didn't really believe it.

After she got engaged, I stopped the affair. Or maybe she did. I don't remember. At any rate, we didn't see each other for a while.

I was the best man at the wedding. And Celia and I started sleeping together again two weeks after they got back from the honeymoon.

That's why I wasn't so comfortable going out for drinks with the two of them. I don't think that makes me a better person or shows that I have scruples. It wasn't that I felt guilty. I just found it unpleasant. I don't have any explanation as to why she always tried to set something up with the three of us, or when she succeeded, why she seemed to enjoy it, except that she is a very twisted woman—in so many ways.

That night we went from the kitchen counter to the couch to the shower and finally to the bed. After we finished, normally she rolled away from me, but this time she wanted my arm around her, and she rested her head on my chest. So I couldn't see her face when she said, "I've missed you. Where have you been for the past month? You can't go disappearing on me like that, damn you."

For most men, that might have made it harder to say what I was about to say. But I was heartless.

"I was in Kansas."

"What on earth were you doing in Kansas for a month?"

"I met someone."

I sensed rather than saw the change, but her tone was still light when she said, "Does she have a dog named Toto?"

"I'm serious," I said. "It's serious."

"What does that mean?"

"It means I'm in love with her."

"You can't possibly know that after a month."

I didn't respond. I wasn't going to argue with her about it.

She sat up and turned around to look at me. The lights were off, but I had a wall of windows in my bedroom, and it faced the towers of the financial district, and there was so much light in the room that I had to lower the shades to sleep. I could see her face in the glow.

"It won't last," she said. "What are you going to do? Go live in Kansas?"

"No. I've asked her to come here."

"So of course she's back home packing." As I watched her, I thought for a beautiful woman she looked rather ugly in that moment.

"Actually, she said no. But I'm hoping she's going to change her mind."

"Do you see a pattern here?" she said. "You seem to fall for women who tell you no."

I saw my opportunity, and I took it. I slid the knife in and twisted it. "Yes, but in every other way, she's as different from you as you could possibly get. And one way it's definitely different this time is that it's the real thing."

Celia stared at me for a moment. Then she got out of my bed and started getting dressed.

"I didn't realize you could be this cruel," she said, pulling on her skirt.

"Oh, come on. I know you didn't think I was a paragon of virtue and consideration."

"You're just trying to hurt me because I wouldn't marry you," she said, buttoning up her shirt. "You're still upset about that."

"I'm not still upset about it. Quite the contrary."

She had sat down on the edge of the bed to put on her shoes. But when I said that, she stopped. She turned around and stared at me hard. Then she said, "I don't believe you."

"Believe what you want to believe," I told her.

I was telling her the truth. I didn't care. You can't fake that kind of indifference. She heard it in my voice.

"So what about us?" she asked.

"Us? Is there an us?"

"Well, whatever it is we do. What's going to happen to that?"

"I suppose we could continue on, sometimes anyway. But we'll have to meet in a hotel since Nora will be living here."

She snorted. "You think I'm going to put up with that?"

"I don't see why not."

"You're in love with someone else," she said, bending to put on her shoes.

"You've been in love with someone else since we met," I pointed out.

She was quiet for a minute. Then she said softly, "No. I never said I was in love with Marcus." She turned around and looked at me, and she looked like someone I'd never seen before.

"I'm sorry for you both then."

I know how that sounds. But for once I actually didn't mean to be cruel. In that moment I was truly sorry for both her and Marcus.

"I'd better go," she said.

"Yes, Marcus will be waiting for you."

"No, he's out of town." She gave a little laugh. "I thought you'd be so pleased that I could stay the whole night."

"I suppose you could still stay." But I made sure that I said it in such a way that she would know I didn't want her to. Well, what can I say? I didn't. It was Nora who I wanted in my bed the whole night. I wanted to see her hair spread out on the pillow next to me. I wanted to see the way her face looked when she woke up from a deep sleep. I wanted to stand behind her and put my arms around her while she was standing at the sink brushing her teeth.

Celia was usually pretty sharp, but she didn't

seem to be picking up on things tonight. She said, slowly, "Maybe I will stay . . ." and she looked over at me.

I shrugged. "Whatever you want. I'm just going to be sleeping. It doesn't matter to me if you're here or not."

That's when Celia, who I always considered hard as nails, actually began to tear. I could see it. Her nose turned pink and her eyes got very bright, though she managed to keep them from spilling over. At least that was something. Part of the reason I liked her so much was that I never had to deal with this kind of crap.

"I'm going to go," she said again.

I know she wanted me to argue with her. To tell her to stay, that it would be all right. But instead I said, "Yes, that's probably best."

I didn't even walk her to the door. I didn't enjoy seeing a woman who had been so strong fall apart right in front of me. When I heard the door close behind her, I got up to pour myself another glass of wine, to celebrate the fact that I wasn't going to marry someone I didn't love. Now I could see that I'd been lucky to escape getting married to Celia, because that's how I found Nora. And I was so sure Nora and I would be different from other couples.

I could look back now and think that was foolish.

But I don't.

No, I think you should celebrate whenever you can. Take that momentary feeling of being lucky, that feeling of being on the right track, and enjoy it. It won't last.

Nora

What Happens When Nora Tells Her Mother and Tammy About Her Decision

I was leaving Kansas.

I had decided, and I wasn't changing my mind. If my deciding to leave was a seed, it was as if it had been planted and had grown into a huge oak overnight. A seed can be blown away; an oak needs a hurricane to uproot it.

My mother was the potential hurricane. I decided not to delay facing the storm. I waited a couple of days for her to recover from the effects of the chemo, and then Monday, after work, I took out the folder that Neil and Timothy had given me. It was my ammunition.

My mother was in her room when I came home. I knocked; then through the door I asked her if she would come downstairs because there was something I needed to talk to her about.

I half expected her not to come down, but about ten minutes later, she appeared.

I was sitting at the kitchen table when she came in. She crossed to the fridge and got out the orange juice. As she was getting a glass down from the cabinet, she said, "So what's this big thing you wanted to talk to me about?"

"You know how I told you that I met someone?"

"Mmm," she said, seeming to pay more attention to pouring her glass of orange juice than to what I was saying.

"I know I didn't tell you much about him—"

"Some slick businessman from New York," my mother said casually, and picked up the glass and took a sip.

"What?" I looked at her blankly.

She licked her lips daintily and said, "Timothy Whitting. Isn't that right? Quite good-looking from what I hear. Though, of course, I wouldn't know since you never brought him here to meet me."

"Wait, how do you know all this?"

"Honey, he's been there every day at the awful place where you work. You think I don't have friends who tell me things? You think I never leave the house?"

That was actually what I thought—because that's what she always said. She always complained to me that she'd been sitting around all day.

"Why didn't you tell me that you knew?" I asked.

"What was the point? He was just going to go back to New York. But now I imagine he's invited you to go to New York with him; is that it?"

This was not at all how I had imagined it going. I had planned out this whole elaborate scheme for how to tell her: I'd carefully explain everything before I told her about him asking me to go to New York. Now I didn't know what to say. So I just said, "Yes, he did."

"And I imagine you're going to do it. You're going to go chase him back to New York."

"It's not like that," I said. "He wants me there."

"Yes, but for how long? Right now you're different from all the New York girls he's known. You're a shiny new toy. But what about when he gets you back to New York, and you don't quite measure up? What happens when he gets bored? It's not like he's asked you to marry him."

"We barely know each other," I protested.

"You think it gets better? You think that's what happens? You get to know each other and you fall more deeply in love?" My mother snorted. "You're going there to live with him without requiring anything from him. Why on earth would he ever ask you to marry him when he doesn't have to?"

"But I don't want someone to ask me to marry them because they have to."

"Which is why you're not married," my mother said. "I would like nothing better than to see you settled and happy with someone. But I have to tell you, I just don't see it happening. Not when you act like this."

"It's not like that. He cares about me."

She rolled her eyes to the ceiling, as if I'd just said the most ridiculous thing she'd ever heard.

"Look what he did for me." I put the manila folder on the table.

I don't know why all of a sudden I had to prove it to her. No, wait. I do know. I had been so certain, and she made me doubt it. So I thought if I could convince her, it would take my own doubt away.

She came over to the table, opened the folder, and looked through the papers. I watched her as she did it—and I swear to you, her face didn't change. Not a muscle. Not for the mortgage or for my loan or for my student loans or for the money in the bank. Nothing.

She closed the folder and looked at me. Then she said, "I'm ashamed of you."

I wasn't expecting it. If she had punched me in the stomach, I think it would have felt better. She went on. "Do you realize what you let him do? You let him buy you. How are you any better than a prostitute now?"

I picked up the folder. I noticed that my hands were shaking.

She went on. "That's pocket change for him. But he knew it would seem like a big deal to a small-town girl like you."

"I don't care what you think," I said—and I desperately wanted it to be true. "I'm going anyway."

"Who's stopping you?" she said. "You think I want you here if you don't want to be here? It's not like I need you. I can get someone else to drive me to the hospital. And it's not like you do a whole lot more than that for me."

This was the opposite of what she'd been saying for three years. I had been prepared for her to do everything she could think of to try to get me to stay. Never in a million years did I think it would be worse for her not to care—or even to pretend not to care.

She said, "Go to New York. See how long it lasts. I bet he's already on to some other girl. You think he's going to sit around and wait for you? You think there aren't a hundred girls, a thousand girls, back there in New York trying to catch him? He came out here, and you're something a little different. But you think he's still going to think you're quaint when you get to New York and he sees you around those New York girls. You think you can hold your own against them? He'll send you packing right back to Kansas. I guarantee you; you'll be back here in under a month. But, please, don't listen to me. Go ahead and see for yourself."

"I will," I said. "Because I think you're wrong." Then I turned and left.

But it was as if every word she said were burned into my brain. I tried to summon up the look on Timothy's face when he'd been about to show me the folder—how excited he'd been. How much he'd just wanted to help me. I remember knowing it, but I couldn't call up the image. It was as if my mother had erased it with her words and replaced it with her version of events.

All I wanted was to get to the one person who I knew would be thrilled for me: Tammy. I had told her that Timothy had asked me to go to New York, and in the same breath I'd said of course I couldn't. Tammy had shown amazing restraint and hadn't said a word, but I knew she almost certainly was thinking I was an idiot for not going. So I was excited to tell her I'd changed my mind.

I drove to Tammy's apartment and knocked on her door. Actually, it wasn't an apartment, it was a room over a garage—her parents' garage. They let her live there for free, and she had her own kitchen, her own bathroom, everything, but she still spent most of her time over in what she called the "big house."

Tammy had a relationship with her parents that was like nothing I'd ever seen. I don't know if it was really disturbing or really wonderful. They did things like smoke pot together, but they also made their own Christmas ornaments and had evenings where they popped popcorn over the fireplace and made hot cocoa and watched old movies on PBS.

Tammy was over in the big house when I knocked on her door. She saw me from the kitchen window, and she opened up the window and said, "Hold on, I'll be right over."

A second later she came out.

"Why don't you come in and have some fudge," Tammy said.

I guessed it was one of their wholesome days—unless they'd gotten high and were making fudge, which could very well have been the case.

"I'm not really in a fudge mood."

"How is that possible?" Tammy said.

"Well, you're looking at the girl who can manage the impossible," I told her.

"Uh oh. Come on in," and Tammy led the way into her living room. Her apartment was decorated in warm colors, red and brown, with pictures of her friends and family, and lots of pillows and always a couple of throw blankets to wrap yourself up in. Tammy swore up and down that she had furnished it, even though I suspected her mother was really behind it. Sometimes I wondered what it would have been like growing up with a mother like Tammy's. Would I have turned out to be just like Tammy then? In my situation, would she have been me? It was strange to think about.

"What happened this time?" Tammy asked me, curling up in her favorite corner of the couch. I took the opposite corner and the red fleece blanket.

Suddenly I got an image of myself of someone who always came to Tammy with some drama. Always some complaint. It wasn't how I usually saw myself, so the sudden flash was disorienting.

As I opened my mouth to tell her what was going on, I got an echo of what I was about to say, and I have to tell you, my problem seemed ridiculous.

"I told my mother that I'm moving to New York, and she said she doesn't care. Or she pretended not to care to hurt me. I don't know which."

Why did that seem like such an awful thing? My mother said she didn't care, and I was free. Whether or not she was right about all the rest of it, wasn't that enough? Free from debt, with money in the bank, and leaving my mother's house. Suddenly I felt buoyant. Unlimited. For a moment. For a split second.

Until Tammy said, "Nora, you can't go."

I felt like my world was turning inside out. Upside down. Nothing was the way I expected it to be.

"What do you mean, I can't go? I thought you'd be ecstatic. I thought you'd be even more excited than I am."

"Nora, did you forget?"

"What?"

"Remember when I made the prediction that you would be leaving."

I laughed. "Oh, I totally forgot about that. You're right. Then again, you're always right."

"Then you have to remember that I said you couldn't go."

"That's a contradiction. If I'm going, I'm going. You can't tell me I'm going and I can't go at the same time."

"Okay, then just let me tell you this. When I held your hand that time, I felt . . . Nora, all I can say is that it's not safe. You've got to listen to me. It's not safe."

"You keep saying that, but you don't tell me anything."

"Okay, how about this? It's the worst feeling I think I've ever felt. It's something that's masquerading as love, but it's not. It's jealousy and resentment and fear, and if you don't act exactly the way it wants you to, I don't know what it will do."

"Why don't you just say it? You mean you don't know what he will do."

"Whatever that feeling will do," she said.

"I thought you liked him."

"This isn't about liking him. Though honestly, Nora, I might like him, but I can't say I exactly trust him. He's not really the trustworthy type, is he?"

"I thought Dan was the trustworthy type. Look how far appearances take you."

"Nora, I'm just afraid you're not going into this with your eyes open. You've got to see who this guy really is."

"Why are you starting to sound like my mother now?"

"God knows, I don't think your mother and I

have ever agreed on anything before. But you might want to listen for a change."

"What do you mean, listen for a change?"

"You pretend to listen, and then you just go do whatever it was that you were planning to do," Tammy said. "I'm just worried you don't take into consideration all the facts."

"Or maybe I'm just thinking about different facts. This danger you're describing to me, honestly I can't say that it scares me. Not like staying here forever scares me."

"That's because you don't feel what I felt," Tammy said.

"Maybe something has changed," I suggested. "Why don't you try again?"

I held my hand out. Tammy hesitated, then took it as if it were a dead fish. She closed her eyes for all of three seconds, then she practically threw my hand away.

"Okay, guess I know the answer to that question," I said.

"Nora, if you could feel what I feel . . ."

"I'd probably still go. Maybe this time you'll be wrong."

"I'm not wrong," she assured me.

"Well, at least my life will be exciting," I said. "Aren't tragedies always the best stories?"

The problem is, even when you think you can see the future, and you're willing to accept the consequences, it's never quite like you think.

THE INVESTIGATION

*P*ractical Homicide Investigation addresses the use of psychics in investigation as follows:

> Practically speaking, police officers are naturally skeptical of psychics and psychic phenomena. However, from an investigative point of view, anything that has proven to be successful in one investigation should certainly be considered in other cases. It should be noted that information provided by the psychic may not always be accurate and in some instances may have no value to the investigation (Geberth, p. 718).

Thus far, the reliability of psychics for law enforcement has not been established. Anecdotal information is sometimes impressive, and even surprising, but nothing can be concluded about using psychics as resources in solving a crime.

Timothy

Nora Comes to New York

I got back to New York on a Monday, and all that week there was no word from Nora. Every day I thought she might call—and nothing.

How do you stop waiting for something? My answer was to get busy with something else. I might have watched a movie or done some work. I would have found something. But it turned out I didn't need to, because Celia showed up at my door a couple of days after her last disastrous visit.

The doorman didn't buzz me. I'm sure she told him not to, and she'd been there often enough that he did what she asked. As a result, I was unprepared when there was a knock on my door. When I opened it, there was Celia. I certainly hadn't been expecting her after the way I'd let her leave on Monday. But it wasn't the Celia I had seen on Monday that showed up at my door—it was the Celia who was so self-sufficient she gave the impression that even if the world's population were wiped out, she would be just fine. It was the Celia I preferred. It was the Celia who, truthfully, I admired.

But I didn't know that right away. I saw her, and I wasn't happy about it. I'm sure she could tell, but she just smiled in that way she always used to smile—as if nothing I said or did or felt could move her in the slightest. She made no apologies; she just stepped forward as if there was no question of whether I was going to let her in. And when she did that, she was right: there wasn't any question.

Within minutes we were in the bedroom, and, I have to admit, I didn't think of Nora even once during the next few hours. You might be thinking, what kind of love is that? After Celia got dressed and left, I know I asked myself that question. I didn't have an answer.

Celia was over every night that week. Don't ask me how she managed it with Marcus. I didn't question it. I needed the distraction. And that's one thing I can say about Celia—she made for a very good distraction. I asked her to spend the weekend with me, and, to my surprise, she said yes.

I felt myself slipping back into my old life. If I could manage to keep my mind from thoughts of Nora, I could almost pretend that whole thing had never happened.

And then she called.

Nora called me Monday morning from work. I could picture her there, in her uniform, behind the counter, picking at a muffin with her fingers. Sometimes she didn't even eat it. I had stood there often enough and watched her just pick one apart.

"It's Nora," she said. Then, almost abruptly, "I want to come to New York if that's still okay."

"When?" I asked her.

"Whenever you want me," she said.

"This week," I said. I was afraid to wait longer. I didn't trust my love to last. I know there had been a long time between the first visit to Kansas and the second, but it still felt so fragile, as if it could disappear at any second. Maybe it already had. When she told me she was coming, I didn't feel the surge of happiness I had anticipated. I felt nothing. No excitement, no dread. It was like dropping a stone into a well, waiting for a splash, and getting just silence.

She said, "I'll book a flight today and let you know."

And she did.

I went to pick her up at the airport on Friday. It was below freezing in the city, with a wind that sliced right through whatever you were wearing. Some people broke out their furs, which was somewhat unusual for New York. The rest of the city shivered in their fashionable and not very warm jackets.

Nora came off the plane in jeans, a big knit sweater, and a parka. Of course she'd worn the same things in Kansas, but in New York they made her look out of place. Provincial. A little awkward and dumpy, though in reality she was anything but.

I couldn't help it—the first thing my mind did was to compare her to Celia, who had continued to come over nearly every night that week. Celia had jokingly said it was like last call at the bar. And like last call, the sex had been better—so much better—because of the very fact that we both knew it was about to end.

So when I saw Nora, my first thought was, "Oh my God, what have I done?" But I put a smile on my face to, hopefully, cover it.

Nora saw me a moment after I spotted her, but she didn't smile. So I stopped smiling as well. And that immediately felt so much better. Then I remembered. I didn't have to pretend with her. I didn't ever have to pretend with her. By the time she reached me, my heart had gone from empty to, well, something else.

When she reached me, I took her hand. I was always surprised by how tiny it was. I held it as we walked to the baggage claim. We didn't have to wait long before the belt started up, and I thought it was an omen that her suitcase was the very first down the shoot. It was one of the old hard-plastic kind, with a handle and four awkward wheels that didn't roll. It was surprisingly light when I lifted it off the belt. I stood for a moment waiting for another when she said, "That's it. I only have one."

I carried her one suitcase to the car I had waiting outside. The driver came around and took the suitcase from me and tossed it in the trunk while we climbed into the back for the drive into the city.

We were silent for most of the drive, but she kept her hand in mine as she looked out the window. She had never been to New York, and as I looked out the window over her shoulder, I tried to imagine what it would be like, seeing it for the first time. In front of my eyes, the familiar disappeared and was replaced with—I'm not sure I can describe it. But I knew then that what I felt in Kansas wasn't a fluke. It wasn't something that would die when transplanted away from wheat fields and open sky. I was addicted to being with Nora. I wanted her with me. I wanted her physical presence, because when I was with her, I felt like there was magic in the world. Isn't that what we all want?

That night I slept with her in my arms, just like I had imagined. Her body was white and her hair spread out like a river of red on the pillow and over the sheets. She wanted to put it up in a braid, but I wouldn't let her. Unlike anyone else I had ever known, her face didn't change when she slept. She wasn't like a child. She was just Nora with her eyes closed.

In the morning I was able to slide my arm from beneath her head and get out of bed, and she didn't even stir. I went to the kitchen and made coffee and brought back a cup for her.

I had to touch her shoulder to wake her, but

when her eyes opened, she went from deep sleep to fully awake in a moment, the way you imagine a trained assassin might.

She sat up and took the coffee from me. She took a sip and immediately made a face.

"You make terrible coffee," she said.

I laughed. "Okay, we'll go out for coffee. There's a Starbucks on the corner. You'll feel right at home. Go on and get dressed."

I watched as she got up and crossed to her clunky blue suitcase. She opened it up and surveyed the contents for a minute. I could tell that she wasn't happy with what she saw. Her movements were hesitant. She picked out a pair of jeans and a turtleneck. But when she put them on, I could see the black pants were the wrong cut— baggy and pleated and tapering to the ankles, so they made her look like a bowling pin. And the turtleneck, though there was nothing wrong with it, couldn't save her from the pants. Plus, the parka was destined to go over it anyway.

She turned around and caught me watching her. And she knew what I was thinking. I could see it. She looked me right in the eye as if to say, Well, what did you think you were getting?

I felt a flood of some emotion. I searched to label it, and I was surprised what I came up with. It was pride. It made no sense, but there it was. She was so genuinely herself. Even here in New York, she was still herself. And at the same time, it made her seem more mine. Everyone in New York was on display, but Nora was different. She was hidden. And I wanted to keep it that way.

The weekend was a dream. I felt like I lived a secret life. I showed Nora a New York I realized I had never seen. When Monday came around, I brought her to the office with me. I had decided she would come in and work with me once she got settled. After I had gotten over the shock of her education, I realized I could share with her the only thing I loved in the world up until that point—my work. There was a conference room I never used, and I could easily make it into her office. I had it all planned.

Nora seemed to like it. She spent all day Monday with me, sitting and listening to my phone calls, looking over the computer systems, talking to Marie, my assistant. But that night, when I said something about going back in the next day, she asked me if she could have a few days to get oriented to the city.

My initial gut reaction was disappointment. I had to admit, I didn't really want to let her out of my sight. If I could have said no, I would have.

Without Nora with me at the office, the week seemed long. The days couldn't quite hold my attention. I looked forward as I never had to leaving the office and going home.

When I got home, Nora would tell me about what she'd done that day. She experimented with the subway and hailing cabs. She walked around Soho and the West Village. She took a trip up to Central Park and got lost wandering along the paths. She said she did some shopping, but I didn't see evidence of any new clothes. For that week, she wore the same sweaters and jeans she had brought with her.

On Friday I asked her to meet Marcus and me for a drink. I told her I'd come home and pick her up, but she insisted she'd meet us there.

I was looking forward to Marcus meeting her. I was sure he wouldn't know what to make of her. I imagined his face when he saw the jeans and the sweaters and the long braid and the parka. I could picture the judgment that he wouldn't be able to hide. All week I had seen it on the faces of waiters and other couples when we went out. They looked at me and they looked at her, and their faces looked like they were looking at a math problem that didn't quite add up.

That was the look I expected to see on Marcus's face. So when we were sitting at the bar and I saw his eyes fix on someone behind me, with the look that he usually reserved for his wife, I didn't even bother to turn around. That was not the look that Nora was going to elicit.

Then I felt a hand on my back, and I turned.

It was Nora, and it wasn't Nora. The jeans were gone; the hiking boots and parka, gone. In their place was a black dress: long sleeved, high necked, but very short. She wore black stockings and high heels. A black coat swirled around her almost like a cape. Her hair was down and straight and stunning against the black. And she was wearing makeup, not a lot but enough to transform her. She was breathtaking. Just as she had been that first night when we had gone out to dinner and she had gotten dressed up. She hadn't done it since—how had I forgotten what happened when she stopped hiding?

"I'm Marcus," Marcus was saying, holding out his hand.

"Nora," she said, and stuck out her hand, straight armed and enthusiastic like a boy. At least she hadn't changed in that way. She was still Nora. But now her beauty was out there for everyone to see.

I could immediately see the effect she had on Marcus. Marcus knew a genuine from a fake. It's true, he had chosen Celia. But before meeting Nora, I would have chosen Celia as well. Celia was what you were supposed to want, what the world held up as success. Nora was what you only dared to dream about.

"How do you like New York?" Marcus asked. "You like it better than Kansas?"

"I thought I would," Nora said. "But it's just different."

"You don't like it better, living here in New York?" I said.

She turned to me. "Of course I do. But you're what makes it better. Not the place."

How can I explain to you how she said that? It wasn't coquettish. It wasn't said to flatter me. It was just the truth.

I happened to glance at Marcus's face, and I saw the admiration that only needed time to turn into envy. Then I saw Marcus look past Nora, and his face changed to a frown.

He turned to me and said, "I'm so sorry, Tim. I told her not to come." I turned around and spotted her just as he said, "But it seems that my wife is here."

When Celia reached us, she kissed her husband, turned to me and gave me a kiss on the cheek, then she pulled back and pretended to notice Nora for the first time.

I did the introductions. "Nora, this is Celia, Marcus's wife. Celia, this is Nora."

Nora stuck out her hand again, and Celia looked at it as if she didn't quite know what to do with it. She ended up taking Nora's fingers in a half shake.

I saw Nora's eyebrows go up a fraction.

"So, Nora," Celia drawled her name. "How do you like New York?"

It was the same question Marcus had asked, but Celia's was dripping with condescension. I saw Marcus wince.

Nora glanced at me, as if to try to gauge how

she should play the situation. I gave her a little nod that I hoped she understood meant she had full permission to defend herself against attack.

She gave the answer that Celia's question deserved—which was barely an answer at all.

"It's fine," Nora said.

"Fine?" Celia repeated. "That's all you have to say about one of the greatest cities in the world. It's fine?"

Nora pretended to think for a moment. Then she said, "Yes, I think that's about it."

"You people from Kansas don't have much to say for yourselves, do you?" Celia said, with a little laugh, as if the laugh would make it seem less offensive. At that moment I realized that Celia was doing exactly what I used to do: she walked a line, staying just barely on the safe side of rude. It usually threw people off balance.

But Nora didn't seem fazed by it at all. She just shrugged and said, "In Kansas we don't spend a lot of time talking about our food. We just eat it."

Marcus and I laughed.

And I have to give Celia credit. She looked over at Marcus, then at me, then back at Nora. And she realized that she wasn't going to win this one. So she gave up with good grace.

"Let's start again. I'm Celia," and she held out her hand again, and when Nora took it, Celia gave a real handshake. Then Celia leaned over and whispered something in Nora's ear.

Nora shrugged and nodded.

Then Celia looked at us and said, "We'll be back in a bit."

She took Nora's hand and started to lead her away.

"Hold on, where are you going?" I called after her.

Marcus wasn't happy with it either. "Come on, Celia, let's just get a table and have some food."

"You get the table. We'll be right back." She didn't even turn around as she spoke.

Marcus and I looked at each other. I shrugged and tilted my head toward the tables. He nodded, and we grabbed our drinks and walked over to be seated.

When we were settled in at a table, Marcus asked, "You think Nora will be okay?"

"I think Nora can hold her own," I said.

"I should say so. Where on earth did you find her?"

"Well, Kansas."

"Are there more of her?" he asked, almost wistfully.

"You've already got one of your own," I pointed out.

Marcus looked at me. After a second he said, "Not really. I think she's having an affair."

I think I hid my reaction well.

"Why do you think that?" I said.

"Just a feeling. But that's not the worst." He

stopped to take a long drink of his beer, as if he needed courage to say what he was about to say. He put the beer down, carefully centering it on the napkin. Then he said, "No, the worst part is that I don't even care. I actually almost hope she is and that she will leave me. She's not . . . It's not like I thought it was going to be."

"How did you think it was going to be?"

"Oh, God. I don't know." He put his hand up to his forehead and held it for a moment, as if his head hurt. "I wanted . . . I wanted something more. More than just the dull routine, you know. I wanted life to be . . ."

"Magical?" I said.

He winced at the word. "I would have settled for glimpses of happy. Is it like that for you?"

I shrugged. I didn't want to rub it in.

"What on earth did you do to deserve that? Even being crazy in love with Celia, I never felt like life was magical. This might sound awful, but it gave me a rush when we were out and I saw how everyone else looked at her. But you must get that as well with Nora."

"She doesn't usually look like this," I said. "She usually wears big sweaters and hiking boots and this big puffy jacket. Then she just looks like a normal girl."

"How could she be just a normal girl?" Marcus looked over at the bar. Celia and Nora were talking as they waited for drinks. In terms of physical beauty, Nora couldn't compete. But she had something else.

Nora happened to glance over and catch me looking at her. Without changing her expression in the slightest, she did that thing with her eyebrows, raising them just a hairbreadth. Then I saw the tiny quirk at the corner of her mouth. And she turned back to Celia.

"She couldn't be just a normal girl," I agreed.

"Anyone could see that," Marcus said.

That started a feeling in me. A flutter of panic. If everyone could see it, that meant that everyone would be trying to take her away from me. After all, look what had happened to Marcus with Celia. Hadn't I done just that? Some guy was bound to try that with Nora. What Marcus said next didn't help either.

"How long is it going to be before she finds out what an asshole you are and leaves you?"

"Oh, she knows already."

Marcus looked at me. "I doubt that."

There was something in the way he said it, and for the first time, I wondered if Marcus knew about me and Celia. The thought had never occurred to me before. I had been certain I was the one with all the information, and he was the one in the dark. In that scenario, he got to be the good guy, but it also made him the dupe. If he knew about the affair . . . I didn't even know how to process the possibility. I would have to completely change my idea of who Marcus was. In that event, I realized that I would have no idea who he actually was. He would be like a black hole. A place where information disappeared. Where the normal rules didn't hold.

We were supposed to stay on for dinner, but you're probably not surprised that I made an excuse and got us out of there. I knew that Nora wanted to have dinner out, but I had the car take us home instead, and I told her I wanted a quiet night in and that we could order whatever she wanted. I just didn't want to take her out looking like that. I wanted her back in her baggy jeans and big sweaters.

When we got back into the apartment, I suggested, "Why don't you change out of that and into a robe or something?"

"You didn't like my dress," she said. It wasn't a question.

"Where did you get it?"

"Barney's."

"I like you better in your clothes."

"I look like a tourist in my clothes."

"Well, that's what you are," I said, maybe a little roughly.

"Oh." She was silent for a long minute. "So when is my visit over?"

"I didn't mean it like that."

"But you could send me back at any time."

"Do you worry about that?" I asked her. It had

never occurred to me to even think about it.

Her voice was quiet when she said, "Of course I do. I'll never measure up against women like Celia. I don't know why you would want me when you could have someone like her."

She was so blind. How long would she stay that way? How long could it last?

I reached out and pulled her in. Wrapping my arms around her, I said, "I don't want Celia. I want you. And you know what else I want?"

"What?" she asked, tilting her head back. Normally she just came up to my chin, but she was taller than normal because of her high heels, and it was easier for her to look up into my eyes.

"I want you to go take that dress off and put on some pajamas or a robe."

"I knew it," she said. "I knew you didn't like the dress. I was so sure you would. I thought I looked good in it."

I didn't want to tell her that that was the problem.

"It's not that. It's just that I like your sweaters."

"If you want, you can come with me when I go shopping and show me what else you like."

She saw my answer in my face.

"In that case, Celia offered to go with me."

"No," I said, probably too quickly. "I don't want you looking like a little Celia clone. I liked the dress. Really. You have great taste."

When I said that I was thinking that if I was

lucky, I would be wrong about her having great taste, and she'd end up with more sweaters. But my hopes of that were dashed when she said, "It's amazing you think so, considering the clothes I showed up in. Those are mostly old clothes from my sister when she was in her outdoorsy phase. I never liked them, but I just never bothered to get new ones. I didn't see the point."

"And you see a point now?"

"Of course I do," she said. "You."

Timothy

Another Family Dinner

The next day was the weekly family dinner.

I told Nora I needed to go out alone that night—to the family dinner. Nora knew all about the family dinners. She grinned, rolled her eyes, and wished me luck.

I hadn't attended a family dinner in over a month. I got there, and the table was set with gold. Yellow flowers, gold tablecloth, and the china that had an inlay of gold at the edge. I wondered if it was in celebration of the fact that our money was intact because I had pulled out of the market. The stocks had plunged yet again the week before as a result of terrible economic data and the inescapable fact that we were headed into the worst recession in decades.

I was late, so everyone was already seated. I went around to kiss my mother hello, and the reception was decidedly chilly. That wasn't a surprise. There had to be some retribution for the fact I had disappeared for so long.

But in the past, no matter what I had done to piss her off the first thing we talked about at dinner was always the portfolio. Of course, I had started sending her an update on Fridays ever since my sister had come to the office and harangued me, but I didn't really think it would be different.

I was wrong.

My mother ignored me, as if I wasn't even there. She skipped right over me and turned to Andrew. It seemed that she had decided Andrew's boys should be homeschooled since they hadn't gotten into the only school she thought was worthy of them. She wanted to talk about the subjects the boys were going to study. She was apparently helping to design their curriculum and had plans for them to get through the subject matter of at least three grades in one year.

Once my mother felt like the path to Harvard had been assured, even though the boys were only four and six, she turned to Edward. Apparently, while I was gone he'd had a story accepted somewhere or other. It was some magazine I'd never heard of, but I guess it was prestigious enough for my mother to approve. I thought about the books Emily claimed he had written. I wondered if it was true. So many people pretended to be successes when they weren't. It would be a nice twist if my brother was pretending to be a failure. I had thought about trying to find out if what my sister had told me was true. But I hadn't. I wasn't sure if I wanted to know. The foundations of my world had been shaken. I wasn't ready for them to come down.

But it seemed like I might not actually have

control over that, because just then my mother did something that truly shocked me. She turned to my sister and said, "How is Alejandro? Can he make it for coffee?"

I couldn't believe it. Not only was my mother saying his name aloud, voluntarily, but even more amazing, he was invited for coffee? No one had ever been invited for coffee.

Then it got worse. I thought certainly when she was done with my sister she would turn to me and chew me out for disappearing, but she somehow never did finish with my sister. They were going over details for the wedding, which I had heard nothing about. It was still over a year away, but they talked wedding and church and reception and food until Alejandro himself arrived.

You should have seen this performance. He was dressed to perfection: perfectly cut jacket, creased pants, shined shoes, and he wore them in a way that seemed perfectly natural—as if he were at home in perfection.

When he came in, he went straight to my mother's chair and bowed over her hand in the way that only a foreigner could really get away with without looking silly. Then he went to Emily and kissed her on the cheek. Then he shook my father's hand, then Andrew's and Edward's. He had obviously met them all before.

Then he came to me. I saw my sister frowning at me over his shoulder. But he was polite when he shook my hand and said, with only the slightest hint of an accent, "Timothy, it's a pleasure to finally meet you."

I had the feeling that he could speak without an accent if he chose, but he knew the accent lent something to his presence.

He sat down in a seat that was brought in for him, right next to my mother. It was, I realized, where I usually sat, but I had been moved further down the table. I hadn't even noticed till then.

That's when my mother finally turned to me, and she smiled. That was never a good sign. My punishment for ignoring her calls and not returning to New York immediately was not over.

"Timothy, did you know that Alejandro manages money as well?" She paused, waiting for my reaction.

I just raised my eyebrows.

She went on, "He specializes in international investments, and his performance has been extraordinary. I was thinking, since you're not doing much with the money right now, that we might transfer some over to Alejandro's fund."

I glanced over at Alejandro. He was very intent on stirring sugar into his coffee.

I looked over at my father, and he shrugged. "Alejandro's performance history does look good," he said.

I had been managing their money for more than

fifteen years, with only two down years, and now I had managed to protect it against losses in the worst financial market in decades, and this was what happened. Even if you did well, people were always looking for someone who might be able to do better—even, apparently, your own family. If Alejandro's performance was much better than mine, then it was because he ran his money with more of a tolerance for risk—unless he had inside information, in which case he would be a very good bet. Cheating always was.

"How much?" I asked.

"Well," my mother said nonchalantly, "I thought whatever you had liquid at the moment."

She knew very well that when we made back our losses, I had divested much of the fund, which meant she was proposing to give Alejandro almost all the family money to manage.

I was suddenly so angry I could barely speak. She wanted to leave me sitting around with nothing, waiting for when they'd throw more money my way.

But my mother was always doing ridiculous things, and I'd always prided myself on the fact that she wasn't able to get to me. What was going on? When had I lost my cool?

I took a deep breath before I spoke, just to check to make sure I wasn't doing something I would regret. But if she moved the money to his fund, I didn't want it back. At the age of forty-three, I suddenly realized it was time for me to be on my own.

I said, "Why don't I figure out what portion of the fund is mine, and then I will turn the rest over to you? I think we should hire someone with no affiliation to oversee the division. Dad, do you have someone you'd like to suggest?"

"Hold on a second, we weren't suggesting that you stop managing all the money," my father said quickly.

"No, I don't want you to do that." My mother sounded angry. "We just were going to take out the money that was liquid, that was just sitting around," she said again, not able to resist another potshot at my investing decisions.

I turned to her. "The bulk of the portfolio is liquid right now, as you know. Not to mention the fact that in taking that money, you would also be taking my money since a percentage is mine and part of the principle is mine, and as talented as Alejandro might be, I would rather continue to manage my own capital. So I think the best thing would be to unwind the finances, and we can revisit it in the future if you want to go another route." I said this as calmly as I could manage.

"I don't understand why we can't just take what you have sitting around, and give it to Alejandro. Why do you need to make it so complicated?" my mother repeated stubbornly.

Alejandro finally stepped in. He turned to my

283

mother and said, "What Timothy says about unwinding the fund makes sense. There are accounting issues and legal issues, and I think it is really simplest this way. You can always reinvest with him in the future, but if you're going to be taking out the bulk of the funds, it makes sense for both you and him to dissolve the arrangement as it stands."

His voice seemed to have a soothing effect on my mother. Like music calming a beast. And even though this bastard was taking my livelihood right from under my nose, I had to admit I had left town and hadn't been in touch. My mother had been unhappy, and he had been there with great numbers and a manner that seemed perfectly designed for ingratiating himself. I had to give the man credit.

My mother obviously did too, because she seemed like she might actually be willing to listen to him.

"Do you really think that might be best?" she asked.

"I do," Alejandro said.

"Would you be willing to work with Timothy to sort that out?" she asked. "I would trust you to see that it's done right."

"I don't know . . ." Alejandro started to say. He had the good manners to look embarrassed.

As far as I was concerned, Alejandro was as good as anyone.

"No, it's fine," I said. "You can come by Monday. Do you know where the office is?"

Emily spoke. "I can give him the address."

I looked over at my sister, and I knew she was thinking about the last time she had seen me there. Instead of being cut off without a cent, in a way she was getting the whole fortune. And from the look on her face, she was definitely enjoying it.

I glanced around the table then, and I didn't see a single friendly face. I knew Emily loved it, and Andrew didn't even try to hide a smug grin. Edward wouldn't look at me, and my father—he didn't look pleased or embarrassed. He didn't even seem to realize anything was at all wrong.

It was very clear I had no allies.

If you think that money brings you safety and security, you should try having a lot of it, along with the feeling that there isn't a single person in the entire world who is there for you.

Except that wasn't true. I had Nora.

The thought gave me reassurance for a split second—until I saw the danger in it. The power to make me feel better also gave her the power to hurt me. With love came fear. It's like sun and shadow. How do you separate them?

THE INVESTIGATION

FAMILY VIOLENCE

In the book *Homicide*, Richard Gelles and Murray Straus are identified as "probably the best-known investigators of family violence in contemporary America." According to Gelles and Straus:

> *The family is the most frequent single locus of all types of violence ranging from slaps, to beatings, to torture, to murder. Students of homicide are well aware that more murder victims are members of the same family than any other category of murder-victim relationship. . . . In fact, violence is so common in the family that we have said it is at least as typical of family relations as is love.*

Timothy

What Happened After the Family Dinner

The only person who said good-bye to me when I got up and walked out of the dinner was Alejandro. He stood, walked me to the door, said he would call me Monday, and shook my hand. No apologies, no fawning—just matter-of-fact and businesslike.

Everyone else sat there like idiots. Except for my mother. She said, "Good night, Timothy. It's nice to have you back." She could afford to be gracious now; she knew that she had won this round. She might even have won the whole fight. I had believed that she depended on me. I was shaken to find that it seemed it had been the other way around all along.

Thank God, Nora was nearby. She was waiting for me at Daniel. We had arranged that I would meet her there after the family dinner. I figured we could have dinner, since I was always hungry when I left my parents' house.

It was only a few blocks away, but I jumped in a cab when I saw one because I wanted to get to her as fast as possible. I was sure the minute I saw her, I would feel better.

But I didn't.

I spotted her right away when I walked in. There

was no way to miss her. She was sitting at the bar, wearing another new dress—this one was red, and with that long red hair, she almost glowed.

She didn't notice me until I was right next to her—probably because she wasn't alone. She had men flanking her on either side.

One of them said something, and she laughed. A real laugh. As she tilted her head back, her hair rippled down her back, and I swear I've never seen anything freer. Or more beautiful.

I can't describe how it made me feel, to see her laughing like that with other men. It took everything in me to keep from taking a swing at one of them. I didn't say anything, but both of the men noticed me, and when Nora saw them staring behind her, she turned around. "Oh, here he is," she said. "Timothy, this is Alex and Stephen. This is Timothy."

I think I nodded at them, but I can't be sure. I had no interest in making nice with two blowhards in suits—they were buy-side or investment banking, from the look of them.

They took one look at my face, and they started backing away. Literally.

One of them, I don't know if it was Stephen or Alex, said to Nora, "Good to meet you."

She glanced at me, then turned back to the one who spoke, and it seemed to me that she gave him an extra big smile and said, "Thank you for the drink and the company while I waited."

I felt wild. At that moment, I wanted to hurt her.

They beat a retreat, and she swung around to look at me. The smile disappeared, and she just looked straight in my eyes as if weighing something. Then she said, "Let's not stay here. Let's go someplace else. I passed someplace I thought looked nice."

She didn't wait for me to agree. She just got up off her chair and headed over to the coat check. She gave the coat check girl her ticket and put some money in the tip jar.

The girl turned and disappeared into the coat room. We stood in strained silence—until the girl came back with Nora's parka.

"Will you help me with my coat?" Nora asked me.

I laughed. I couldn't help it. She had gone out wearing that awful parka over that dress. And I knew she had done it for me.

"Well, you said you liked my parka," she said, smiling.

"I love your parka," I told her. And I took it and held it out for her to slip her arms into the sleeves.

We walked east over to Third Avenue, to a dive bar, and ate chicken fingers and drank Budweiser on tap. I probably had too many beers. When we left, I had the feeling that I needed to concentrate in order to walk straight. We hailed a cab and I pulled her against me, her and her big marshmallow parka.

I waited until the door of the apartment closed behind us. Then I practically leapt on her. She tried to push me away and take off her jacket, but I wouldn't let her. "Leave it on," I whispered.

I made her sit down on the sofa. I pulled off her shoes. I rolled down her stockings, then I took off her underwear. And I made love to her in that silly jacket and that stunning dress. Halfway through, I let her take off the jacket. Then the dress. And it was just her body, white against the leather of the couch, and her hair. That hair spread out over her shoulders. It wasn't just long; it was heavy and thick and it felt like strands of silk when it slid over my skin.

I ran my fingers through it as she looked up at me.

"I love you," I told her.

"I love you too."

I searched her eyes. I couldn't see it.

"I need you to prove it," I told her.

"What do you mean?"

I stood up and held out my hand. She put her hand in mine, and I pulled her up and led her down the hall and into the bathroom. I opened up the bottom drawer and took out my electric razor and handed it to her.

She held it for a moment, as if she didn't know what I wanted.

I took the cord and plugged it in.

She just looked at me blankly.

I reached out and lifted a lock of hair from her shoulder, and I said, "I want you to prove it. I want you to cut off your hair."

Her expression didn't change, but her eyes were wide and dark. Her pupils seemed to have expanded to take up the whole iris, so they were just a well of black. She glanced at herself in the mirror. Then she looked back at me.

"You're really asking me to do this?" she said.

"Yes."

I don't know if you'll understand, but the thrill I felt at that moment was like nothing I'd ever experienced. This was it—it was what I wanted. It was what I needed. I needed proof, and this would be it. This would give me what I'd been looking for. I would know for certain how she felt.

"How much?" she asked me.

"Everything," I told her.

I don't know what I expected. Tears I suppose. Or protest. Or questions. I got none of it. She looked at me with no expression at all. At least none that I could read.

She said, "I'd prefer to do it alone, if you don't mind."

I did mind. I wanted to watch, but I couldn't quite bring myself to say it. So I nodded and turned around and left the bathroom.

She closed the door behind me, then I heard nothing for a long time.

I lay down on the bed and waited. Eventually I

heard the buzz of the razor when it was turned on, then the higher pitch of it as it was set to work. I lay there listening to the whine of it.

I closed my eyes and I imagined the heavy strands of hair falling to the floor. I saw it as something sad and beautiful, like the autumn when the trees drop their leaves and cover the ground with a carpet of color.

It went on much longer than I thought it would. But finally the noise stopped. And the silence afterward was almost a palpable thing.

I opened my eyes. But a long time went by and nothing happened. Then, finally, the handle of the door turned. And she came out.

Nora

*What Nora Thought of Coming
to New York*

I admit it. I thought New York would be the answer to all my problems. I thought it would be a wonderful adventure. I thought I would feel like I was living for the first time.

But from the moment I stepped out of the cab, I knew I didn't fit in there. The airport was fine—maybe because in the airport I was surrounded by people who weren't from New York. But the minute I got onto the streets, I knew I didn't belong. Everyone seemed to have some sort of handbook on how to dress, how to walk, how to appear sophisticated and aloof.

I never paid much attention to my clothes in Kansas. I mean, you might dress up when you were going out at night, but during the day it was really more about being comfortable. Here the way everyone else dressed made me feel like a lumberjack. I looked around and there were so many beautiful women in New York. I had no idea why Timothy had asked me to come. What was he doing with me? I couldn't answer the question. He had invited me to live with him, but the thing that we never talked about, that was left unsaid, was what would happen if it didn't work out.

So in some ways that first weekend was an agony. Funny, right? I'd gotten everything I wanted, everything I'd been waiting for, and I was miserable. All my money worries—gone. I had met an amazing man. I had escaped my mother's house and a dead-end job. I'd come to New York. And I was miserable.

For the first two days, the thought that haunted me was that I wanted to go home. But that was also my greatest fear—that Timothy would send me back.

What I wanted and what I feared were the same. It seems so obvious, but it took me two days to realize it. But when I finally saw it, it made me laugh. And when I did, everything was better.

That's also when I started actually doing something to change what had made me so uncomfortable. During that week on my own in New York, I discovered some things about myself. I found I always turned in the wrong direction when I came out of the subway. I found I loved walking around the city, even when it was bitterly cold. I found I liked shopping. I always assumed I hated it, but it was a bit different when you had money in the bank and you were in New York. I found my attitude had changed—I didn't mind feeling out of place, and the looks other people gave me when I was out with Timothy just made me laugh.

When I was feeling more secure, I started to see his insecurities. Aren't relationships like that? It's like being on a seesaw. There are those precious moments when you're just even with each other, but you move through that, and then one person being down by definition means the other person is up. I knew he loved me, and I knew he was afraid. I discovered that, if you look, you can actually see everything. All you have to do is clear away your own fears. The things you think are so well hidden: we can all see them. That's the secret. Everyone can see everything.

But, even though I could see what he was feeling, I didn't see what was coming. So I ended up standing in the bathroom with an electric razor in my hand.

What can I say about the moment when I understood what he wanted from me? He wanted me to cut off my hair to prove I loved him.

It wasn't a fair test.

The truth was, I had wanted to cut off my hair for as long as I could remember. I would have done it, but I was afraid no one would want me without my hair. My mother had taught me that it was my beauty. Without it, I would be nothing. I resented it, I wanted to be rid of it, but I felt like I needed it. And here was someone telling me they wanted me without it. He was standing there, thinking he was asking for the greatest sacrifice, but with that request, he was giving me the greatest gift.

I also knew that if he didn't think it was a sacrifice, he wouldn't have his proof. And I wasn't sure if I could convince him of it if he watched me. I didn't ask him to leave the bathroom so he wouldn't see how upset I was; I asked him to leave because I wasn't sure I would be able to hide the opposite.

After he left, I stood in front of the mirror and looked at myself for a long time. Then I took the electric razor and I turned it on. I stood with it buzzing in my hand for a long time before I finally raised my arm and used it. The hair that had taken me thirty-three years to grow took me about three minutes to shave off. That's how quickly it goes.

What is the thing you think gives you value? What makes you feel most yourself? What is it that you identify with? What is it that you think makes you, you? Find out what that thing is, and then give it up. It is only then that you will be able to see what is left. And you won't be the same. You will be irrevocably, irretrievably changed. I know I was. When I walked out of that bathroom, I was not the same girl who had walked in.

He was lying on the bed, and when I came out, he sat up and stared at me. I wondered what he saw. I had left an inch or so of hair. It was shorter than most boys'. The only people who had less hair were bald men and the military. It was a harsh haircut. Unforgiving. There was nowhere to hide, but for the first time, I didn't feel like I needed to. I knew I was beautiful.

"Come here," he said—but the way he said it sounded more like a question than a command.

I walked to the edge of the bed and stood there. He pulled me down next to him, then folded me into a fierce hug. He held me longer than usual, but finally he let go and pulled back to look at me again.

He searched my face for something. I don't know what he found.

Then he said, "Nora, will you marry me?"

I said yes.

Two Months Later

Timothy

The Day Before the Wedding

It was the day before our wedding, and everything was set. We had opted for something very simple—or, rather, I had, since Nora insisted she would be happy with whatever I wanted. So I decided to have a small ceremony and a dinner at my family's house in the Hamptons, mainly because it seemed the fastest and easiest way to do it—fastest being the most important attribute.

I wanted to be married to Nora as soon as possible. Well, that's not exactly true. She would have gone down to city hall with me any day of the week, but I didn't want that. I wanted to mark it. I wanted it to be important. I wanted it to be witnessed—not by a lot of people, just by the significant ones.

My parents' house was on the beach, and we planned to have the ceremony there, just before sunset. We were going to have dinner outside, on the deck looking over the ocean, if it was warm enough, inside if it was chilly or raining. It was the time of spring when it could go either way. We hired a catering company to come in and do the dinner.

The nearby town was small and quaint, and since it wasn't summer, it was also relatively quiet. So, for accommodations, we rented out almost all the rooms in a good-sized bed-and-breakfast—one of those huge, sprawling old houses with a wraparound porch and four-poster beds in each room—and we invited our immediate family and a handful of friends. Nora's mother and sister (neither of whom I had met) had been picked up at the airport and driven out that morning. Tammy and Neil were the only friends Nora had invited, and they were arriving right before the rehearsal dinner.

My family was coming out as well: Andrew and his wife and two kids were going to stay at the house with my parents. Emily and Alejandro and Edward had opted to stay at the B&B. The only friends I invited were Marcus and Celia. Though I would have loved an excuse not to have invited them, I had been the best man at their wedding, so I couldn't think of any way out of it.

I wondered how most people felt the day before their wedding—though I doubted if one out of a hundred would give an honest answer. People like to report feeling the way they think they're supposed to feel. They say they were excited, happy—most probably would admit to being nervous, because that's acceptable—but would a bride, who has been looking forward to the day her whole life, admit it was a disappointment? Or would a groom admit to having a feeling in his gut that it's really a huge mistake? I didn't think so.

Though I shouldn't be so hard on people—they might not actually be *able* to tell the truth. Scientists have done studies on people's abilities to predict what they will feel when they get something they want—and their ability to recall how it really was. It seems that people expect to feel elated when they get the thing they most wanted in the world, but when the event happens, they almost never feel as good as they hoped. The crazy twist is that, if asked long enough after the event, they remember feeling how they *thought* they would, rather than how they actually felt.

So you keep running after the things you want, because you think they will satisfy you—and you truly do think that in the past they gave you satisfaction. But the satisfaction itself, the real feeling of it, somehow slips the net. It's anticipated and remembered but almost never experienced.

I was certain it was going to be different with Nora. My wedding day would be everything I imagined. I was sure of it.

I don't know how to describe how I felt about her. "Love" isn't the right word. It sounds too peaceful. What I felt was more like a hurricane. I felt buffeted, blown apart by it. I wanted to reach the eye of the storm—the peaceful place in the center, the place of safety. When I felt that, I knew I would have what I wanted.

I was sure that's what the wedding day would give me.

I had thought that shaving her hair off would do it. I thought it would give me what I was looking for. But that wasn't what happened.

This is what happened.

She came out of the bathroom. At first I couldn't see her. She was backlit, framed by the doorway. And it felt as if another person had come out of the bathroom, and it wasn't that she looked different, because I couldn't really see her. Rather, it was something harder to pin down. She stood differently. And when I asked her to come, she walked differently. When I was able to see her face, it was different too.

I had had an image of what she would look like. I thought she would come out shorn and vulnerable. When I think of it, I always imagine that the shaving of someone's head is a humbling—a stripping away of something.

First of all, she didn't shave it all off. She came close, but she gave herself a short and, I swear to God, almost chic haircut. The vulnerability simply wasn't there. If anything, it was the opposite. All the neediness I had sensed in her, all the timidity, all the uncertainty—they were all gone.

But the biggest problem? She came out of that bathroom looking more gorgeous than when she went in. Before, I thought her hair was what brought out her beauty. Maybe it was her hair, but

I found it didn't need to be long. It was the same amazing color and now, being so short, it emphasized her face. She had incredible cheekbones—I had never even noticed. And her eyes, which had just seemed normal before, now looked huge. Her chin came to a delicate point. She was even more a creature of fairy tales. I had thought it was the hair. Apparently, it was just her.

I wanted a sacrifice, and it turned into a makeover. It would have been funny, if I could have laughed.

But it wasn't funny for me. It still left me in that awful place where I couldn't feel her love. I still needed proof.

I told myself that when we said our vows I would feel it. That's the moment when the peace would come.

Now it was the day before. It was almost here.

And I will tell you the truth about how I felt the day before my wedding. I couldn't wait.

Nora

The Day Before the Wedding

I went in the car to pick up my mother and sister at the airport. But not because I wanted to. Lord knows, I was dreading being trapped in a car with the two of them. But if comparison makes people feel better, I could at least console myself that it was better than being trapped in a car with Timothy's mother.

I had met his mother a grand total of once. She invited me over for tea. I was met at the door by a butler. At first, I thought the butler was his father. When you're not used to butlers, and a man opens the door, it's just logical to assume that he lives there. If he's the right age, he's the man of the house.

But when I held out my hand and said, "I'm Nora," he just looked at me, then looked at my hand like I was presenting him with a dead fish. Then he said, "Mrs. Whitting is waiting in the salon."

He turned around, walked across the foyer, and opened a door.

When I went through the doorway into the salon, I walked into a room so formal it looked like something out of a museum. All the chairs were stiff-backed brocade and they were lined up along the walls—not in a configuration that makes you think of people sitting and talking.

There was a woman sitting in one of the chairs, next to a table with two teacups and a pot of tea. She looked tight. Not just the tightness of too much plastic surgery, though there was that. There was a deeper tightness. I recognized it. It was unhappiness.

She tried to hide it under a mask of disapproval. She watched me as I walked across the room, and I could see her nose wrinkle slightly.

I might have felt self-conscious, but Timothy, though he hadn't warned me about the butler, had told me plenty about his mother. He'd prepped me for what to expect from this visit, and he'd even gone shopping with me, picked out an outfit for me to wear, and told me that I shouldn't worry about anything because whatever I did it would be wrong. I laughed, thinking he was making a joke. But he quickly let me know that he was being completely serious.

It seems that, even after all he told me about his mother, I still didn't quite understand. But, sitting there with her, I suddenly got it. And in that moment, I realized that the stories never quite captured it. It was almost certainly the same when I told my horror stories about growing up with my mother: someone else might hear and take them in and still not understand what it was like—how bad it really was.

Now, sitting there in front of her, I saw that truly there was no "getting it right" with this woman. I have to say, it made me feel very relaxed. If you really believe that there's no way to do it right, then you just don't worry. And one look at Timothy's mother and I could see he was right.

I was going to hold out my hand, but when I thought of what the butler did, and also what that woman Celia, his best friend's wife, did, I thought better of it. I wondered if I should wait until she invited me to sit down. But then I had the thought that she might never invite me to sit down, and I imagined just standing there awkwardly while she talked to me. So I looked for a place to sit. There was no way to sit facing her since there was no chair facing her. In fact, there wasn't even any chair near her. I chose one on the other side of the table with the tea, but it was facing in the same direction, and it was far enough away that I would have to get up to get a cup of tea.

Still, since it seemed the best option, I took it.

"So you're going to marry my son," she said.

The way she said it, it wasn't a question.

I answered anyway.

"Yes."

She picked up the teacup sitting next to her, and took a sip. I waited for her to offer me some tea, but she didn't.

"I asked you here because I was curious as to how you caught him. Are you pregnant? Though I didn't think Timothy would be the type to marry someone just because she was pregnant."

I laughed. I couldn't help it.

She stared at me like I'd just brayed like a donkey.

"Did I say something funny?" she asked.

I didn't even bother to answer. "No, I'm not pregnant," I told her.

"Then how did you manage to get him to ask you to marry him? I was certain that Timothy would never let himself get trapped like this."

I heard the words she used—"caught," "trapped"—and I thought that she and my mother seemed to have the same idea of marriage.

"I didn't do anything," I said.

"Then how did you get him to ask you?"

"I didn't. He just asked."

"Ah." She nodded. "I think I see."

I had no idea what she "saw."

"The subtlest of traps," she said.

"What?" I was completely confused.

"The woman who doesn't care."

"But I do care," I said.

"Of course you do," she said, as if that closed the case—in her favor.

I felt a little dizzy. This woman would skewer you with a question thrown at you like a spear, and then start talking in circles.

The next question was another spear lobbed at me.

"So how do you feel about the fact that you're about to be very rich?" she asked.

"I don't know. I haven't thought about it."

It was true. I hadn't thought about it at all. In fact, there were times in the past month when, purely out of reflex, I had the thought, "I have to pay the bills." Then a split second later I would remember that Timothy had paid off all my debt. I can't describe the relief that would wash over me. But as for how much money I would have by marrying Timothy, that thought never occurred to me. In my head it was his money.

Apparently, that also was the thought his mother was having, because she said, "You do know you'll have to sign a prenuptial agreement, don't you?"

"I hadn't thought of it."

"There's nothing to think about. You don't have a choice," she said.

I wanted to argue with her just so I wouldn't give her the satisfaction of agreeing, until I realized that my arguing with her would give her more satisfaction than anything. So I said, truthfully, "I don't have a problem with it."

"Just because you have my son fooled with some innocent Midwestern act doesn't mean I'm going to fall for it," she said tartly.

"Okay," I said. I didn't know what else to say.

"I wanted you to know that," she said.

"All right."

"And that I know this won't last more than six months. I know my son. As soon as he gets you, he won't want you anymore."

"Maybe," I said.

"You know I'm right, don't you?"

"You could be, but if that's the case, that's what divorce lawyers are for."

"Are you being flip with me?" she demanded.

"A little," I said.

"Well, I don't like people being flip with me in my own home. I think we're done here."

And that had been it.

I left without even getting tea.

Timothy's mother called him while I was still in the cab, so he knew all about it—her version at least—by the time I came in the door. He made me tell the whole thing over again, from my side, and as far as I could tell, he loved every minute of it.

He kissed me and said, "I would have been really worried if she actually liked you. Hearing how much she didn't like you reassures me immensely."

Now I was on the way to meet my mother at the airport, and I was dreading it. I knew the first thing she would say when she got off the plane and saw my hair. I still remembered her reaction when I was eight and I decided to cut myself some bangs. I was so proud of my new haircut, so I went to show her, and she took one look at me and slapped me across the face, dragged me to a mirror, and said, "Look at what you did. I'm ashamed to be seen with you looking like that." That's how I remembered it anyway. My memory from when I was eight might be a little suspect, but I knew the sort of reaction my mother was capable of. Though, honestly, even without having cut off my hair, I would still dread seeing her.

Sure enough, my mother stepped off the plane, took one look at me, and said, "Oh, Nora. Oh, what did you *do*? What were you thinking?"

I'm sure she would have gone on and it would have gotten much worse, but my sister came to my rescue—just like she used to when I was little.

"I think it looks amazing," she said. "*You* look amazing."

I had sent her fifteen thousand out of the fifty that Timothy gave me, so that might have been part of the reason why she was being so nice. But I could tell she also genuinely meant it. In fact, she was looking at me like she'd never seen me before. Then I realized she had never seen me in makeup like this or in the new wardrobe I'd gotten in New York. I had to smile when I thought that, to her, I must look exactly like all the other New Yorkers looked to me when I first arrived.

"Thanks," I said.

"Jeez, I need to find myself a rich banker," she

said. "It seems to really be the way to go. And now you're going to be set for life."

"What do you mean?" my mother said. "You think life is some fairy tale? Rich men do whatever they want. He'll get bored with her and leave her in a year."

At least my own mother gave me six months more than Timothy's mother, I thought wryly.

"Well, at least she'll still get some money," my sister said.

"Do you think, on the day before my wedding, we could maybe not talk about my getting divorced?" I asked. "I have to manage to get married before I can get divorced."

"Is he having second thoughts already?" my mother demanded. "Did we fly all the way out here for nothing?"

"No, he's not having second thoughts, not that I know of. Anyway, Mom, are you feeling okay? How are you doing? You're not too tired, are you?" I looked at her more closely, and I had to admit to myself that she didn't look so good. She'd been so sick for so long, but she never actually looked sick. Now it finally seemed to be catching up with her. She had dark circles under her eyes, and it looked like she had lost weight.

"Oh, I'm . . ." and I saw my mother glance over at my sister, and my sister shake her head ever so slightly. "I'm fine. Doing fine."

I glanced at Deirdre.

"She's fine," Deirdre said. "Really."

The more they talked, the less I believed them.

And then my sister very deliberately changed the subject. "So, is his parents' house amazing? What's his family like?"

"I don't know them very well," I said.

On the ride back, I told them who was who in his family so they would know who everyone was at the rehearsal dinner. Then I heard about the twins and how Boyd had only seen the kids once in the past two months. Somehow the drive from the airport passed, and finally we arrived at the B&B.

We all dispersed to our rooms to get ready. I took a shower (I loved that all I had to do to my hair now was rub a towel over it and put some gel in it). I got dressed and was putting on my makeup in the dresser mirror when I heard a voice call out from the hall, "Yo, I'm here. Where the hell are you, Nora?"

"Here," I called.

A second later, Tammy burst into my room.

She still had her coat on, and she was lugging her bag with her—she hadn't even gone to her room.

"You won't believe what—" she started, then she saw me. "Holy crap! Your hair!"

"What about it?" I said.

"I can't believe you didn't tell me you did that!" She paused and looked again. "It looks good. It looks really good. Has your mom seen it? Oh my God, she must have had a fit."

"It wasn't that bad, actually."

"Fuck me, I think I'm about to start believing in miracles. You cut off your hair, your mom's not acting crazy, and you're getting married tomorrow. I think the world might be coming to an end."

"Oh, shut up," I said, but I couldn't help smiling. "How's everything back home?"

I felt a little guilty as I asked the question. I hadn't really kept in touch since I'd left. We'd exchanged some e-mails, but Tammy's usually went something like, "Have the funniest story to tell you. But have to dash now. Write more later." And of course later never came. Though I can't say my e-mails were a lot more descriptive.

"You won't believe it." Tammy pulled off her coat, tossed it on the bed, and flopped down on top of it. "I've got the best gossip ever."

"What?"

"Jeanette has got a man."

I have to admit I was a little disappointed. "That's the best gossip ever?"

"Wait a second, missy. You don't know who the man is." She was smiling like the proverbial cat.

I searched my mind for the man that would put a smile on her face like that. I came up with the person I thought might be the least likely. "Neil?" I guessed.

"No. Neil's got a terrible crush on me. Don't you know that?"

"Yes, but I thought he might have figured out that you'd never give him the time of day."

"You never know." She shrugged.

"Do you have something else to tell me?" I demanded.

"No. That would only be if I got desperate. Guess again."

"I don't know. I give up. Tell me."

And she did.

"Dan."

"No," I said. "No way."

"Yes way. Dan's leaving Stacey for her best friend."

I started to laugh. I couldn't help it. "Dan and Jeanette," I said.

"Seems like you and Jeanette have the same taste in men."

"Lord help me," I agreed. "Well, I wish them the best."

"Oh, don't lie. You just love it that you know he's going into an even worse disaster than the other one."

"Maybe just a little. But I feel like taking delight in their misery is probably bad luck."

"It's just fucking human," Tammy said. "A little justice in the world."

"I thought you were an anarchist."

"Oh shut up and let me enjoy it."

"Okay. You've got five seconds, and then it's going to be time to go to the rehearsal dinner."

"Holy shit, I'm totally not ready." She leapt off the bed. "I knew I shouldn't have flown in so late, but Neil wanted to share the car to the airport, and this was the cheapest flight. Fucking Neil," but she said it with affection. "I've got other news, but I'll tell you later. Maybe after dinner."

"If I survive the dinner," I said. "I just hope everyone's going to be on good behavior tonight."

"Oh, I hope not. A wedding that goes smoothly isn't really a wedding at all. Family drama is, like, a requirement."

"Don't jinx me," I said.

THE INVESTIGATION

MOTIVES

Excluding cases with no apparent motive, the victim is more likely to be male when the motive is linked to revenge, money, or alcohol-related arguments.

Female homicide victims are most likely to have been killed as a result of a domestic argument and/or the breakdown of a relationship.

Timothy

The Rehearsal Dinner

In the weeks leading up to the wedding, Nora was really nervous about the families coming together for the rehearsal dinner. It wasn't like her.

When I tried to ask her what she was so nervous about, she said it was her mother. I understood what that was like; I had my own mother to deal with. But I was certain that her mother couldn't possibly be as bad as mine. And I was right. When I met her mother and sister for the first time, I thought her sister seemed reserved, almost a little suspicious, but her mother was charming. She smiled and took my hand and told me how long she'd been waiting to meet me and how delighted she was.

Afterward, I admit, I made fun of Nora for being nervous. I didn't see what could go wrong at dinner—well, what could go wrong with her family anyway.

We'd chosen a small Italian restaurant along the main street in town, with a private room at the back and a patio. It was old, with dark wood and low ceilings. My mother, of course, when she came in, declared it "oppressive and dreary," but her taste usually ran to floral chintz, so that was no surprise. I had thought that Nora and I would sit at the head of the table, but when we arrived and people started to sit down, my mother ignored the place cards and appropriated one end, installing Alejandro at her side, and my father took the other end, though at least he had the courtesy to invite Nora's mother to join him. (Though maybe it wasn't just courtesy. Nora's mother was surprisingly attractive, and my father was an old letch.) Nora and I sat in the middle, next to each other, and everyone else was left to fend for themselves.

The seating mix-up was just the first indication of the chaos to come. The first course had just been served when my mother stood with her wineglass raised.

I glanced over at Nora, and she looked at me with her eyebrows raised.

My mother cleared her throat and started: "I know we're gathered here to celebrate Timothy's upcoming nuptials, but I also just want to say a word about another new era that's beginning. I'm going to have a new son-in-law soon," she smiled at Alejandro, "and he's going to be taking over the handling of our family's financial health. I think we should be celebrating that new beginning as well." And she raised her glass.

It was a good try, but she didn't realize that after telling me she was taking the money away, she had emptied that particular clip of ammunition. I didn't care. So I was able to sit there and smile while she made that ridiculous toast. My family understood what was going on, but I saw Tammy turn and whisper something to Neil.

As soon as my mother sat down, Nora's mother popped up with her glass in hand too.

"I don't have anything prepared," she said. "But since Mrs. Whitting was so gracious as to start, I'd like to make a toast to new sons-in-law, since tomorrow I'll have one as well. And a toast to all kinds of health, not just financial. Health is a blessing we tend to only think about once it's gone."

Everyone raised their glass to that as well, and my father said, "Hear! Hear!" Well, almost everyone raised their glass. I noticed that Nora's sister, Deirdre, didn't. She just sat there scowling.

I had a feeling we were treading a dangerous line, and I wasn't sure what it was. I thought I would try to head this off, so I got up.

"I just wanted to say thank you all for coming to celebrate with us. I hope you enjoy the dinner and the company."

I was trying to head off more speeches. It didn't work.

My brother Andrew decided to get up next, though I really couldn't tell you what he said—something about hoping I would be as happy as he was, and have children as great as he had, and that my marriage would go as smoothly as his. He went on for a long time. He was one of those people who, when he gets up and has the room at his mercy, it goes to his head.

He was still going when the staff started clearing the appetizer plates. I decided to step out to the patio to get a little air. I was only out there a few minutes when Alejandro joined me.

I had gotten to know Alejandro a bit better over the last two months because my mother had insisted on having him check up on the dissolving of the family fund. He had proven to be reasonable and rational, and most importantly he had run interference with my mother. I had come to have a grudging respect for him.

I knew he must have a reason for following me out to the patio. That was part of what I respected about him—everything he did had a logic behind it. And he didn't beat around the bush either; he was a straight shooter.

He took out one of those long, thin cigars that looks more like a cigarette. He offered one to me silently, and I shook my head.

He lit it and took a deep inhalation and let it out, as if he had been holding his breath for a long time.

"I'm not going to be managing your family's money," he said.

I turned to look at him. He was staring out into the darkness.

"I'm a businessman. I have to assess the cost-benefit analysis," he said. "And I've decided that the amount of time and attention and care that would be required in this scenario is . . . more than I'm willing to undertake. I'm sorry, Timothy. I've known for a little while. I thought I'd wait until after your wedding, but it didn't seem right not to let you know. Sorry to cause you the inconvenience of doing all the work to unwind the fund, and then not to go forward with it."

He had no idea, but he had just given me the best wedding gift I could have imagined. My mother was going to be beside herself.

"Alejandro," I said. "I completely understand. You've been fantastic. If you ever need anything, just let me know. Like a kidney, or anything like that."

He laughed. "I like you, Timothy. I didn't think I would, but I do."

"What's going to happen with you and Emily?"

He took another puff from the cigar, and narrowed his eyes as he blew out. "I don't know."

I nodded. "Sorry about that."

"Well, we'll see what happens. Anyway, I wanted to tell you."

"Thanks again," I said. I turned and held out my hand. He took it and held it.

"If you would consider working in a team, give me a call. And just to sweeten the pot, I'll take care of your mother for tonight and tomorrow. I'd really like to have you on board. I'd give you your own fund to manage."

"I'll think about it," I said.

"Good." He nodded, stubbed out his cigar, and went back inside.

I stood out there a moment more, breathing in the night air, hearing the murmur of voices through the glass doors. Then I turned around and looked back inside. Andrew was still talking, but he didn't seem to notice that no one was listening to him. People had broken out into little conversations. The most disturbing development was that somehow Tammy and Edward had shifted seats and were now sitting next to each other, shamelessly flirting. I thought that might happen, and had hoped to prevent it, but I should have known better.

I looked around the table. It seemed that Marcus had taken on my sour sister. But my favorite pairing was Neil and Celia. I saw Celia trying her tricks on Neil, and Neil simply wasn't biting.

I took a breath and went back inside.

As at all rehearsal dinners, everyone drank too much, ate too little, and stayed too late. It was past eleven when we left the restaurant. Only Andrew, his wife, and my parents, who were staying at the house, had to drive, and I'd hired a car for them. For the rest of us, the B&B was only a few blocks away, so we walked—though some of us not so steadily.

I had my arm around Nora. She had been so

quiet all night. She was normally quiet, but this was even quieter than usual.

"Are you okay?" I asked.

"Sure," she said, without looking up at me.

"You nervous about tomorrow?"

"I was nervous about tonight."

I noticed that she hadn't answered my question—and I wasn't happy about it. But I had discovered that when I pushed her, she tended to shut down. So I only said, "You don't seem very excited."

"It's having the families around. It's a little stressful."

"But look how well it went tonight."

"It went all right," she said.

"All right? It went better than all right."

She didn't answer me because at that point Edward spotted a bar and said, "Hey, who's game for getting another drink?"

"I'd be up for that," Tammy said, almost immediately and not surprisingly.

Everyone else offered a low murmur of negatives until, very surprisingly, Celia said, "I'd like another drink."

You should have seen the look Tammy turned on her. I could tell that in high school Tammy was one of those girls that was truly feared. She was tiny, but with an arsenal of looks like she had, she *must* have been feared. Celia pretended not to notice.

I imagined pitting Celia and Tammy against each other. Who would win? I would have bet on Tammy in the ring, but in this situation there wasn't much she could do. Tammy and Edward and Celia headed off to the bar, while the rest of us continued on to the B&B.

We said our good-nights in the lobby. I played the gentleman with Nora's mother and sister, then I walked Nora to the door of her room. I had decided to go with tradition and get separate rooms for the night before the wedding.

Nora stood with her back against the doorsill, looking up at me.

"I love you," I told her.

"I love you too," she said.

I kissed her, and her lips were as soft as ever.

"Guess what?" I said.

"What?"

"We're getting married tomorrow," I whispered.

But it was like so many things in life that we think we know for certain—they're not so certain at all.

Timothy

Timothy Gets a Visitor
as He Gets Ready for Bed

I went back to my room, brushed my teeth, washed my face, and was just getting out of my clothes when I heard a soft knock on the door.

I was sure it was Nora, and I loved the fact that she couldn't stay away.

"Come in, door's open," I called.

The door opened, and I discovered it wasn't Nora. It was Celia.

She closed the door behind her and leaned against it, with a smile that I knew well.

Now I realized why she had said she wanted to go for a drink with Tammy and Edward. It was an excuse not to go back to the room with Marcus, so she could slip away and come back here.

"Celia, what are you doing here?" I asked her.

After Nora came to the city, I ignored Celia's calls for a few weeks, until I realized she wasn't going to stop calling. I finally picked up and told her it was over with us. She seemed to take it well. She said only, "Too bad. Let me know if you change your mind." And that was it. Until now.

In answer to my question she said, "What do you think I'm doing here?"

"Celia, for God's sake, I'm getting married

tomorrow, and your husband is just two doors down."

"I know," she said, her smile getting wider.

I couldn't resist.

It wasn't about Celia. I didn't actually care about Celia. It was the thrill of doing something you're not supposed to do—something that would shock and appall other people. I had never been able to resist that.

"Come here," I said.

And she came.

When I made the decision, Nora didn't enter into it. I know that sounds strange, but I loved Nora. It seemed so clear to me that what I did with Celia didn't affect how I felt about Nora. If anything, it made me love Nora more.

Celia was a noisy lover. It was part of what made it so exciting. And she was louder that night than usual.

I tried holding my hand over her mouth, but that only muffled it. She was so loud I didn't hear the door (which was still unlocked) when it opened.

Celia's head was thrown back and her eyes were closed. Then she opened them to look at me, and her eyes slid past me, then they widened in shock.

It was instinctive—I didn't even think; I just turned my head to look.

Nora

The Rehearsal Dinner

Timothy was so pleased with how the rehearsal dinner went—but he didn't know everything that happened. It didn't go quite as smoothly for me. In fact, my whole world blew apart right before the tiramisu was served.

The waitstaff was clearing the plates from dinner, and pouring more wine, and the room was loud with all the conversations—and not with yelling. It was going well, and I was just starting to relax and think that a miracle might happen.

I slipped out to go to the ladies' room. I heard the door open and someone else come in while I was in the stall. When I came out, I found my mother waiting for me by the sinks.

"So, what do you think of the dinner?" I asked, trying to be upbeat. It didn't work.

She ignored my question completely. She said, "Nora, I have something to tell you."

I had just turned on the faucet to wash my hands. "What is it?"

"I'm dying."

I shut the faucet off and turned to face her. "*What?*"

Now that she had my attention, she was suddenly very busy rummaging in her purse. She pulled out a lipstick, opened it, leaned into the mirror, and then she paused and said, "I've stopped the chemo. There's no point in continuing on with it."

"Is that what the doctor said?"

She applied the lipstick and pressed her lips together. When she spoke again, she didn't answer my question. Instead she said, "Honey, you knew this was coming."

"No," I said. "No. You told me that you were getting better."

"Well, I didn't want you to worry."

"How much time do you have?" I asked again.

"I don't know," she said, and I heard her voice getting thick. She put her lipstick away carefully as if that simple action needed all of her attention.

"We'll find another doctor. Timothy and I will help with this. Don't worry. Okay? We'll be here for you."

She looked up then—looked intently into my face and said, "If you really want to help, you'll come home."

I felt sick to my stomach.

"Of course I'll come home to see you, and you can come to New York, if you feel well enough," I told her.

"No, I mean move back home."

This was it. This was the nightmare I had been dreading without even knowing it. I thought I was afraid of disagreements or unpleasantness but, no, it was this. This tidal wave of guilt. What are you supposed to do in this situation? I felt like the right thing to do would be to go back home and be there for my mother. Of course that was the right thing, wasn't it? And yet, I couldn't do it. I didn't even need to think about it to know I couldn't.

"I'll be there for you, but I can't move back home again."

She fumbled in her purse and pulled out a tissue. But again she wouldn't look at me.

Then, almost desperately, I said, "Mom, I'm getting *married*." It was an appeal. I knew it as I said it. I wanted her to let me off the hook. I wanted her to tell me it was okay.

She didn't. She was clutching the tissue when she said, "Nora, I don't want to die alone."

"What about Deirdre? Can't Deirdre move in with you? Then you'd have the kids there as well. You wouldn't be alone."

"And I'd have no peace. Her kids scream all the time, and anyway Deirdre won't do it. She doesn't care. You know that."

"But you two seemed to be getting along so well recently."

"Deirdre's fine when you give her what she wants, but forget it if you actually need anything from her." My mother took the tissue and blotted her lips.

"Did you ask?"

"Yes, I asked," my mother snapped, tossing the

tissue angrily into the wastebasket. "And if you can do one thing for me, I'm asking you not to bring this up to her. She didn't think I should tell you at all, and the last thing I need on top of all this is a lecture from her."

So that was the look my mother and Deirdre had exchanged when I picked them up at the airport.

It might be a terrible thing to think, but I wished that my mother hadn't told me. During all the years I was home, I wanted so much to know what was actually going on. And now, I wanted nothing but *not* to know.

My mother recovered quickly from her little spurt of anger. She looked at me again, with that look I couldn't bear.

"I need you, honey. I need you with me."

"Mom, I . . ." and I couldn't go on.

But she knew without me having to say it.

She turned on a dime, from pleading to vicious. "You think you've found it, don't you? You think now you're going to live happily ever after?" my mother said. "You've found Prince Charming, with looks and money and charm, and you're just going to ride off into the sunset?"

"I just want a life."

"I'm sorry, I didn't realize that living with me was like a death. Is that what you're trying to say?"

"No—"

But my mother wouldn't let me get a word in edgewise. "You don't have to tell me. I know my life is like a living death. Ever since I had you girls, and you tied me down, and you took everything from me. You were why your father left. When you were born, you cried all the time, and he couldn't take it. You took my life from me, and now you won't even be there for me at the end of it. Forget I even asked."

It had been a long time since I'd heard the story of how I was the reason why my father had left. She used say it to me all the time when I was growing up—that I was the reason my father left, that I was the reason she was all alone. It used to really upset me. I found it still did, but not enough to get me to change my mind.

My mother went on, "Just forget I said anything. And, for God's sake, don't say anything to your sister."

As if she had been summoned, the bathroom door swung open and we both turned as if caught. Deirdre took one look at my face, and she knew. She rounded on my mother.

"Don't tell me," Deirdre said to our mother. "I can't believe you did this. And *tonight*."

I tried to smooth things over. "It's okay. It's fine. Really."

"It's not fine. It's *not* fine," Deirdre said.

"Stay out of this, Deirdre," my mother said. "I swear to God, you stay out of this."

"No way. I've had enough." Deirdre was obviously furious. "I told you I'd keep my mouth shut, but it was on the condition that you didn't pull something like this. You're sick, you know that? You're really sick."

I broke in, "Deirdre, it's okay. I know you were trying to protect me, but maybe it's best that it's all out now."

"You don't even know the half of it," my sister said.

At that moment the bathroom door swung open again, and Timothy's sister, Emily, came in.

"Wow, crowded in the bathroom," Emily said in that way she had; the words were normal enough, but there was hostility beneath them.

Even my mother could hear it. "We were just going," my mother said. And she looked pointedly at me.

"Yes, right," I said. But as I followed her out, Deirdre grabbed my wrist.

"I need to talk to you," she whispered.

"Okay. Later," I said, but I was thinking that it was the last thing I wanted. My sister and I would probably just get into a big fight over it as well. I thought if I could, I would avoid her until after the wedding.

"Where have you been?" Timothy asked me, when I got back to the table. "You were gone for ages. I think I want to add something to the vows tomorrow—I want to put a five-minute cap on your abandoning me at dinner parties we're hosting."

He didn't know that my mother had been trying to convince me to abandon him for a lot longer than five minutes. I decided I wasn't going to tell him. Not tonight.

"I saved your tiramisu for you," he said. "Well, most of it."

I looked down. Someone had eaten half of it.

"Now I know why you wanted the tiramisu," I said. "Didn't you get one yourself?"

"I told you it was my favorite dessert."

"You can have the rest of mine." I pushed my plate toward him.

"No, you should have it. I think it's the best tiramisu I've ever had."

But then, somehow he did end up eating the rest. He was drunk, like everyone else at the dinner table at that point. I think I'd been on my way to nicely buzzed before my trip to the bathroom. But that had sobered me up, and after that I felt left out, the way you do when you're sober in a room full of drunks. It was a relief when, soon after that, the party broke up.

Most of us ended up walking back to the B&B together, but on the way Tammy and Edward and Celia decided to get a nightcap. Timothy murmured to me that he was worried about Tammy and Edward, but I didn't worry about that at all. I thought if anyone was at risk, it was Edward. It surprised me that Celia wanted to join them for a drink, though I didn't really spend too much time thinking about it.

We all said good night. I could see that my sister was trying to catch my eye, but I avoided her, and Timothy was my bodyguard; he walked me to my room. Outside the door, we both stopped. I turned around to look up at him.

He touched my face. "I love you," he told me.

"I love you too," I said.

He kissed me and said, "Guess what?"

"What?"

"We're getting married tomorrow."

I smiled.

Then I went into my room and closed the door behind me. I lay down on the bed, still in my dress and shoes and coat. And I closed my eyes. I didn't go to sleep. I just lay there.

I don't know exactly how long, but it didn't seem like a very long time before there was a knock at my door. The last thing I wanted to do was to talk to anyone right then, but I got up and went over to the door and opened it. I was sure it was going to be my sister. Or my mother. The last person I expected to see standing there was Celia.

"Celia, is something wrong? Are Tammy and Edward okay?" I couldn't think of any other reason she'd come knock on my door that late at night. It's not like we were good friends or anything. I'd met her only that one time, with Timothy and Marcus, for drinks.

She looked at me, and she had the strangest smile on her face. Then she said, "Come to Timothy's room in about fifteen minutes. Don't knock. The door will be open. Just come in."

Then she turned around and walked away.

It might have sounded mysterious and cryptic, but it wasn't. As soon as she said it, I knew.

I closed the door and went back over to sit on the edge of the bed. I checked the clock. It was three past midnight.

It was my wedding day.

I waited until the clock read eighteen past, then I got up and climbed to the upper floor.

I walked past Timothy's room and down the hall, and I knocked at another door. It took a few minutes, but Marcus opened it, wearing a robe.

Then I said to him, "I think you should go down the hall to Timothy's room and get your wife. You don't have to knock. The door will be open."

He just stared at me. At first I thought maybe he didn't understand, and I was about to say it again, when he asked me, "Which room?"

I pointed.

He brushed past me and went to the door I had pointed to. He hesitated a moment before putting his hand on the doorknob, and I realized he was listening to something. A moment later it was louder, and I could hear it too. Then he turned the knob, went inside, and closed the door behind him.

Then there was silence. Just breathless, absolute silence.

Celia came out first. She was wrapped only in a sheet, and she was clutching her clothes. She was almost next to me before she saw me standing there. When she did, she stopped short.

"Why did you send *him*?"

I didn't answer her.

"I wanted you to see," she said. "If you saw, you'd understand. He doesn't love you. He couldn't do that with me and still love you."

She waited for a moment for me to say something, but I just looked at her. And finally she turned, took another few steps to the door of her room, and disappeared inside.

It took longer for Marcus to appear. But eventually he came out too. He walked down the hall, and when he reached me, he stopped as well. He said, "I'm sorry Nora."

I don't know why he said that. He didn't have anything to apologize for. But I guess that's just what people say when they don't know what else to say. Then he disappeared inside their room as well.

I walked down the hall to Timothy's room. The door was slightly ajar, so I reached out and pushed it open.

338

Timothy was sitting on the edge of the bed in his boxers. His head was down, but he raised it when I came in and he looked at me.

He didn't say he was sorry. He just said, "Nora."

Just my name. Just like that.

I closed the door behind me. There was a chair over by the window. I walked to it and sat down.

He followed me with his eyes. When I sat, he said, "You're not going to marry me now, are you?" He looked hollowed out.

"I don't know," I told him.

"You don't know . . ." he echoed. "So there's still a chance?"

"I don't know," I said again. It was the truth.

There was a long silence.

Then he asked quietly, very quietly, "Do you love me?"

When he asked me, I simply asked the question of myself. And I was surprised at the answer I got.

"Yes," I said. "I love you."

It was so strange. I didn't understand it. But I loved him more than I ever had.

I watched him as I said it. Would my words have any effect? They were just words, after all. How can you give someone else a feeling in words? It's like trying to capture a symphony by describing it.

"Nora . . ." he said.

I waited for what else he was going to say.

There was a long pause, and he said, "Please. Please."

Please what? He didn't say. And I didn't ask. I knew some questions didn't have an answer.

I stood up and walked over, and I kissed him on the forehead. Then I left.

Timothy

After Marcus Walked In

It sounds like it would be an awful experience—to have your best friend walk in on you having sex with his wife. And I can't say it was pleasant, but because it was Marcus, it wasn't as bad as you might think.

Marcus was true to form. He was not someone who pretended to be one thing most of his life, and then turned into another in a crisis. I had never seen Marcus anything but collected, and now I think I never will.

He came in the door, and Celia saw him first. Then I saw him.

We were both there, naked on the bed, staring at him. And he simply stood there.

I rolled off her and reached over to the floor for my boxers.

No one said anything for a moment. I was waiting for something—some recriminations. You know the things you imagine people saying, like "How could you?" or "I trusted you," or "I never thought you'd do something like this." Maybe cursing or even for Marcus to hit me. Lord knows, I deserved it.

The first thing he said was directed at Celia. "Get your clothes and go back to the room."

His voice was eerily calm.

She didn't argue. As quickly as she could, she wrapped the sheet around her, gathered her clothes in a bundle in her arms, and then paused by the door.

"You go on; I'll be there in a second," he said.

Without a word, she opened the door and went out.

He looked at me. Then he said, "Nora's out in the hallway. She was the one who asked me to come in here and get Celia."

When he said that, I wished he had hit me instead.

"We'll be leaving tonight and driving back to the city," he added.

There were so many things he could have said. But he didn't. I have never respected a man more than I did Marcus at that moment. The word "character" came to my mind. And I knew Marcus had it—and I didn't. I realized that, before, I'd always put Marcus down in my mind as a sucker. As a patsy. Now I saw that that was my way of not being the bad guy. Of making it somehow his fault. Suddenly I saw how ridiculous that was. If he'd said anything to me, anything at all, I think I might have been able to twist it somehow so he'd be implicated as well. It was his weakness that allowed me to do that to him. I would have jerry-rigged some excuse like that. But by not saying anything at all, he'd left the whole where it belonged—in my lap.

He looked at me for a moment; then he turned and left the room. And when he left, I felt something I hadn't felt since I was a child. It was shame.

I sat down on the edge of the bed and waited.

When Nora came in, I forced myself to look at her, and I said her name: "Nora." But that's all I could manage.

She crossed to the chair and sat down. She didn't say anything. Finally, I couldn't stand it anymore.

I said, "You're not going to marry me now, are you?"

It seemed like an eternity went by before she answered.

"I don't know," she said.

"You don't know . . . So there's still a chance?"

"I don't know," she said again.

There was another long silence.

Finally, I asked the question I could never seem to get an answer to, no matter how many times I asked it. I said, "Do you love me?"

There was no pause. There was no hesitation. She just looked at me and said, "Yes. I love you."

And, I can't explain this, but I finally believed her. I had never believed her when she said it before, but I believed her now. Why now? Maybe because there was no reason for her to say it. Maybe because I knew I didn't deserve it. Maybe it was true for the first time. How can I know?

"Nora," I said. "Please . . ." Please what? I didn't know. "Please . . ."

I think I meant to say, "Please marry me. Please don't leave me. Please forgive me." But I realized that I had everything I wanted. She loved me. What else was there to ask for?

She got up, kissed me on the forehead, and left.

I sat there for a moment. And I felt the most wonderful sense of peace. This was it. This is what I had been looking for. And it came in the way that I would have least expected it.

I lay down. I would have thought that I'd lie there wide-eyed for hours, but surprisingly I felt myself drifting into sleep almost immediately. Then a thought pulled me back from the very edge of unconsciousness. I thought of Celia. What if she hadn't left? What if she tried to come back to see me again? When she got something in her head, there was no stopping her. She had talked her way past my doorman. She had called me ten times a day for a week until I picked up. I couldn't be sure what she would do.

I got up and locked the door and went back to bed. And I was asleep in seconds—the kind of deep, dreamless sleep where everything is lost but nothing is missed.

THE INVESTIGATION

HOMICIDE

Socrates had this to say about death: "To fear death is nothing other than to think oneself wise when one is not. For it is to think one knows what one does not know. No one knows whether death may not even turn out to be the greatest of blessings for a human being. And yet people fear it as if they knew for certain it is the greatest evil."

Timothy

The Next Morning

I went down to breakfast the next morning. There was a spread set out in the dining room: coffee, tea, fresh orange juice, muffins, cereal, all laid out along the table.

The dining room opened onto the morning room at the back of the house, where there were armchairs and couches—and where everyone from the wedding party was scattered. I scanned the group. It looked like almost everyone was there (except for Marcus and Celia, of course). But the one person my eye scanned the room for was missing. Nora wasn't down yet. I wondered what that meant.

The morning room was aptly named: the morning sun poured in and everyone seemed to glow just a little. Except Tammy and Edward— they looked like hell. They looked like I should have looked. But I had woken up feeling great. The disaster of the night before seemed like a dream. Had it even happened? I had woken up with the sense that anything was possible. (It turned out that sense was exactly right—but not at all in the way I had imagined it.)

I was about to head over to say good morning to Nora's mother and sister when Edward ambushed me in the doorway.

"Holy shit, Timothy, that little girl . . ." And he glanced over at where Tammy was sitting across the room.

"She's not so little," I reminded him. "She's Nora's age. She's thirty-three."

"Whatever. But I have to tell you, last night—"

"Listen, spare me the details, okay Eddie?"

He didn't even seem to notice that I had called him Eddie.

"Okay, fine. I just want to know, what's her deal?"

"Forget about it, okay? That's Nora's best friend. You did whatever you did last night, but past that, she's off-limits."

"I have the best sex of my life, and you tell me it's off-limits? That's not right," he protested.

"Oh, come on. I know how much sex you've had, Edward. You're exaggerating."

"I'm not. I swear to God, I'm not. You don't want to hear the details, but—"

"I really don't. Listen, I'm going to take a breather from this discussion, and I'm going to go get my breakfast, okay?"

I escaped from Edward by retreating back into the dining room. As I was getting my coffee, Neil came up to refill his cup.

"So I guess you guys are keeping it formal?" Neil asked. "Not going to see Nora before the wedding?"

"No, we're going to see each other," I said. "I

guess she's just sleeping in." At least I hoped that was it, and it wasn't that she was avoiding me.

Tammy joined us over at the buffet: "You mean I drag my ass out of bed, and she's sleeping in?" she demanded, overhearing my explanation to Neil.

"By the way," Neil interrupted. "Did you hear who my new manager is?"

I looked over at Tammy. "I don't believe it."

Tammy shrugged. "He begged me. I told him I'll probably quit after two weeks."

"So you're going from working at the Box to working at Starbox?" I said. "One box to another?"

"Actually," Neil said, "I'm changing the name."

"What's the new name?"

"Neil's," he said, with an embarrassed smile.

"Of course it is," and I nodded, remembering Joe's and Mike's.

"I think it's time to get the lazy bride out of bed," Tammy said. "Shall I fetch her, or do you want to?"

"Why don't we both go," I suggested. I wanted to see Nora, to try to gauge how things stood between us, but I didn't want to go up alone and put her on the spot. I was well aware I didn't deserve to demand anything of her after what had happened the night before.

We climbed the stairs and walked down the hall to Nora's room. Tammy knocked on the door.

"Nora? Time to get your lazy ass up and get married," she called out.

There was no answer.

Tammy knocked again, harder. "Come on, Nora. We're waitin' on you."

She waited for another moment, then she tried the knob. I saw it turn in her hand, but she didn't open the door. Instead, she called once more, "Nora? If you're not gonna come answer this door, I'm just gonna come in."

Still no answer.

She glanced over at me, rolled her eyes, and said, "Just give me a second." Then she disappeared inside.

I waited outside in the hall. I had woken up feeling so peaceful, but right at that moment that felt light-years away. I was anything but peaceful. I could feel my heart pounding in my chest.

It felt like I waited outside the door for an eternity, but it was probably less than a minute before Tammy came out again. The moment I saw Tammy's face, I knew what people mean when they call someone's face a mask. Everything seemed frozen except her eyes, which I can't describe. They were the eyes of someone who has just seen something awful, something horrific, and just by looking at their eyes, it is as if you can see what they have seen—not the actual image, but the feeling. The feeling was beamed out like a laser.

All she said was, "Oh, God" and her voice was shaking so much I barely recognized it.

I didn't wait to hear the rest. I pushed past her to go in the room. I heard her say, "Timothy, don't." That's what people always say in these situations, and it never stops anyone.

I don't know what I expected. My first thought was, "What kind of bed-and-breakfast puts brown sheets on the bed?" What a stupid, trivial thing to think. But there it is.

Of course they weren't brown. It was Nora's blood, which had soaked the sheets and then dried. And later I found out the grizzly detail that the darkness of the blood was a result of where she'd been stabbed—in the right side of her chest, the chamber where the blood had just returned to the heart.

Details like that haunted me later. I couldn't get them out of my mind. But the worst was seeing her face. I wish more than anything I had left without looking at her face. For the longest time afterward, I couldn't remember her face as it had been when she was alive. Whenever I tried to remember what she looked like, I saw her as she looked that morning. It didn't look like she was sleeping. It didn't look like her. We don't know it these days, because death is so hidden from us, but death has a face. It has a look all its own.

THE INVESTIGATION

EXCERPTS FROM POLICE INTERVIEWS WITH TIMOTHY'S FAMILY AND FRIENDS

Excerpted from the interview with Timothy's mother:

> *She had something over him. She must have, to make him agree to marry her. Timothy is like me: he's not sentimental. I promise you, if he did anything, she drove him to it.*

Excerpted from the interview with Timothy's brother, Edward Whitting:

> *What do you want me to tell you? I didn't see anything; I didn't hear anything. It could have been anyone. I mean, I know I didn't do it. And her best friend spent the night with me, so she couldn't have either. Could Timothy have done it? Like I said, in my opinion it could have been anyone.*

Excerpted from the interview with Timothy's sister, Emily Whitting:

> *It doesn't surprise me. It doesn't surprise me at all.*

Excerpted from the interview with Marcus Franklin:

I thought I knew who Timothy was. He was the best man at my wedding, for God's sake. But it turns out I didn't know him at all. Beyond that, I really don't know what else to say. I don't know what he is capable of doing. I don't know anything anymore.

Excerpted from the interview with Celia Franklin:

I loved him. No, I don't think he knew it. Most of the time I tried to play it cool—he preferred it that way. But there were a few times when I couldn't manage it.

Yes, I realize that admitting this gives me a motive. I don't care. I've decided to finally tell the truth.

Excerpt from interview with Alejandro Cordoba, fiancé of Emily Whitting:

I don't believe Timothy is capable of this . . . It's true, I don't know him well, but it's the sense I have. His family thinks he did it? That doesn't surprise me. Why? Well, you would have to know his family.

Timothy

After Finding Nora

I don't even remember leaving the room. That was the first of a number of blanks I experienced in the next few days. One minute I remember standing over Nora's bed; then I found myself outside in the hallway.

For a split second, it was like waking from a dream, and I wondered if I had only imagined what I'd just seen. Maybe I was about to wake up in my bed, and it would be the morning of my wedding, and this would turn out to be a nightmare. That was the only thing that made sense to me. But then I looked over and saw evidence of the reality of the nightmare; Tammy was standing there crying—great shuddering sobs.

I didn't know what to do. I didn't know what to say. I had the thought that I should get the situation under control, even though at the same time, I had a sense that nothing would ever feel under control again. But, still, I played out the role. I said, "Tammy, you'd better sit down. Is your room along here?"

She nodded and pointed. And I walked over and opened the door. She went in and sat down on the bed. I stood in the doorway for a moment. My brain had frozen, and I had no picture of what I should do next. I realized that usually there was a chain of events in my mind stretching into the future, so I was almost never at a loss for what to do next. But right then my mind was a total blank. I had no idea which direction to move. Then the phone on the nightstand caught my eye.

"I'm going to call the police," I said. I walked over to the nightstand and dialed 911. They asked me the nature of the emergency. I don't remember what I said. But I know I gave the address. Then they tried to keep me on the phone, but I hung up. I think I said, "I can't talk to you now," but I'm not sure.

After I hung up, I looked over at Tammy. She was still sitting on the bed, crying. "You should lie down," I told her. "I'm going to go downstairs and . . . I'm going to go downstairs. I think we should try to keep the others from finding out until the police get here, so you should probably stay here. Will you be okay?"

It was a stupid question. Of course she wasn't going to be okay, but she nodded.

Then she said, "I told Nora this was going to happen. I told her. Why didn't she listen to me?"

I didn't know what she was talking about. For a moment I thought she was saying that she had threatened Nora. Did that mean—had Tammy done it? A second later I knew that was ridiculous.

But the question had come to my mind, and I couldn't get rid of it: maybe Tammy hadn't, but *someone* had.

In this situation, I would have thought that would be the first question in anyone's mind. But reality never matches imagination, especially in extreme situations. Seeing Nora like that was such a shock that no thought found a foothold in my brain except for the one that I didn't want to believe: the thought that she was gone.

I left Tammy's room, shut the door carefully behind me, and went downstairs. I knew I couldn't go back into the morning room. I couldn't face it, but as I was walking past, I glanced in.

The scene there looked exactly the same. Everyone was sitting, drinking their coffee and eating their muffins. It was surreal. How could they be sitting there so calmly when upstairs—my brain shied away from the image of those brown sheets and the face that wasn't Nora's anymore. What if it was someone sitting in there who did it? I found myself searching their faces. Then I remembered who was missing. Marcus and Celia. Celia. Of course it had been Celia.

Strangely, the realization didn't bring relief. But it did bring the first emotion I could remember feeling—it was rage.

My face must have reflected what I was feeling because at that moment Neil glanced over and caught sight of me, and whatever he saw made him get up and follow me out of the room. It was my one piece of luck that whole awful day.

Neil followed me out and found me in the foyer. "What happened?" he said point blank. Not, is something wrong? Not, is something bothering you? He knew just by looking at my face, as I had by looking at Tammy's.

I said, "Nora's dead."

His face went very still, and he blinked very rapidly, but thank God he didn't make me repeat myself, he didn't ask me if I was kidding, and he didn't try to tell me that it wasn't possible. He reached out and gripped my elbow hard, but he didn't say anything for a second. Then he asked, "Did she . . . ?"

"No. Neil, there was a knife . . . There was a knife . . ." I couldn't finish. "I've called the police."

He said, "Timothy, I think you should sit down. Maybe you want to go up to your room?"

It was exactly what I had said to Tammy.

"But the police—"

"I'll wait down here for the police."

"I was thinking we would wait to tell everyone else until after the police are here," I said.

"Agreed. I'll do the best I can."

"Okay. I think I will go up to my room then." The very act of talking was difficult for me. Words seemed inane.

Neil seemed to understand, and he didn't say anything else. He just laid a hand on my shoulder as I went past.

I climbed the stairs again, went to my room, opened the door, then closed it behind me. I went over to the bed and lay down. How on earth had I imagined I could wait downstairs for the police? As soon as I lay down, I knew for certain I couldn't have remained standing another second. I wondered if I would cry. I couldn't even remember the last time I cried. But I just lay there. It was quiet for a few minutes. Then I heard footsteps running up the stairs to the third floor, where Nora had her room. Someone screamed. Actually, it was more like a wail, rising like a siren. And that wailing went on for I don't know how long. Neil must not have been able to keep it a secret, and I wondered briefly who had insisted on going to look.

It was so bright in my room. I got up, pulled down the shade. I realized my teeth were chattering. When I got back into bed, I got under the covers. I didn't even take my shoes off. Within a couple of minutes, I was sweating, but my teeth were still chattering.

I lay in bed, sweating and shivering. I heard when the police arrived. Their footsteps were like sledgehammers on the stairs. I couldn't hear what they were saying, but I heard their voices out in the hall above.

A few minutes later there was a knock on my door.

I didn't get up. I didn't feel any desire to move.

Then Neil's voice came through the door, "Timothy, it's Neil."

I got up and opened the door for him. He came in and shut it behind him.

Neil said, "I'm sorry, I had to tell them downstairs what happened. Nora's mother was asking about what was keeping Nora, and she was going to go upstairs to get her. So I told her to keep her from going, but then she ran upstairs anyway before I could stop her . . ."

So it had been Nora's mother who had screamed.

"It's okay," I said. Then, because it seemed like the thing you're supposed to do in this kind of situation, I asked, "How is Nora's mother?"

Neil shook his head. "Don't ask. But Deirdre is with her now. So hopefully Deirdre will calm her down a little. And the police are here now. They've got the room cordoned off, and I think the detectives are coming soon."

"And where is everyone else?"

"They asked everyone to go back to their own rooms and wait there to give their statements."

I nodded.

"But I thought I'd come see how you were. I was thinking I could sit over here by the door. Not to talk. The police don't want us to talk to each other about the events. But I don't think they could object if I just sit here."

"You don't have to do that," I told him.

"I know," he said.

He took a seat by the door anyway.

So I went back over to the bed and lay down.

It was only later that I realized he must have sensed that I was worse off than anyone else, even though I wasn't screaming or crying.

Over the course of the next hour or so, there were a couple of knocks on the door, but Neil slipped outside and dealt with them, and then came back in alone. At one point he came over and said, "Nora's sister really wants to talk to you. Do you want to talk to her?"

I said no, and Neil went out to the hall and came back in alone.

A little while later there was another knock on the door, but this time Neil couldn't send them away. He came over and told me there was a policeman who wanted to talk to me. He paused, then he asked me, "Timothy, do you need to have a lawyer here?"

It took me a second to realize what he was asking.

"No, Neil," I told him.

"It might be a good idea anyway."

"No, really. It's okay. I'll talk to them."

He nodded and went to let the policeman in. The officer was about my age, and he looked embarrassed to take the statement from me while I was in bed, but I didn't care. He asked me if I wanted to get up, and I said no. Then he asked a few questions, wrote down what I said, and went away. But not for long.

Timothy

The Day

How did that first day pass? I have to admit, I escaped into my imagination. As I lay in bed I could hear the noises in the bed-and-breakfast. I could hear the voices of the policemen, and the specialists they brought in to work the scene, and the detectives, and God knows who else. There was practically constant activity, but I was somehow able to block it out for long periods of time.

In my mind, I created another reality. I imagined that Nora and I were married, that I was lying in bed, and she was next to me, sleeping. With my eyes closed, how could I know the difference?

The problems started when I had to open my eyes.

I had to answer more questions. A woman came in—I think she was a detective because she was wearing a suit instead of a uniform—and she asked me a set of questions nearly identical to the first set of questions asked by the policeman. And then, some hours after that, another man in a suit came in and did the same.

Neil didn't stay in the room. The woman detective insisted that Neil had to leave. She said that in order to get the clearest picture of what had happened, it was vital that people not talk to each other. She told us that when people talked, they often unknowingly changed their story to fit what someone else had said. They sometimes confused something that actually happened and something they just heard had happened. So it was important to keep people separated. They couldn't absolutely demand it, but . . . And she left us to finish the sentence for ourselves.

I didn't care. Having Neil there was fine, but mostly because he didn't try to talk to me, and he kept everyone else away.

After Neil left, I locked the door, then lay down again. A little while later, someone knocked. I didn't answer. I didn't even get up. My mother's voice came through the door.

"Timothy. I need to talk to you."

I didn't answer her.

After that my father gave it a try.

"Timothy. Timothy, we need to talk about getting you a lawyer. And how you're going to proceed with this. Timothy?"

I didn't answer him either.

It was quiet for a while.

There was another knock on my door. I waited, but no one said anything. The knock came again, even more hesitantly. I wondered who it was—but not enough to get up and look. They must have gone away since I didn't hear anything else.

Some time passed; I don't know how much.

Maybe I slept. When I next opened my eyes, the room was dark. Something had woken me. I heard a knock, then Neil's voice.

"Timothy?"

I got up cracked the door for Neil. He said, "We've ordered food. I though you might want to come downstairs for a little while and get something to eat."

"Why on earth would you think that?"

He made a grimace of apology. "Let me put it another way. You're going to have to face everyone at some point, and I thought you might want to get it over with."

He had a good point. "Aren't we not supposed to speak to each other?" I asked.

"They took everyone's statements. They're asking us to stay for another night or two if we can, but they lifted the no-talking ban. I can have some food brought up to you. Unless you want to come down . . ."

"No, I don't want to. But I will."

"Are you ready now?"

"Sure. Might as well get it over with."

Neil led the way, and I followed. It was strange. As we went down the stairs, I felt like it had been days since I'd been downstairs. Weeks even. I felt like I'd been caught in a time warp and had been up in that room for eons.

The setup was the same as in the morning: food spread out on the dining room table and people gathered in the morning room on the couches and chairs. The minute I stepped into the room, I saw that my mother and father were there. If I had known, I probably would have opted to stay upstairs. But it was too late now.

My mother spotted me across the room, and she made a beeline for me.

"Do you want me to stand by?" Neil asked.

"No, that's okay," I told him. "There are some things that are too much to ask."

"You're making jokes now," Neil observed. "You must be feeling better."

"That wasn't a joke," I told him.

I heard him laugh as he turned away and went over to the table for some food.

My mother walked over and stopped in front of me. She was, of course, perfectly dressed in a black skirt and black blazer and black heels. I realized I almost never stood next to my mother. She was always seated at the head of the table, where she seemed to take up so much space. But standing next to her, I realized how small she was. Nora had at least come up to my nose. My mother barely reached my chin. She had to tilt her head back a little to look up at me.

I braced myself for what I knew was coming.

Except that it didn't come.

She asked, very calmly, "Are you all right, Timothy?"

"No. Not really."

She nodded. "Your father and I, we'll do whatever we can to help. You know that, don't you?"

"Yes. Sure."

"The police told us that you've got an interview scheduled for tomorrow morning. Your father and I arranged for a lawyer to be there. But if you'd rather arrange something else, or if you already have, just let us know and we can change it."

I wasn't excited about my mother picking my lawyer, but I hadn't done anything about it myself, and I knew it would be stupid not to have one there.

"No, that sounds good," I said.

"There will be other things to deal with, but one thing at a time," she said. "Right now, you should probably try to eat something. We're right over there if you need us."

"Um, thanks."

Then she turned to go. But she stopped and looked back at me. And she said, "Sometimes we do things, and we don't want to, but we don't seem to have control. I understand that."

At first I didn't know what she was talking about. Then I realized she thought I had done it—she thought I had killed Nora. I didn't know whether to be angry that she assumed the worst or touched that she seemed to be trying to tell me that she didn't care.

I didn't have to think of an answer because she

didn't wait for one. She just went back over to where my father was sitting.

I saw that Tammy and Edward were sitting over on the couch near my parents. Edward had his arm around Tammy's shoulders, and he seemed to be consoling her.

After hearing my mother, and now seeing Edward like that, I knew that the world had ended. It had turned into something unrecognizable. Things do go on, but they are not the same. The world turns upside down.

I went to get some food, and Edward came up while I was spooning mashed potatoes onto a paper plate.

"Tim, I just wanted to say . . . I'm really sorry," Edward managed to get out. "If there's anything I can do . . ."

I looked at him. "Yes, there is something. You can tell me, have you published books under a pseudonym?"

He blinked. He hadn't been prepared for my question, but he answered me.

"Yes," he said simply. "I have."

I nodded. "Congratulations. If you wouldn't mind, I think I'd like to read one sometime."

"Sure. I'd like that."

I looked around the room. "Do you know where Nora's sister and mother are?" I asked him.

"No. They haven't come down yet," he said.

"And Andrew and Emily?"

"I think they're heading back to the city. Andrew and his family, the police told them that since they weren't even here at the B&B they didn't need to stay in the area. They asked Emily and Alejandro to stay, but . . . well, you know Emily."

"No, I don't think I do know Emily," I admitted. "But if she wanted to leave, it's probably for the best. When are you headed back?"

"I'll stay as long as you need me here," he said.

"Thanks. I'm sure that has nothing to do with the fact that Tammy is still here," I said.

He smiled, and it was a smile I don't think I'd ever seen on his face before. It was almost shy. And suddenly my heart hurt. I could see on Edward's face the dawning of that feeling I'd had for the first time with Nora. I felt something rising in my throat. To my horror, I realized I was about to start crying. I put down my plate.

"I can't . . ." I said.

That's all I could manage. I turned and escaped from the room. And, thank goodness, no one came after me. I broke down while I was climbing the stairs, and I completely came apart when I shut the door of my room behind me.

That night—I don't really want to talk too much about that night. It was supposed to have been my wedding night. It was supposed to have been the best night of my life—instead it was the worst, and I hope to God it will be the worst I ever have. I can't say anything else about it. These things are beyond description. But after it was over, I got up the next day, knowing that I was not, and would never be, the same.

The brain rebels against finding reasons for that much pain, but they are there. With Nora, all I wanted was to feel truly loved. And I had gotten a taste of it after Nora caught me with Celia and told me she loved me anyway. I thought that was it; I thought that was what I had been looking for all my life. But after that awful night—the first night in a lifetime without Nora—I realized I had been so concerned with *being* loved that I never asked myself if I knew how to love. I simply assumed I did. But that night, I discovered the truth—that a heart unbroken doesn't know how to love.

It was only now that she was gone that I understood how to love her.

THE INVESTIGATION

HEART WOUNDS

Heart wounds cause instant and alarming symptoms: pain; hemorrhage, often copious, sometimes slight; palpitation; dyspnea; syncope. The symptoms depend on the site and extent of the heart wound. Death is instantaneous if the ventricle is torn widely open or the center for heart-block is damaged, or the auricles injured. Fortunately, the ventricles are the parts commonly injured—the left ventricle much more often than the right. A bullet or knife may wound the heart wall without perforating the ventricle. This superficial wound may bleed profusely and confuse the diagnosis. A perforating wound, if small, may bleed but little, owing to its being closed with every systole by the interlocking of the heart's muscles. Often there is but little external bleeding.

—From *The Practice of Surgery*
by James Gregory

Timothy

The Day After

The next day, when I finally left my hotel room, the machine of procedure really started for me.

A policeman came to my room first thing in the morning to escort me down to the station for more questioning. They brought me into a room with my lawyer (the one arranged for me by my mother) and three detectives. Two I recognized from the day before—the woman and the man in suits who had questioned me—and another man from the district attorney's office who was there to oversee.

I can't speak to what other detectives are like, but mine were nothing like you see in the movies or on TV. There you always have at least one suspicious, hard-nosed cop who gets aggressive with the suspect: the "bad cop." But I had three cops in the room, and not one of them took on the "bad cop" role. They all talked to me normally, even respectfully. First, the woman detective told me that they were going to tape our conversation if that was okay with me.

My lawyer jumped in and said, "Of course it's not okay with us. But since we can't stop you, we'll just have to make sure that there's nothing on that tape."

My lawyer, unlike the detectives, was a completely stereotypical top-drawer (and top-dollar) defense lawyer: shrewd and shifty. I had disliked him on sight, and he was not doing anything to change my opinion of him.

The woman detective, who seemed to be taking the lead on the case, just said, "Of course." Then she turned to me. "We can't make you talk to us. Of course we know that. But we're hoping you'll answer some questions."

I nodded.

She started asking questions, and I answered her. She started off with the same general questions both she and the other detective had asked the day before—the sequence of events starting from when I woke up and leading up to when the police arrived on the scene. I tried as best I could to answer all the questions. There were some spots that I simply couldn't remember, and I told her that. She just nodded and marked it down.

Then she asked me to take her through the events of the night before.

I did. And I didn't leave out the part with Celia and Marcus. It would have been silly. I could tell by just looking at the detective that she already knew anyway. I was sure she had talked to Marcus and Celia the day before. One of them must have told her.

I could also see that she was a bit surprised when I volunteered the story without her having to pull it out of me, and my lawyer just about had a heart attack trying to get me to shut up. But I didn't listen to him. I told the events as simply as I could. I reported it like a stripped-down newspaper story: I had slept with Celia the night before my wedding. Marcus had come in. Nora had also known about it. We hadn't fought about it.

The only problem was that I don't think anyone in the room believed me.

Then all three detectives started a volley of questions. At that point my lawyer had completely given up trying to get me to be quiet, and though their voices were still calm, the questions from the detectives came at me rapid-fire.

No, I said I didn't know if we were still going to get married.

No, I hadn't killed her.

No, I hadn't gone to her room.

I paused for a second when they asked me who I thought might have done this.

Celia, I told them. Celia had done it. It couldn't be anyone else.

Then they started asking me the same questions all over again.

I gave them the same answers.

When they started for the third time, my lawyer finally broke in again. "I think that's enough," he said, and I found myself agreeing with him.

My lawyer gathered his papers, put them in his

briefcase, and we both stood up. I found I'd been sitting there long enough for my legs to get stiff. But as I was leaving, the woman detective said, "If you honestly didn't kill her, why don't you want to find her murderer?"

I admit, I was annoyed by that. "Why do you think I've been sitting here answering all these questions?"

"Right now, you're our suspect," she said. "You haven't given us anything that changes that."

"But what about Celia? I told you, she did it."

She hesitated. I could tell she was deciding whether to reveal something.

Then she told me.

"We don't think Mrs. Franklin is a viable suspect," she said. And then she blew apart my theory—and my world—in a few words. "Mr. Franklin and his wife both say they weren't out of each other's sight that night after they left you in your room. They both claim they left the bed-and-breakfast less than ten minutes after the . . . encounter. And we were able to get pictures of their car going through the tollbooth on the highway, and the time corroborates their story."

I knew if Marcus said he hadn't let Celia out of his sight, it was the truth. That meant Celia couldn't have done it.

I was shaken, but I tried to hide it. "I don't know what to tell you," I said to the detectives. "I don't know who it could have been."

"Help us figure it out," the woman detective urged.

"I would strongly advise you leave now," my lawyer interrupted.

It was my turn to hesitate. I didn't know what I wanted to do. As calm and as friendly as the detectives seemed, I knew they were probably just trying to keep me talking in the hope I would slip up and implicate myself. As she had said, I was the prime suspect. I wanted to help them find the murderer, but if they were just going to try to pin it on me, I didn't want to help with that. Not because I cared about what was going to happen to me. At that point I felt like I would have happily died if it would help Nora. But if they pinned it on me, whoever did it would get off scot-free.

"Aren't you supposed to be able to figure it out from evidence?" I asked the detective.

The day before she had demonstrated her willingness to explain the philosophy behind separating witnesses before talking to them, and now she explained to me the problem with the evidence in this situation. She said that the scene had been compromised by so many people entering the room. Tammy and I had gone in. Then Nora's mother had gone in, and apparently Neil had gone in to get Nora's mother out. Not only that, the trace evidence was complicated by the fact that it was a hotel room: so many people had passed through it.

I went back over to the table and sat down. "How can I help?" I asked.

And she told me how. She told me about victimology and how the best help they could get would be from the clearest and most detailed picture of the victim's life. That was the only way they could get insight into possible motives. For that, they had to rely on the people close to the victim. And I had pieces of the story that no one else had.

I said I had given them everything I knew.

The detective told me I had given them facts, but they needed more than just facts. They needed feelings, my impressions. She said that no thought was too insignificant.

I thought about what she said. And I knew she was right. So I sent my lawyer home. And I told them my story. This story.

But the story I told them wasn't complete. First of all, it was missing Nora's side. I wished more than anything I had that. It really was only half a story without it.

And, for my half, there was one more piece of the story yet to come.

THE INVESTIGATION

EXCERPTS OF INTERVIEWS WITH NORA'S FAMILY AND FRIENDS

Excerpted from the interview with Tammy Phillips:

> *I knew it. I knew this was going to happen. I told her, but she didn't listen to me. She should never have left Kansas. I warned her. Why didn't she listen?*

Excerpted from the interview with Neil Robeson, friend and former employer:

> *I don't understand, what is it you're asking me? Who would have wanted to kill Nora? God, that sounds like the most ridiculous question to me. Why? Well, you would have had to know Nora. No one could have wanted to kill her. No one. Yes, I know, someone obviously did. I don't have an answer for you. Timothy? No. [Interviewee paused.] No. I believe he loved her. I believe what they had was the real thing.*

Excerpted from the interview with the victim's mother:

I warned her. It was too good to be true. Big shot from the city coming with all these promises. All these lies. He did it. He took my baby away from me. He took her away.

Excerpted from interview with the victim's sister, Deirdre:

[After a long period of crying, the interviewee finally speaks, almost inaudibly.] I have something to confess . . .

Timothy

After the Interrogation

I didn't hide anything when I talked to the detectives; I told them the whole truth.

It's a powerful thing to tell the truth. To truly tell everything. I don't know if they believed me, but when it was finally time for me to go, they all stood and shook my hand. The woman detective thanked me for my help and asked me if there was anything they could do for me.

I said yes.

Even though things had gone well when I had seen my family the night before, I didn't want to test my luck. So I asked them to help me get back into my room without seeing anyone. And they did. They took me out of the station the back way, and they got an officer to take me in an unmarked car. He went inside the bed-and-breakfast and came back out to let me know the coast was clear.

I managed to get inside and up the stairs, and I was just opening the door to my room and about to slip in when I got caught.

It was Nora's sister. She must have been sitting in her room with the door cracked open, watching for me.

She said urgently, "I need to talk to you."

"Now's not a good time." And I stepped into my

room and tried to close the door, but she put her foot in the gap.

"Timothy, I have something to tell you."

I could have managed to shut the door on her, but something in her voice stopped me. "Come in then."

She came in. I shut the door behind her and locked it.

She crossed to the chair by the window—the chair where two nights ago Nora had sat when she told me she loved me.

I took a seat on the edge of the bed.

Deirdre glanced at me once, quickly; then she looked away. And she didn't look at me again.

She stared down at her lap, her fingers so tightly twined they were white and bloodless at the knuckles and bright red at the tips.

"I've been trying to talk to you. I wanted to tell you . . . I haven't said anything to the police yet . . . I'm supposed to go for an interview tomorrow, and I don't know what to do. I don't have anyone else to talk to. Tammy always hated me, and I think that Neil, Nora's boss, does too . . ."

She was disjointed, not making any sense. I said, "Okay, slow down. What haven't you told the police?"

"I think it might be my fault. I don't know for sure, but I think if I'd told Nora the truth this wouldn't have happened."

My heart sped up, but everything else seemed to

slow down. I heard my own voice say calmly, "What do you mean, the truth? What truth?"

Deirdre took a deep breath, and I saw her clasp her fingers even tighter.

She said, very slowly and deliberately, "My sister gave up her life, and I let her do it."

"Gave up her life? What do you mean, she gave up her life? Are you saying she wasn't killed? That *she* did it?"

"No, I'm not talking about that. I didn't mean her *life*. I meant three years ago . . . three years ago when she moved home to take care of my mother."

"That didn't have anything to do with you," I said. "That was her choice."

"I'd love it if that were true," Deirdre replied quietly. "But how can you make a real choice when you don't know the truth?"

"What was the truth?" I asked.

Deirdre's lips were trembling.

"The truth . . . the truth is my mother isn't sick. My mother was never sick."

"I don't understand," I said, even though her words were very clear.

She tried again. "My mother lied about being sick to get my sister to come home."

"Are you sure? How do you know?"

She made a little movement with her head. "I just knew. I don't know how Nora didn't see it. It was so obvious to me."

380

"How could something like that be obvious?" I asked. "If someone tells you they're sick, tells you they have cancer, you believe them."

"I know. I can see how you'd think that. But you'd have to know our mother. I don't believe anything she says. And there were other things. The timing of it was one. She got sick right after Dan, Nora's fiancé, broke up with her. Before they broke up, Nora came home all the time. And it looked pretty certain she would move back to town after she graduated. But then Dan broke up with her, and she not only didn't have a reason to come back, she had a reason to stay away. And then, suddenly, our mother gets sick? It didn't feel right. And then after Nora moved home, our mother wouldn't let her go with her into the hospital. She made her wait in the parking lot. Nora never met her doctors. She wasn't allowed. Who does something like that?"

"That's all just suppositions," I said. "How can you know for sure?"

"I checked. Of course I checked. I called the hospital where my mother was supposedly getting chemo, and they didn't have any record of her. They told me that no one by that name had ever gotten treatment at their hospital."

"So you knew all this, and you didn't tell Nora?"

Deirdre didn't exactly answer my question. She said, "I thought for sure that she would start to suspect something."

"But she didn't," I said.

"No. She didn't."

"And you didn't say anything."

"No." Deirdre still didn't look up. She seemed to be staring at my feet, but I could tell she wasn't seeing anything—she was looking inside, and as I watched, I saw her face twist with disgust. She didn't like the view. I felt a flash of pity. I knew that landscape. I had traversed it the night before.

Her voice dropped so low I had to strain to hear her when she said, "There was a part of me that was happy about it when she moved back. I was jealous of her. I was jealous of how well she was doing. I hadn't even finished college, and she was in grad school at Chicago. I was happy that finally she seemed to be having a hard time. Finally. I was the one who had the hard time growing up. I was the older one. I took the brunt of everything. My mother took it all out on me. I was the one who got punished, even when it was Nora who'd been the one to do something wrong."

I had a flash of memory: a story Nora had told me about her mother locking Deirdre in the closet to punish Nora.

Deirdre went on: "It felt good that Nora should suffer like I had. I know it sounds awful. But that's how I felt. I felt like it was a kind of justice. But then it went on so long . . . and I knew it wasn't fair. I was going to say something, I really was . . . but then my husband left, and I was in a bad way with the kids. I needed some money to keep my apartment. I swear, I needed it. Without it we would have been out on the street. I asked Nora, but she didn't have it because she was supporting Mom. So I confronted my mother. I said if she gave me the money, I promised I wouldn't tell Nora the truth. She gave me the money—and more when I needed it. But then you came along . . ."

"And Nora came with me to New York," I said.

"It was okay for a while. My mother was sure you'd leave Nora, and then Nora would come back home . . . but then you proposed."

I said, "I would think your mother would have been happy for Nora."

"How can you be happy for someone else if you're miserable? If you've been that miserable for so long? When you're that unhappy, that's all there is for you. Seeing other people happy . . . it just makes your unhappiness worse. It's not the way it's supposed to be, but it's the way that it is."

She paused, then asked me, "Did Nora tell you what happened at the rehearsal dinner?"

"No, she didn't say anything. Something happened?"

"Our mother ambushed Nora in the bathroom and told Nora she was dying. She said Nora had to come home and take care of her. I thought she might pull a stunt like that, so I warned her that if she tried anything, I was going to tell Nora the truth. But she did it anyway. I don't know what she was thinking. I don't know how she thought it was going to work out. Obviously, she *wasn't* thinking. I had no idea how far gone she was."

"What did Nora say when your mother told her that?" I asked. I didn't realize until I spoke that the anxiety would come through in my voice.

"Nora told her no. Nora chose you."

It should have made me feel good. But it was a pleasure that was intense anguish at the same time. What else could I feel when I discovered all over again how much I had lost?

Deirdre went on. "I was trying to talk to Nora. I was trying to tell her . . . but I didn't get a chance, and I figured there was time. I thought there was plenty of time . . ." She started to cry. "I don't know what to think. I don't know if my mother did . . . did this thing. I tried to talk to her, but . . ." Deirdre wiped her nose on her sleeve, took a shuddering breath, and went on, "I don't know if my mother is pretending or if she's really crazy. She says that it's your fault. That you did it. She says that Nora changed her mind and told you she was moving back to Kansas and that you couldn't take it. I don't know what to believe. I think I know, but there's still a part of me . . . She's my mother. But I know . . . I don't think . . . I wanted to ask you . . . Did you do it?"

"No," I said.

She lifted a hand to her face and covered her

eyes, as if by covering her eyes she could take away sight and knowledge.

"I don't know. I don't know who to believe . . ." She stopped talking then because she was crying so hard.

I knew Nora would have tried to comfort her. But Nora wasn't there.

We sat there for a long time. I listened to Deirdre cry, but all I could think about was my own pain. I wondered how it could hurt so much. How long could I sit there and take it?

The answer was, not very long. I couldn't just sit there and take it. I had to do something.

I stood up and asked Deirdre, "What room is your mother in?"

She looked up at me. "What are you going to do?"

"I'm going to ask her myself."

"I don't think—"

"What room is she in?" I said again. There was no way I was going to let it go. I was ready to go and bang on every door until I found her. I think Deirdre could hear that in my voice.

"Five. She's in room five," Deirdre said.

I could hear Deirdre following me as I got up, opened the door, walked down the hallway, and stopped in front of the door to her mother's room. I rapped my knuckles against the door.

"Who is it?" her mother's voice asked.

"Timothy," I said.

There was a pause.

"I have nothing to say to you," the voice came through, sounding closer.

"I suggest you open this door. Now," I said. A flimsy lock was not going to keep me out. I was ready to bust right through that door if I had to.

But I didn't have to.

She opened the door, and then beat a hasty retreat across to the other side of the room, putting the bed between us.

I stepped inside, and Deirdre came in after me and shut the door.

"What do you want? Did you come to finish off what you started?" Nora's mother demanded. "I'm half-dead already. You might as well finish the job," her voice was high-pitched, edged with hysteria.

Even angry as I was, I could see that she did look terrible. But I felt no pity. My only thought was that if she wasn't strong, that would make her easier to break. And I was ready to do whatever I needed to do to make that happen. I had come to get an answer to my question. But as I looked at her, I knew. I can't tell you how, but I knew without even having to ask. In that moment I knew what it felt like to be angry enough to kill.

"You are sick. Do you know that? What kind of person kills their own child? What kind of monster must you be to have done that? And how can you even live with yourself?"

As I spoke, she backed up until she was half-cowering in the corner and her whole body was shaking. She pointed a wildly trembling finger at me. "It was you. You did it. It was your fault. You took my daughter from me."

I stepped closer. I wanted to hurt her, and I used words instead of fists simply because I knew that would cause the most pain. "You know I didn't take her," I said. "That's what you couldn't stand. You knew that she couldn't wait to get away. Nothing in the world would have convinced her to go back with you."

"Lies. It's all lies. Nora changed her mind. She said she was going to come back with me, and when she told you, you killed her."

I pounced. "How do you know that she was going to go back with you? Deirdre was there when you told Nora you were dying and asked her to come back with you at the rehearsal dinner, and she said no. When did Nora change her mind? When you went to her room later that night?"

Nora's mother didn't answer me. She just shook her head.

I went on, twisting the knife of my words deeper. "You know that Nora loved me. That Nora chose me. Even when you told her you were dying, she still chose to stay with me."

I had never seen someone come apart quite like she did. She was trembling so much it was as if someone had her by the shoulders and was literally shaking her.

I don't know what made me say it. It just burst out of me. "What I can't understand is how you could be so sick as to kill her. It's monstrous. Why not me? Why wasn't it me?"

It was like hitting the magic button.

"It was supposed to be you," she half shrieked. "It should have been you. But I couldn't get the door open. The door wouldn't open. It was your fault. Your fault. The door wouldn't open."

As she spoke, I remembered. Just before I'd fallen asleep, I'd had the thought that Celia might try to come back, so I had gotten up and locked the door.

I had come to get a confession. I hadn't bargained on this. This last piece. This twist of fate that made her mother's accusations true. It was true: it was my fault. It should have been me. I would have done anything for it to have been me. And it was my betrayal that had caused me to lock that door. One little action, done on the verge of sleep, turned out to be the difference between living and dying.

I would never lock another door in my life. Not even the door to my heart. Believe me, I tried—but it turned out that the lock had been broken.

THE INVESTIGATION

STATISTICS

Parental murders of children have occurred for centuries and have been documented in virtually every known society, from advanced, industrialized countries to indigenous groups.

—From *Why Mothers Kill: A Forensic Psychologist's Casebook*, by Geoffrey R. McKee

Nora

Postmortem

The story has ended for me, as it will end for everyone. I suppose it's somehow fitting that I should end this story as well, even though I have never liked endings—not in movies or books or life. My favorite endings were always the ones that gave me the illusion of things continuing, on and on, forever. Happily ever after.

But even after everything has been told, there are always more questions. The questions are the heart of the story when we're alive. We think the answers matter. We think the facts add up to something.

Timothy wanted my side of the story, and so I have added it to his. I believe he will be able to hear me if he listens. And here is the rest.

After I left Timothy's room, I went straight back to my room. I took off my clothes and put on my nightgown. I did it automatically, my mind a blank. Then I had the thought, "Timothy was having sex with Celia." There was a kind of clutching pain with it. It passed, and I went into the bathroom to wash my face. Then I had the thought, "I have to decide if I'm going to marry him tomorrow." That brought with it a kind of panic. Then it passed as well, and I put toothpaste on the brush, ran it under the sink, and brushed my teeth. Then the thought came, "I can't marry him after what he's done." That came with a wave of rage. And I got out the night cream and put it on my face and hands. Then I had the thought, "I love him." I can't describe that feeling. I guess it was love. I turned out the light and went and climbed into bed.

Then came the knock on my door.

I thought about pretending to be asleep, but I hadn't yet turned out the lamp by my bedside, and I knew that the line of light would show under the door, and I didn't want Timothy to think I was ignoring him. I didn't even consider the fact that it might not be Timothy.

I climbed out of bed and went over and opened the door. My mother was standing in the hallway, and she was crying.

"Mom, what happened?"

She didn't answer me. I'm not sure she could have, she was sobbing so hard. She was having those shuddering heaves when you can't quite seem to get enough breath.

"Come in, come in," I ushered her in. "Lie down, okay? I'm going to get a wet towel."

I went into the bathroom, took one of the washcloths, and ran it under cold water. Then I wrung it out, laid it on the counter, folded it, and brought it back out. She was lying in the middle of the bed, but she was still crying as hard as before.

I sat down on the bed, and I leaned over and was about to put the towel on her forehead.

Her face twisted as I watched it, and she raised her hand and pushed me violently away—at least that's what I thought at the time.

If I'd had to imagine what it was like getting stabbed in the heart, it would have been completely different. I would have predicted a sharp, piercing pain. But there was only a pressure, like she had thumped her fist against my chest. There wasn't even any pain, just a kind of thud, but the kind of thud you feel rather than hear. And I had the thought that I needed to put my head down on the pillow for a moment.

I would have guessed that dying by bleeding to death came with dizziness and cold sweats, like the one time I fainted at the doctor's office while getting blood drawn. But it wasn't like that at all. I lay there, and a kind of warmth spread through my body, like being immersed in warm water, but from the inside.

At the time I didn't know what was happening.

But now I know everything. I could even tell you what my mother was thinking. I can see the thoughts from here. It's like being on the top of a tall mountain; you can see vast distances, but it's all very small and far away. I can see thoughts, see intentions, see past and future—though with past and future sometimes it's hard to tell the difference and get the order right. It's like with

392

things way off in the distance: it's hard to get the proper perspective and see which are farther and which are closer.

The police came and did their investigation. The forensic team arrived to work the scene. They took a lot of pictures of the knife that had slipped easily through my ribs and pierced my heart. They were careful with the removal of my body, and they took the sheets as well.

Of course, it was all for nothing, since my mother had come into the room before the police arrived. She said later she didn't know what she did or what she touched—so the prints on the knife (which were hers), the hairs and fibers on the bed (also hers), all those things that help build a case, they were all useless.

The evidence might not have been quite so useless if it had pointed to Timothy. Because that's what usually happened. That's what made sense. Men kill their girlfriends; husbands kill their wives. Mothers don't kill their children. That's what we think anyway, even though it's not true. And as the police have discovered again and again, people don't believe the facts. They believe what they believe. And when the facts contradict belief, belief usually wins.

The only reason they were able to get an indictment was the confession my mother made to Timothy and my sister. My sister was the one who told the police the truth. She went down to the station and told them everything she'd told Timothy, and then she described the scene afterward between Timothy and Mom. At first they didn't believe her, but she told them things they could check: like how my mother had lied to me about having cancer to get me to come home, and about the weekly trips to the hospital, where I would sit in the car, and my mother would go and sit in the waiting room until it was time to come out. And it was only after they started to check out the things Deirdre told them that they started to believe.

Now I can see the things that even Deirdre didn't know. How my mother would sometimes, on her way out of the hospital, stop a passing nurse and tell her she was dizzy. They always got a wheelchair and wheeled her outside. And how my mother would search the Internet for little things to tell me, to keep me worried and convinced. That's also how she picked the type of cancer to get: leukemia so it would make sense that she didn't look sick or have surgery. But the truth was, it never even occurred to me to question whether she was sick. As my sister said, my brain just didn't work that way. In life, what we see is limited by what we believe. It is a justice that needs no laws to enforce it.

So now I have shared what I can see of the past. The future is more dangerous to visit, but there are a few things I can reveal, make of them what you will.

My mother would be charged, but the case would never go to trial. Sometimes life has a dark sense of humor. The whole time she was pretending to be sick, she didn't ever go to a doctor. How could she? So the real cancer that it turned out she actually had—one that would have been treatable—went undetected. She died before her trial date.

Not long after that, Timothy's father died of a heart attack on a Monday morning. He hadn't been expecting it, and he hadn't taken care of his estate planning. The government took a huge cut. And then the rest went to Timothy's mother, who finally got to try her hand at investing. She lost half the principal within six months, before she learned her lesson. The family dinners came to an end, and when that happened, they became what they always were: strangers.

And Timothy?

For years he kept a shrine in his heart for me. He was so certain he would never get married. And he held out for a long time. Then he met someone at a charity event for the prevention of family violence. She was twenty years younger than he was, but she'd had more tragedy in her life than he had. She'd lost her three children when her ex-husband set their house on fire, and she'd been badly burned where her nightgown caught on fire. Despite all this, she still smiled and laughed and lived more than most people who were healthy and had every reason to be happy and still weren't. It took another five years, but Timothy eventually married her.

But in his heart, he was faithful to me. For years he thought about me every day. Then, eventually, less often—and he felt guilty for it. After days of happiness, he would lash himself for forgetting. He'd ask himself how he could be happy when I wasn't there? He told himself that I was the one who should be alive and that he should have died. But I can tell you that any sentence that starts with "should have" is a lie.

Timothy carried with him the certainty that I was his true love. And that was the real tragedy. Because the fact is, he was actually happier in his life the way it was than he would have been with me. It's true, he loved me more—in the way that the world thinks of love. But that kind of love consumes you. It eats you up; it gives you no rest. He loved his wife in a gentle way and if she had died before him, he would have mourned her in the same way—gently, with fondness, but without the tearing sorrow he felt for me.

Those are the facts, and in life we always seem to want the facts. We look at statistics. We seek out explanations and hard evidence. We hope, with facts, that we will be able to control the events in our lives, or that if we can't control them, at least the facts will explain them. We hope they'll help us understand. That suddenly it will all make sense. That the mystery will be revealed. But have you noticed that the facts are like a blanket that's not quite big enough? There's always something of the unknown that's left exposed.

Now that the story is over for me, I can see that the unknown isn't something frightening. It is love itself. And when it comes, it is the one thing that is uncontrollable, unpredictable, unlimited. Even from here, where everything makes sense, that remains a mystery.

Center Point Publishing
600 Brooks Road ● PO Box 1
Thorndike ME 04986-0001 USA

(207) 568-3717

**US & Canada:
1 800 929-9108**
www.centerpointlargeprint.com